Jeff Dawson is a journalist and author. He has been a long-standing contributor to *The Sunday Times* Culture section, writing regular A-list interview-led arts features (inter-viewees including the likes of Robert De Niro, George Clooney, Dustin Hoffman, Hugh Grant, Angelina Jolie, Jerry Seinfeld and Nicole Kidman). He is also a former US Editor of *Empire* magazine.

Jeff is the author of three non-fiction books – *Tarantino/Quentin Tarantino: The Cinema of Cool*, *Back Home: England And The 1970 World Cup*, which *The Times* rated 'Truly outstanding', and *Dead Reckoning: The Dunedin Star Disaster*, the latter nominated for the Mountbatten Maritime Prize.

Also by Jeff Dawson

An Ingo Finch Mystery

No Ordinary Killing
The Cold North Sea
Hell Gate

HELL GATE

JEFF DAWSON

CANELO

First published in the United Kingdom in 2020 by Canelo

This edition published in the United Kingdom in 2021 by

Canelo
31 Helen Road
Oxford OX2 0DF
United Kingdom

A CIP catalogue record for this book is available from the British Library.

Print ISBN 978 1 80032 036 9
Ebook ISBN 978 1 78863 973 6

Look for more great books at www.canelo.co

Printed and bound in Great Britain by Clays Ltd, Elcograf S.p.A.

To my family, as always

Three may keep a secret if two of them are dead.

Benjamin Franklin

Based on a historical event

Part One

Chapter 1

The body bobbed on the spring tide.

'The oar, use the oar.'

'Boat hook's fine,' muttered the constable.

'The *oar*,' urged the harbourmaster. 'Some goddamn respect!'

He nudged the tiller and rubbed his eye. Two days on and the smoke was still curling, funnelled down the channel between Manhattan and Queensborough. Acrid, stinging, it rose thick to screen the noonday sun.

The constable shrugged and shouted forward.

'You heard what he said. Use the oar.'

'He has a name – *Tobias*.'

Pressing a kerchief to his mouth, the constable edged towards him, careful not to tread on the rowing boat's grim cargo.

Tobias rolled his eyes. He lay prone at the bow and reached out, smacking the blade down hard.

'Again…' barked the constable. 'Too far to the right.'

Gentle waves lapped the hull. A bell clanged on a buoy. Somewhere in the distance a foghorn droned, sound muffled by the smog. Ahead, in the Hell Gate strait, the waters swirled white. They could not afford to drift.

The oar went closer and flicked the leg.

'Couple of inches... *There!*'

The white pinafore dress billowed like the dome of a jellyfish.

'Female... juvenile...' muttered the constable.

'Some compassion,' scolded the harbourmaster. 'It's a *little girl.*'

He gave himself a moment.

'What d'ya think? Nine years old... ten?'

The constable shrugged again.

'Okay,' said the harbourmaster and nodded to the shore.

The constable waved landward, signalling no room for any more. He was not sure if they could see him through the smoke.

From the plane trees that lined the river path, before the grand timbers of the Gracie Mansion, the man with the grey silk suit discerned the rowing boat turn.

'How many?' he asked.

His colleague scanned with binoculars.

'The negro fellow just pulled out another. Small. A child. That's five, I think.'

Most of the bodies had washed up round the bend, on the rocks of the Brothers Islands, but some were still drifting down.

'I mean, *how many in total?*'

'Twelve... fifteen hundred...?'

The man in the suit exhaled a whistle. Ash was still falling and he brushed it from his shoulder. He nodded back up to the sidewalk where his valet stood by the idling red Ford – dutiful, alert.

A slender man of near seven feet tall, he had the pock-marked skin and high cheekbones of his First Nation forebears. His black hair was worn symbolically long – bunched and beaded. He stooped to open the door.

Back at the low-tide mark, desperate men waded to their chests. They hauled the boat onto the shingle. Tenderly the bodies were laid next to the others, a row that already stretched ten yards.

Policemen logged the details. Someone from the coroner's office set up a camera. One angry man threatened to wrap the tripod round the photographer's head. Women dressed in black sniffled quietly.

In the June heat, the scent of death oozed along the waterways. No posy of flowers – and there were many strewn – could mask the stench. At the recognition of her child, a mother's legs buckled and she released an animal moan. Others rushed to support her.

In the distance, the huge pleasure steamer lay part submerged, like a fat man wallowing in a bathtub. Pitched to one side, a giant paddle had lifted near clear of the water. From the portholes the black cloud billowed, the heat still too intense for the Fire Department tenders.

–

After dark, the orange glow from the Arlington Hall windows drew the public. In the warm night air they came, black-clad, ambling across Tompkins Square Park – 'Der Weisse Garten' as everyone still called it – the Schwartzmeiers and the Lindemanns; the Goehles and the Steins; the Lüchows, the Geigers, the Allings; all greeted with lingering, cupped handshakes and consoling hugs.

Some arrived in buggies, clopping across the cobbles of St Mark's Place. Others trudged out of the Atlantic Garden *Bierhaus* – sorrows drowned like their loved ones

– while the 'El' trains clattered on the tracks above the Bowery.

Inside, the tension was palpable, the hall packed – men standing, lining the walls beneath the black crêpe frieze, while their womenfolk squeezed in to take the seats. As the speakers began, a crush swelled around the doorway, latecomers unwilling to divert from the tide of emotion that poured with every oration.

The pastor spoke first, his face lined, drained. Up on the stage he looked lost, a ghost behind the lectern. It was members of his own congregation – the St Mark's Evangelical Lutheran Church – who had chartered the pleasure steamer for the annual day out, he explained. It had been a regular treat for the families, the seventeenth such excursion, heading for a picnic at Locust Grove off Long Island Sound.

Wisely eschewing his profession's convention that God's will might have been responsible for the boat then catching fire and sinking, he gave a meditation on grief. He could still not believe it: that it could happen to his own flock... that tomorrow alone would see a cortege of two hundred hearses...

Then he sat back down, broken.

The President of the District Bund went next, with far less room for tolerance. Not three hours ago, he told them, he had received information from a reporter on the *New Yorker Staats-Zeitung* who had been scouring the city archives. He waved a sheaf of papers for effect.

The steamer, the *General Slocum*, had had its career as a pleasure boat punctuated with accidents, he revealed – beached twice off Rockaway; again at Coney Island; collisions in the East River and off Battery Park – mishaps that had been hushed up by the Port Authority.

A murmur swept the room.

The boat, grossly overcrowded, was a death trap — straw and oily rags left lying around; storage areas full of gasoline; a lamp that was knocked over; a captain who ignored word of a blaze. A 12-year-old boy — *a 12-year-old boy!* — had been left to raise the alarm.

The chorus of disapproval swelled.

The *General Slocum*'s crew had never conducted a fire drill, for heaven's sake. Not once. The lifeboats were wired to their housings. The fire hoses were rotten and had crumbled to dust. Mothers placed children in life preservers and threw them into the water only to find they had been padded with iron bars — *iron!* — to cheat on the inspector's weight specifications.

His voice began to crack.

'The children. *The children…*'

Someone came to ease him from the lectern, prising away his fingers.

'Thirteen hundred. *Thirteen hundred,*' he wailed. 'Burnt, drowned, all gone. Our people, our community… *Gone!*'

The room hummed, buzzed. Grief had turned to anger — a force, the next speaker knew, that could be harnessed, captured, utilized.

A community elder held two palms aloft, an appeal for calm, before his sombre introduction to a special guest, a man who had dropped everything to rush here from Ohio. 'Head of the American National Party — some say the next resident of the White House — Senator Abel Schultz.'

Polite applause rattled in expectation.

If there was one thing clear it was that Senator Schultz knew how to work a room. He entered at the back, such that news of his advent rippled forward, adding a choreographed sense of theatre as heads spun this way and that.

He was a man of modest height, around 50 years old, with craggy features and piercing blue eyes, oiled hair only slightly greying. He took his time, moving down the aisle, clutching hands, laying palms.

As he mounted the steps, slowly, deliberately, a spotlight fizzed into life. It cut through the fug of tobacco smoke to cast the Senator in a pool of light, throwing his silhouette onto the velvet curtain behind. The pastor blinked in the glare. The President of the Bund hoisted his papers to shield his eyes.

'Ladies and gentlemen, *Damen und Herren*,' Senator Schultz commenced. 'I have the dubious distinction of having grown up during the Civil War, the greatest tragedy ever to have befallen our great nation.'

He took his time, his tone flint-sharp, piercing… stabbing out every syllable, his enunciation crystal clear.

'But in the 40 years that have ensued, a time of peace and prosperity, not one calamity – the Great Chicago Fire… the Galveston Hurricane… or the Johnstown Flood – has touched me, touched this *community*, in the way that this… this damnation on the East River that has come to pass.'

There were shouts of 'Amen', shouts of '*Ja*'.

'But, my friends, do you know what is just as tragic? It's that not two days into this abomination – *two days* – while bodies are still being identified in the morgue on the Charities Pier, heartless landlords have already begun exploiting this community's loss to further their own ends, seizing property, raising rents. I say shame on them. SHAME!'

He leaned forward.

'Here in Manhattan, Little Germany, our own dear *Kleindeutschland*, was already being squeezed by the Italians, the Irish, the Chinese and the Russians. Alas, this… this "*Slocum* Disaster", marks the day that our walls were breached…'

He hung his head, shaking it in disbelief.

'…breached *terminally.*'

A smattering of handclaps followed. A recognition. There were words exchanged between neighbours. Schultz had tapped into something.

'A curious thing. But for one vote in Congress in 1776, the language of our United States would have been German, not English. Did you *know* that?'

Some nodded, some shook.

'Did you know, too, my friends, that, after Berlin and Vienna, New York is the third-largest German city on God's earth? *The third largest.*'

He quickened the pace and scanned the room.

'Not coolies or navvies. Not scroungers or drunks. No. *No!* Just humble, honest, hard-working folk who settled here in pursuit of a better life… a dream.'

He waved a hand towards them.

'Tradespeople, *family* people…'

The hand picked out faces at random, as if he knew them personally.

'…engineers, architects, machinists, boilermakers, road-builders, teachers, tailors, bakers, shoemakers, dressmakers…'

The applause came back stronger.

'Fathers, mothers, sisters, brothers…'

He thrust his index finger skyward, as if channelling a higher power.

'The founders, the forgers of this young nation. *Model Americans*.'

He nodded theatrically at his own truth, puffing out his chest, looping thumbs into lapels. He left the sanctity of the lectern, pacing, turning on cue as the rehearsed thoughts struck him.

'Oh yes. Right across the land, my friends. In New York City as it is in the mighty Steel Belt which stretches clear through the Middle West – in Pittsburgh, in Scranton; in Cleveland, in Toledo; in Fort Wayne, in Chicago, in Milwaukee – where the hands and brains of three million German-born sons, German-born daughters, stoke the industry, the *engine*, which drives America...'

He quickened the pace.

'...a land whose very liberty was preserved by the bravery and courage of German–American soldiers – men who fought for the Union Army in that great and terrible war of which I just spoke – 200,000 warriors...'

The clapping grew furious, rapid.

'...heroes of the 9th Ohio, the 74th Pennsylvania, the 9th Wisconsin... and, of course, *the 52nd New York*!'

An old man with a chest full of campaign medals rose to his feet, tears streaming down his cheeks. There were shouts of encouragement. Schultz was working up a head of steam, forgoing his soliloquy to bark his sentences in stentorian tones.

'And what thanks do we get? Not that we ever asked for any... *None*.'

His face was a nickelodeon star's rictus of exaggerated disgust.

'NONE!'

He slammed his hand down hard on the lectern's wood.

'Our *Volk* are being demonized. Hell, and if you'll forgive such a word, Pastor...'

He turned for effect. The pastor nodded his pardon. There was a release of guilty laughter.

'...even Anglicizing their names – Schmidt to Smith, Braun to Brown – ashamed of their heritage! *Ashamed* of our Old Country. That one across the water...'

He pointed to the distance. It might as well have been to somewhere across the street.

'...ashamed because the US Government, be it Republican or Democrat, has no time for people of German stock, wherever they may be.'

The nodding continued.

'Too busy sucking up to Great Britain,' he mused, before shifting again to the shake of incredulity. 'Whose yoke crushed this land till we threw it off in pursuit of our own manifest destiny.'

He threw his palms up in utter disbelief.

'And to the decadent *French*...'

He nearly spat the word out.

'And the casualties in all this? People like *you*. The people grieving in this very room.'

The jerk of his head made his hair flop forward. He smoothed it back.

'The same people who will, sure as damnit, have to suffer in silence through any so-called "inquiry" into this travesty, be it State or Federal, while the perpetrators of this crime, aided and abetted, wriggle themselves off the hook with a litany of cockamamie excuses.'

He took his time.

'But we say "No"!'

He waved both fists in the air, roaring for all he was worth.

'NO!'

He stood still now, waiting for calm, waiting for the punch.

'I want to remind those men in New York City Hall...'

The pointing resumed.

'...those men in Washington, of words decreed by another, a man far wiser than I...'

He issued a smile of self-deprecation, his head bowed, humble.

'...*that all men are created equal.*'

There came further murmuring, nods of approval. He tripped round the acclaim with staccato jabs, finding gaps to punctuate the applause.

'We Germans will not be bowed. We will fight back! And seeking justice for *this* catastrophe, this slaughter, this *massacre* aboard the accursed *General Slocum*... This will be our beginning!'

He was straining to be heard now, just the way he wanted it.

'*Your* loved ones. *Our* loved ones. As God is my witness, I make a solemn promise to you this day. WE WILL NOT LET THEM DIE IN VAIN!'

The room was on its feet – every last person cheering, hollering, exhorting.

At the side of the stage, the man in the expensive grey suit nodded discreetly at the triumphant Senator, arms thrown wide, basking in his glory. With his angular Amerindian accomplice in tow, he slipped out through the stage door into the night.

Chapter 2

Ingo Finch leaned on the rail and pinged the stub of a Navy Cut out into the breeze. From up high on deck he watched it dance downwards, not sure if it ever hit the water.

He gazed up again.

'I didn't know she was going to be blue.'

'I'd say more *green*,' replied the gent next to him.

'In all the pictures, the illustrations, she's a copper colour.'

The man, a New Yorker, smiled.

'When the French gave it to us – a gift – it was just that, copper... *literally* made of copper. But the air, it oxidises, creates a coating... a *patina*.'

He dragged on his cigarette and spluttered a bit.

'They were gonna paint the thing, restore it to the original colour, but folks kinda got to likin' the lady the way she is.'

'Blue,' teased Finch.

'Bluey green, I'll give you that,' the man chuckled. 'One thing's for sure, you can't miss her.'

He coughed again, harsh.

'Holy Moly, your English smokes!'

The Statue of Liberty continued to slide past on the port side, staring her dull-eyed stare, waving her golden torch to all incomers – *'your tired, your poor, your huddled masses yearning to breathe free'* as the inscription put it – most of whom, observed Finch, seemed to be straggled in miserable-looking queues on Ellis Island just behind her.

The wind kicked up and the American clutched his homburg.

'What's your name, friend?' he asked.

'Collins,' replied Finch. 'Bradley Collins.'

They shook.

'Glad to make your acquaintance, Mr Collins.'

There was a swell of excitement, the decks packed, the air peppered with the audible gasps of those viewing the Manhattan skyline for the very first time. Finch was not immune. Superficially, it was just as he'd seen in the photographs, in the moving picture shows and imagined in every novel – so familiar it felt like greeting an old friend. But the majesty, the sheer scale eclipsed all expectation – from the towers springing up around Battery Park to the turrets of Midtown and the cranes and skeletal steel of visions still in progress.

The American pointed.

'The Flatiron Building, see it? Damned near 300 feet high. I tell you, Mr Collins, you think you've seen it all, then, sure enough, the city goes and outdoes itself.'

To the right lay Governor's Island, the Brooklyn Navy Yard and the massive suspension bridges – parts still under construction – that spanned the East River. To the west of Manhattan lay the Hudson.

Where the Thames was an artery, the Hudson was like a giant arm, mused Finch – gently crooked around the island, shielding it from the Atlantic. On it, the river traffic ploughed up and down – the freighters, the steamers, the barges. Across the Hudson's lanes cut the ferries, bobbing on the wakes, plying their trade between the city and New Jersey, both shores an endless row of docks, wharves and jetties.

In early spring, the air was crisp but the sky bright blue. As they sailed upriver, closer to the detail, Finch watched the steam rise from seemingly every flue and chimney stack of every single building in the city, swirling past the barrelled water towers teetering on struts way up on the rooftops.

The ship had been slowing since the Narrows and gave a sharp, deafening blast on the horn, which elicited a tangible fairground thrill. The black smoke from the twin funnels began wafting erratically, confused by the change in wind and direction.

As it executed its turn, the ship started to roll, a burst of spray slapping up and catching them all unawares, something which only added to the exhilaration. You could feel the turbines dropping in pitch, the hiss of the wash at the stern. Gulls squawked over it, scanning for titbits. The pilot's cutter appeared and a gaggle of blunt-nosed tugs grunted out, belching soot, ready to shepherd *RMS Baltic* to the White Star quays.

–

Finch edged down the first-class gangway, gripping the rope more tightly than he had imagined. The riot of sounds, colours and smells hit him smack in the face. His legs weren't yet steady and his left knee was always a weakness. After nearly eight days at sea, he had been warned it would take time to recover his land legs. The sensation reminded him of his first ocean voyage, some six years ago now, when he sailed from Southampton to Cape Town.

Six years…? *Jesus.*

The White Star quays were bespoke – three large docks to accommodate the never-ending expansion in the size of the vessels. The *Baltic* was, currently, the world's biggest ocean liner. But between the White Star Line and its rival Cunard, whose quays were right next door, size and speed seemed mere records to be broken – and broken frequently. Throw in Manhattan's 'skyscrapers', thought Finch, and the Western World seemed engaged in some internecine trouser-dropping, countries contesting the prodigiousness, the prowess, of their respective manhoods.

Huge red-brick buildings lined the quays. Railway tracks ran across the cobbles to the yards beyond where mounds of coal and stacked crates for the outbound passages were being marshalled by teams of longshoremen.

Below was a sizeable number of excited locals, there to receive home their loved ones – waving handkerchiefs, hollering up names. They were for second class or steerage, knew Finch – they would have to wait. Behind them on the road purred the limousines of the first-class passengers – himself among their number – all feigning nonchalance at global travel, and whose expensive tickets came with the privilege of disembarking ahead of the hoi polloi.

Despite the furs, silks and fineries of the VIPs, there was still the grubby business of passports to deal with. Finch produced his dark blue British one and took his place in the queue while uppity customs officers proceeded with a sadistic slowness in applying their stamps, causing the patriarchs and matriarchs to mutter.

In the high-ceilinged customs hall, hung with a huge Stars and Stripes flag, the chatter echoed, the city lying tantalizingly beyond the far open doors.

'Collins… Mr Collins!'

Finch hadn't fully adjusted to his new name. It took him a moment.

'Mr Collins,' it went again.

Standing off to the side, a thin man in a brown suit was beckoning him.

Finch gestured that he had yet to clear immigration, but 'brown suit' shook his head at the absurdity of the notion.

There was no handshake, no smile. He had a pinched face, a sharp nose.

'National Bureau of Criminal Identification,' he said and discreetly flashed a shiny agency badge. A customs official waved them both through.

Added the man, matter-of-fact: 'We got your luggage taken care of.'

He led Finch out into the late-morning sunshine. Passengers and goods carts bustled round the ticket offices for the Troy Line and Central Railroad ferry over to New Jersey. An assignment of timber set for the South-west service to Jacksonville, Florida, was being loaded. A saloon across the road boasted a tempting sign proclaiming the merits of its cold 'lager beer'.

There were other vessels moored – a paddle steamer, a smaller passenger ship and still some grand sailing ships, clippers, whose days, Finch fancied, must surely be numbered. He cast an eye back at the good old *Baltic*, his recent home, and wondered when he would be boarding for his return.

The man uttered a curt, insincere enquiry as to the comfort of 'Mr Collins's' voyage, though didn't listen to the answers, then steered him towards a black open automobile waiting at the far kerb, driver standing next to it, a squat man who avoided eye contact.

'Hop in,' said the agent.

'Where are we headed?'

'No need to be suspicious. To your hotel, Mr Collins. Not far. And don't worry, the Bureau's really pushed the boat out...'

Did Finch detect a faint smile?

'...in a manner of speaking.'

The name on the radiator grille said 'Cadillac'. It was sizeable and, Finch noted, well-sprung. The driver wound the engine with a hand crank. It coughed into life and he climbed behind the wheel. He released the handbrake lever and they turned inland, picking up Tenth Avenue, heading north.

Finch had had ample time at sea to study the maps and guides; to familiarize himself with the layout of the city; but he hadn't bargained for its sheer assault on the senses, from the laundry flapping from the tenements on high, all the way down to the street-corner hawkers with their handcarts of roasted peanuts and pretzels.

The further they penetrated, the greater the noise, the greater the colour, the whole of Midtown coming across like one giant billboard – huge signs for *Coca-Cola*, *Kellogg's Toasted Corn Flakes*, *Palmolive Soap* and *Folger's Golden Gate Coffee*. New York seemed as riotous as London, but in concentrated form, everything crammed onto the bottom end of a not especially big island.

Like London, the majority of the traffic was still horse-drawn, but there were red electric trolley buses ploughing up and down and quite a few motor cars, their horns honking more for the hell of it than for anything in particular. Just like London, at the intersections, white-gloved policemen waved arms and blew shrill whistles, more in hope than expectation. The uniforms and domed helmets were not unlike that of a British bobby, but bigger, such that each police constable, down to his big copper buttons, seemed like a boy dressed up in his father's clothing.

About 50 yards back, Finch noticed, was a silver automobile, not dissimilar to their own, which slalomed in and out of the traffic in their wake. The agent gave it a glance, tapped his driver on the shoulder, who then appeared to deviate off the designated route. They zigzagged north, past cigar stores, knife sharpeners, Italian barbershops, delivery boys scurrying hither and thither, and firehouses with bright red shiny engines.

On the broad avenues it was sunny, even warm. On some of the cross streets, in the shade, there was still ice – dirty ice – like it had sat there all winter.

They took a right on 42nd Street, heading east, where the 'mom and pop' stores gave way to oyster bars and chop houses as they moved up to cross Broadway. Finch tried to suppress a thrill at just reading the names on the street signs. To the south, a few blocks down, sat the new Palladian edifice of Macy's department store, which dwarfed anything back home on Oxford Street. He noticed the silver car again, just hanging back.

They turned up through Times Square with the famous tall newspaper headquarters at the far end. The area was wall-to-wall with theatres.

'The Great White Way, Mr Collins… Because of all the lights.'

'The lights aren't on.'

'They will be.'

Huge marquees jostled and vied for the public's attention – a matinee for *Who Goes There?* at the Princess Theatre; Ethel Barrymore playing Ibsen at the Lyceum; a production of *Twelfth Night* at the Knickerbocker.

Finch wondered whether the Bard could have envisaged anything like this. Or, for that matter, Robert Louis Stevenson. Outside the New Amsterdam, two men trudged up and down wearing sandwich boards – one dressed as a city gent, the other with fiendish fur and fangs, extolling the dramatic transformation of the new hit show, *Dr Jekyll and Mr Hyde*.

They headed up Seventh Avenue towards the grand Carnegie Hall, the road unfolding onto the open land of Central Park, then turned right along Central Park South where the sightseeing buggies queued for holidaying punters, the aroma of idling horse dung suggesting that business was seasonally slack. There was clearly money along the park's edge – every apartment building, every hotel, adorned with gilded decor.

At the eastern end of the street, scaffolding framed the huge, near-complete Plaza Hotel, the air rent with the *rat-a-tat-tat* of pneumatic-driven jackhammers billowing clouds of dust. Across the corner junction rose the slender structure of an apartment hotel, a green awning with gold lettering proclaiming, 'The New Netherland'.

'Here,' instructed the agent and the car came to a halt.

He gestured up and indicated for Finch to alight.

The silver automobile slowed past them, then accelerated off. The badge on the trunk said 'Buick'. There were two men riding in it, but beneath their baggy caps and goggles, they were anonymous.

'I'm not being funny,' spluttered Finch, 'but were we…?'

'…being *followed*?' said the man. 'The big surprise would be if we *weren't*, Mr Collins. You're a stranger in town – a lone-travelling "businessman" – people want to know *what* business. We got the mobs – Italian, Irish, the Jews; we got the socialists, the communists, the anarchists; all of them looking for leverage. You've had people checking you out for a week at sea. New York City's a big town, but it's also a small town.'

'Should I be concerned?'

'Just a welcome wagon,' he said. 'Someone lettin' you know that *they* know. Believe me, they meant harm, they wouldn'a showed themselves.'

He nodded again at the hotel.

'Like I say, your bags will be along soon.'

Finch slid across the leather and eased down onto the sidewalk.

'One more thing, Mr Collins. Listen good. You're to make a rendezvous with a colleague of mine, a fellow who will look after you from this point on. You're to meet him at 1.52 p.m. precisely, Columbus Circle.'

'That's pretty specific.'

'I don't make the rules.'

'Columbus Circle? Where's th—?'

'You'll figure it out.'

Finch sighed.

'What's your name?'

'I don't have a name.'

'What's *his* name, the one I'm meeting?'

The agent shrugged and tapped the driver on the shoulder. The engine revved and they pulled out into the traffic.

A liveried porter wandered over, all top hat and tails. He seemed disappointed at Finch's lack of luggage.

'This way, sir,' he said.

Chapter 3

The building stood tall on St Mark's Place. With its Renaissance revival adornments and mansard roof, it was conspicuous among the row of town houses – a little piece of *Mitteleuropa* on the Lower East Side. Home of the German–American Shooting Society, its facade was dominated by an imposing terracotta emblem – of crossed rifles, a target and eagle wings. Underneath ran a motto, '*Einigkeit macht stark*' ('Unity makes strength') – a threat, mused Sammy Proctor, as much as an imploration.

By day, the *clack-clack-clack* of air guns, BB pistols and .22-calibre weapons issued through open windows. With its gymnasium and punchbags, there was an added smack of glove on leather. The club exuded a disciplined virility in a part of town that was uniquely devoid of evidence of misspent adolescence.

By night, and by contrast, the place betrayed a distinct Grimm menace. Sammy had taken extra care as he jemmied open the fifth-floor window and began his descent – treading softly, careful not to ping any stray bullet casing across the parquet floor. He was drawn all the while to the incessant, curious humming, a low resonant chant of human voices, male voices, emanating from deep within the bowels of the building.

He had heard rumours of the strange comings and goings in the dead of night – of flickering lights, of furtive entries and exits via the basement. There had been whispers… of events within… of weird things… *very* weird things…

Sammy pressed his face against the ornate iron grille of the air duct. Whilst he could not yet divine the source of the strange cantillation, what did lie before him certainly aroused his interest – the subterranean changing room where, under dull electric light bulbs, members of the St Mark's Youth League were stripping to their underwear.

Not yet 20 years old himself, Sammy could not deny a certain prurient interest in a score of hard-bodied young men. It had been the reason behind his sessions with the psychiatrist; behind the searing pain of the electro-convulsive therapy that still affected his speech and made him appear slow – *dim* to others.

Despite his mother's efforts to inveigle Sammy into the company of society debutantes, even being dragged by an uncle to a house of ill-repute to see if the ladies there might 'fire up the engines', the forbidden impulses remained.

For over a month, he'd been venturing Downtown – sitting on a stoop or mooching in an alleyway, close to the waft of sweat, oil and cordite. Sammy knew enough of the layout to seek out the ventilation shafts and had located the horizontal duct behind the ground-floor wall – its dimensions as tight as a coffin's, forcing him to shuffle his slight frame along on his elbows.

He watched as the lads wisecracked and jostled and flicked each other with wound towels. Yet, the boasts of sporting and sexual prowess, it was all just gallows humour. As they arranged themselves on the benches, they too could not ignore the ongoing resonant hum. It was coming from somewhere close… very close.

The door opened, then slammed shut, giving the boys a start. Two men stood before them. Sammy shuffled, rapt. They were dressed in full-length velvet robes of forest green – on the left breast, woven in gold, a sort of broken Maltese cross. Their hoods were pulled down over bowed heads, obscuring their faces – sacerdotal, like monks…

Sammy watched as the boys stopped and stood to attention.

Sure that he was commanding the room, the first man spoke deeply and methodically, at pains to be crystal clear in his instruction, never once revealing his face in full, affording only occasional glimpses of his mouth or the tip of his nose.

'If none of you has the stomach for what is about to happen,' he warned, 'he must leave now.'

Sammy watched as the youths cast furtive sideways glances, but none demurred.

'Very well,' he said, and pointed to a trestle table, upon which lay folded a pile of similar robes.

There was a flail of limbs as they wrestled them over their heads.

'Like *this*,' corrected the second man and showed them how to tie the braided gold cord around the waist. The detail was specific. Then they lined up, standing to attention like soldiers. Once inspected, they were told to sit back down.

Sammy twisted in his vantage point.

'Here…'

The second man produced a goblet of sorts – medieval-looking, wooden with gold rivets – and poured a cloudy liquid into it from a copper jug.

He handed it to the first youth.

'Three long sips. Pass it on.'

The youth did as he was told. The next one did the same.

Sammy felt a pang of cramp in his left calf and fought to stretch his leg.

'It goes without saying,' said the first man, 'that what you are about to witness tonight shall remain privileged. Never to be discussed. Not even amongst yourselves. Not a word. This instruction shall come only once.'

There were nods.

'It has been made patently clear to all of you of the penalty, the *ultimate* sanction… We have eyes and ears.'

They nodded again.

'Very well.'

The second man cast an eye to a clock on the wall. It was just before two in the morning.

'Another minute while it takes effect.'

The cramp had not subsided. Sammy stretched his leg again but his foot connected with a drainage pipe, giving a sudden metallic clang.

He froze.

It was not loud, but enough for the first man to prick up his ears.

Sammy clamped his hand to his mouth. He pulled his face back into the darkness. The searing pain in his calf demanded his body correct his alignment. But he remained stock-still.

For a brief moment, the shadowed eyes of the first man were cast up in his direction, unconsciously locked on his. Sammy felt something primal – a terror. His heart thundered. The pulse rapped in his ears.

The second man rushed to the changing-room door. There was a flash at his hip – a glint of metal as he pulled out a pistol. Sammy recognized it – a Luger – sleek, black. The man hurried into the corridor.

Sammy used the commotion to twist for relief. He had taken great care, even entering the duct backwards should he need to effect a quick escape. There was no obvious evidence of his passage through the building. But... the prised-off mesh covering the shaft? Should anyone look closely...

His mind raced. His breath came in sharp pants. There was a foul taste in his mouth.

The shaft he was situated in was linked to a central vertical one, running up the building like a chimney. There were outlets on other floors. If he could *just*...

And then, below, the man returned.

'Rats,' he said. 'Just rats.' And he tucked the Luger away.

Sammy exhaled his relief in instalments.

But... the human voices from elsewhere, locked in that distant chant, were beginning to rise in volume. And there was a smell now, of burning... of evergreen... pine... like Christmas...

He peeked back through the grille. The youths sat glassy-eyed, trance-like. Instructed to rise, they did so wearily. One of them wobbled.

The two robed men arranged them, each youth with a left hand placed on the shoulder of the one in front. Though it was beyond Sammy's field of vision, it seemed another door was opened. There was a sudden blast of incantation and smouldering wood.

To investigate further required Sammy to inch himself backwards, slowly, into the dark and the filth. He heard the scuttle and scrape of rodents. He gritted his teeth and reversed. The further he went, the louder the chanting. He edged his way until he found another grille.

The room below him was large – the gymnasium. And it was crowded, with maybe up to 100 men, all dressed in the same green robes, heads bowed, gently swaying in unison, issuing the resonant mantra.

There was no artificial lighting, only candles, which lined a circle of open space in the centre. At one end was a large chair – roughly hewn from dark wood and, in the middle, an imposing wooden slab, chest high, constructed of the same material. Both were adorned with forest greenery – ferns, pine fronds, mistletoe… There was no mistaking their purpose – a throne and an altar.

A man moved among them swinging an incense holder, wafting more smoke. It was a sign that something was afoot.

Sammy manoeuvred himself to watch the youths from the League ushered in – some of them seemingly more conscious than their fellows and with noticeable glances of consternation being shared by the more alert.

Three loud bangs. The room fell silent.

The blows had come from a wooden staff, a weighty gnarled rod. The man who wielded it wore the same robe, face similarly obscured, but with a V-shaped gold sash that hung about his shoulders. He was stout. Slowly he took his place on the throne, then banged three more times on the ground.

'I command the room to silence,' he boomed.

The man's voice was full, orotund.

'Brothers,' he bellowed. 'We are gathered here once again to invoke the spirits of the ancient land of Thule and avow the quest for purity bequeathed by the elders of the Order of Teutons.'

A call and response ritual followed. It was in German. Sammy couldn't understand. And then came three sharp blows again. The room fell silent – so quiet you could hear the candles flicker. Sammy held his breath.

The man rose off his throne.

'Bring in the traitor!'

Added now was a human whimpering. Directly below Sammy, snivelling, his body bleeding and bruised, was a naked man. Bound at the wrists and ankles by what appeared to be vines of some sort, he was being dragged by two men. The others parted, allowing the poor soul to be flung into the middle, pitched onto his belly.

The man was possibly in his 30s, his slick dark hair dishevelled. And his white, vulnerable flesh was a contusion of welts, cuts and grazes, particularly on his back. There was some muttering in the ranks from the new initiates.

'Silence!' came the roar from the throne.

He turned to the wretch before him.

'This man, prostrate before us, whom we treated like a son, a brother, has chosen to betray us – to strike us low while we are in pain.'

There were nods, murmurings of assent.

'He must atone for his errors.'

The man had a badly injured right leg – possibly broken. His attempt to claw his way to his feet, clutching at the altar, was pathetic. He collapsed back down, groaning, wincing.

Sammy fancied he could smell the man's fear… But it was his own.

On a nod from a subaltern, the man was scooped up and thrust onto the altar, tied so that he lay face up, arms and legs spreadeagled, rendering him utterly exposed. He shrieked when they bound his broken leg. Sammy could see that one eye was completely shut, swollen and black.

There were three more blows with the staff. From behind the throne emerged another man, impossibly tall, his cloak barely big enough to conceal him. The pitiful creature on the altar squirmed and squealed.

From an ornate leather scabbard, the tall man slid out a long, curved knife – shiny and oiled. He raised it high. Upon its rune-etched blade the candlelight glinted. The chanting rose both in pitch and in volume – not controlled now but spontaneous, a lusting…

He turned to the throne and a head was dipped in approval, at which, with one swift arc, the tall man sliced the victim from breastbone to navel.

The act seemed frozen in time, a full second or two before near-black blood started rising up through the slash. The man screamed in agony, still alive, but with his life now spurting away rhythmically from just below the ribcage.

His assaulter turned to salute the room, raising his weapon high. Blood ran down the hilt. The sea of green parted and he extended his hands towards the room's new recruits… bowing, offering up the blade on open palms.

And then it dawned on them – he was inviting them each to add his own handiwork. One of the boys fainted, another vomited.

It was all Sammy could do to stop throwing up himself.

Chapter 4

The North Atlantic — two days before disembarking

Finch lay on his bunk and eyed the opened envelope. He had promised to burn the letter upon reading. That was before he boarded in Liverpool. Technically, the ongoing act of refusal had not just compromised his mission but downright invalidated it. Given the consummate ease with which his controller, Mr Melville, was given to liquidating non-compliant MO3 agents, he considered that he should perhaps take matters more seriously.

Finch poured himself another shot of Talisker in one of the White Star's fine crystal tumblers and lit himself a Navy Cut. He turned the paper in his hand, marvelling all the while at how, in the middle of the Atlantic, he should feel only the slightest motion. The engineers had stabilized the *Baltic* with ingenuity. He wondered if they were of the same opinion down in steerage.

And then he did what he should have done days ago. He grabbed the ashtray and took his lighter to the letter's thin paper. Sure that every last scrap had been cremated, he walked into his bathroom and pulled the chain on the embers. Then he donned his camel-hair coat, turned up his collar and stepped through the thick teak door to the first-class passenger deck.

The cold salt air and a blast of spray shook him out of his reverie. But it was preferable to the stifling steam-driven heat of the interior. On the starboard side he was currently leeward, screened from the whistling wind. He leaned on the wet rail and watched the ocean. How like a landscape it seemed – gentle hillocks and sculpted valleys, mere foothills to the more ominous dark crags on the horizon with their white-capped peaks.

After the daily long lunch (following elevenses, following a cooked breakfast), there were few people about, the first-class clientele having taken to their post-prandial snoozes. It was all so tiresome to Finch – donning a dinner jacket every time he wanted to eat; a constant process of enforced formal dining. Eat and sleep. It was all there was to do in the rarefied air of 'luxury travel'. No wonder the rich grew fat and lazy.

The deck chairs were stacked and tied down, a sign of bad weather ahead. On deck, with the horizon visible, the ship was pitching more than he had felt. He took a stroll regardless, the better to flex his problematic knee. A middle-aged couple bade him a queasy good afternoon. The woman looked like she'd just been sick. If Finch were wearing a hat he would have doffed it, but he knew better by now than to sport one on deck.

Towards the bridge, beneath the telegraph office, was a noticeboard. In the absence of newspapers, the daily bulletins were of interest. Beyond reading H. G. Wells or Jules Verne in his cabin, they were the only diversion – the rest of his time aboard spent stoically ignoring every invitation for a hand of bridge or to sit through the third-rate cabaret acts in the lounge.

All he knew, according to that letter, was that someone on board was supposed to make direct contact. Meanwhile he was to keep up a pretence. He was Mr Bradley Collins of London, an importer/exporter of some unspecified produce.

He thanked his new coat for its deep pockets. He pulled out his whisky bottle, squeaked out the cork and took a generous swig. The latest telegraphs, he noted, had come via St John's, Newfoundland. This was the sixth day at sea. By tomorrow, Wednesday, they would be skirting the eastern seaboard. By Thursday morning they would be in New York.

The pinned notices made for sombre reading. In Russia, the proletariat were in open revolt. The strikes, the civil disorder, had spread even sooner than Melville had predicted. In response, the Imperial cavalry showed no mercy, chopping down protestors at will, signs that this great Russian uprising – or this *stage* of it – was going to be short-lived.

Incredibly, in the ongoing Russo–Japanese War in the Far East, the Russian fleet was still labouring in the Pacific after the long journey from its Baltic base. It had been its passage across the North Sea five months earlier – mistakenly firing upon British fishing trawlers – that had set in train the series of events which had brought Finch here today. If the Tsar's military forces were *that* incompetent, it seemed the old regime *could* ultimately be overthrown. If not this time, then later. Melville had foreseen that, too.

Elsewhere, Morocco was shaping up to be a new crucible of confrontation. The Germans were backing its independence from France, with a pledged royal visit by the Kaiser to underscore the claim. On seemingly every international issue, positions were becoming entrenched: Germany on one side; Britain and France, the Entente

Cordiale, on the other... with a weakened Imperial Russia to be added, *if* it survived.

'Mr Collins?'

It was a steward, a fresh-faced, straight-backed young man, whiffing of health and vitality. Finch tucked away the bottle. He hoped he hadn't seen it.

'Sir,' he added and whipped out a small silver salver, his thumb securing a piece of white card upon it. Finch read it. It was an invitation to dinner this evening, in the Versailles lounge, at the behest of Lady Belinda Brunswick.

Finch was already regretting his stroll.

'Would you like me to respond, sir?'

Finch let out a sigh.

'Very well. Tell Lady Brunswick...'

The steward produced a notepad.

'...that it will be my pleasure. I look forward with great...'

'Great what, sir?'

'Great... *enthusiasm*. Yours sincerely, etc.'

The steward didn't budge.

'Oh, of course...' said Finch and retrieved some pennies.

'Very good, sir,' said the young man and marched off briskly, untroubled by the ship's motion.

Finch wandered back, reaching occasionally for the rail. The canvas awnings of the lifeboats rasped in the breeze. He wondered, in an emergency, whether they could realistically accommodate 3,000-plus passengers and crew.

Above him, the two yellow funnels pumped their smoke into the air. At the stern, the blue ensign flapped furiously. The sky was leaden.

Back in his cabin, Finch ran a bath – salt water but piping hot. He took his dinner suit off the hanger, lay it on the bed, and swore that he would get rid of it at the earliest opportunity.

Then he took another swig of Talisker and wondered why an elderly *grande dame* should have sought him out… particularly as 'Mr Collins' didn't exist.

–

What Finch knew of Lady Brunswick came from the society pages. She was a textbook Dowager Countess, one of that new Anglo-American upper class, a friend of the Astors and the Gettys; one who summered with the Vanderbilts, took Thanksgiving with the Rockefellers, and whose trans-Atlantic status was secured by the dinner parties that continued in transit on liners like the *Baltic*.

The door to the Versailles lounge was opened by a steward dressed unnecessarily in tropical whites, with gloves to match. It could have been a salon lifted from any of Europe's courtly homes – Queen Anne chairs, a chaise longue, bucolic landscapes on the walls, potted palms, a baby grand piano, and a tail-coated young man running through some muted Debussy upon it.

There was a huddle of guests, the hum of polite conversation, though when Lady Brunswick saw Finch she greeted him personally and enthusiastically and pressed a champagne flute into his hand.

'Mr Collins, so *delighted* you could join us.'

She was dressed in widow's black, a long evening dress, offset by an ostrich feather in her blue-rinsed hair and heavy pearls around her neck. She was in her 70s, Finch supposed – short, stoutly built, with a soft, kind face and a pair of lorgnette spectacles, whose stick she wielded with long black velvet gloves.

Finch stooped to kiss her hand. The collar studs dug into his neck.

'The pleasure is all mine, Lady Brunswick.'

He was introduced to the others, a selection of dinner suits and gowns, British and American, whose names he forgot instantly. He wondered whether one of them was his contact.

Lady Brunswick had saved her best guests till last.

'May I introduce Mr Morgan.'

Finch shook his hand. He was a short, bald man with a bulbous nose and a droopy moustache. It was only when she added his initials 'J. P.' that Finch understood the kind of company the fictitious 'Mr Collins' evidently kept.

For the most famous financier in all of America, John Pierpoint Morgan cut a modest figure.

'The new owner of our White Star Line,' added the man next to him.

'Now now, Bruce,' joshed Lady Brunswick and introduced: 'Mr Ismay, the White Star chairman.'

He was a man of around 40 with a mischievous face and handlebar whiskers.

'I've been hearing all about it,' lied Finch.

'Not *too* much I hope,' quipped Morgan. 'You in the shipping business yourself, Mr Collins?'

Finch pulled at his collar. He couldn't remember clothing as uncomfortable. And it was making him sweat.

'Indirectly. You know... importing... exporting...'

'Jolly good,' said Ismay and placed his arm around Finch's shoulder. 'You must tell me more.'

The round dining table was through a set of double doors and laid for ten. Were it not for the chandelier that swayed gently over it, its movement reflected in the mirror over the fireplace, you would never know you were at sea.

Finch found himself honoured with a seat next to Lady Brunswick herself. To his great relief, he was one space removed from the inquisitive Ismay, who tapped on his glass and proposed a toast to his hostess.

The chair to Finch's right was empty, though barely had the first course been served – salmon mousse – than the late arrival was announced. It was the ship's skipper himself, Captain Smith – 'Edward John' as Lady Brunswick called him – who hustled in, still in uniform, carrying with him the cold and tang of the sea. He was greeted with enthusiastic applause and seemed embarrassed by it.

Smith had a bushy white beard with a genial yet pragmatic air about him – one not *of* the social class by whom he was being feted, but indulging its company all the same. In his sing-song Potteries accent, he excused himself in advance should he be called away.

Finch survived dinner – a sublime batch of Maine lobster – by parrying interrogations as to Collins's professional dealings with a faux-dismissive, 'Please, let's not mix business with pleasure,' or variants thereof, a tactic which worked rather well.

Politics and world affairs got their inevitable outing. Mention of the Boer War brought the usual opinions out into the open. Captain Smith recognized Finch's wince of a veteran – even though it was never stated. He discreetly tapped a red-and-blue ribbon on his chest, the Transport Medal. When he confided that he, himself, had been involved in the conflict, running supplies to and from South Africa, Finch warmed to him further.

Ismay, who'd been availing himself of the Bollinger, declared that with J. P. Morgan's investment, White Star would soon be able to announce it was laying down hulls at Harland & Wolff on two new super-liners, whose size would eclipse even *this* vessel. They were to be called *Olympic* and *Titanic*.

He clapped the skipper on the back.

'As fleet commodore, of course, Captain E. J. Smith could have his own pick.'

'Well,' blushed Smith. 'I do say I've got one big command left in me.'

There was still no hint of a contact. But, when it came time for the gentlemen to adjourn for cigars and brandy, with the ladies heading for the lounge, Lady Brunswick laid her hand on Finch's arm.

'Mr Collins, if I might have a word.'

She led him into a smaller parlour, a private room with a pair of high-backed chairs, a roll-top desk… and, eyed Finch, a drinks cabinet.

'Whisky, Mr Collins?'

'Don't mind if I do, ma'am.'

She poked and rattled at the decanters and glasses.

'Talisker, isn't it? Neat?'

'How did you…?'

And then the penny dropped.

Finch smiled and took the tumbler. She poured one for herself.

'Chin-chin,' she said and they clinked glasses.

They sat opposite each other, a small coffee table between them.

'Surprised?' she asked.

'A little.'

'A Grand Dowager. What better entrée into the corridors of power?'

'I can see the logic.'

'Born in England, raised in America, and with a home in both, a foot in either camp... I say, do you have a cigarette?'

He pulled out his Navy Cut, lit one for her – which she inserted into an ebony holder – then one for himself.

'I'm old enough to have worked for the Union intelligence services in the Civil War... to have eavesdropped on the French during Napoleon III's little Mexican adventure. You've met "M", of course.'

'"M"?'

'Mr Melville.'

Finch nodded.

'Believe it or not, I trained the little whippersnapper. And, trust me, he's every bit as ruthless as you think – *more* so. If he knew, for example, that you'd held on to that letter...'

'How did...?'

'Captain Finch – *Doctor* Finch – I know *everything*.'

She gestured towards the door. They didn't have much time.

'I know your history – South Africa... then that business with the Bolsheviks in London...'

'None of it was through choice.'

'*Choice* has nothing to do with this, Captain. You were not selected without good reason.'

Finch sipped his whisky. Not a day had gone by without reflection on his lot. Back in '99 he had been a small-town doctor, one whose sense of duty saw him volunteer for Boer War service in the brand new Royal Army Medical Corps. Until that night, in Cape Town, on leave from the battlefields, when he found himself – entirely unwittingly – embroiled in a case of espionage; ensnared in the machinations of military intelligence.

Last October, having forsworn such activity and long settled back into civilian life in England, trouble had sought him out again, this time on the home front. His involvement had placed him at the mercy of the so-called powers that be, a hostage to their whims. He was now, like it or not, an official MO3 operative.

'So what is it *this* time?' he asked.

Lady Brunswick lifted her lorgnette glasses and looked him up and down, her tone unsympathetic.

'Sarcasm will get you nowhere, Captain. Need I remind you that a typed order for your "termination" still sits in M's filing cabinet. It awaits but a signature.'

She uttered it in the perfunctory manner of a bored employer discussing a contract. Finch, head bowed, studied his cigarette. He said nothing.

'It's the Germans,' she then added.

'Germans?'

'More specifically the German–Americans.'

She cleared her throat.

'You're a reader of newspapers.'

'When they're available.'

'Then you'll be aware there's a movement growing in New York City, indeed across the United States, something neither Britain nor our allies in Washington like very much – what you might call an appeal to "isolationism", an "America First" movement.'

'I'd seen something to that effect. I hadn't appreciated the gravity.'

'Well, that movement... it's building momentum... coalescing. It's found an outlet in a new political group, the American National Party, and it's capitalizing on disaffected working-class voters, especially of the German–American variety, tired of the White House and its newfound imperial ambitions.'

Finch signalled his understanding.

'Don't underestimate the United States. Britannia may rule the waves for the moment but America is fast becoming a crucial player, a new 20th-century Power… alongside, in the East, I might add, the Japanese.'

Finch tugged at his collar.

'Discomfort is a giveaway, Captain Finch,' she tutted. 'For you to succeed, you have to be at ease in your new skin.'

He sat up straight, like an admonished schoolboy.

'Lady Brunswick, I've *never* underestimated the Americans.'

'And so we shouldn't. Since the Spanish–American War, the USA has been expanding, particularly in the Pacific – the Philippines, Guam, annexing Hawaii. As you know, it's now taken over construction of the Panama Canal. If you'll forgive them their frightful habit of assassinating their Presidents…'

She turned wistful.

'Poor Bill McKinley. It's clear his successor, Teddy Roosevelt, now that he's won an election in his own right, has further international designs, even though he's making it all sound so bloody reasonable.'

'You mean, "Speak softly and carry a big stick"? His famous words.'

'Indeed… In fact, he's about to position himself as peace-broker between Russia and Japan in that nasty little war they've been conducting in Manchuria.'

'I didn't know that.'

She tapped her nose.

'Privileged information.'

Finch swirled his glass and studied his drink.

'So, a conservative – *nationalist* party – one operating within the democratic structure? Hardly earth-shattering. Pales compared with some of the stuff going on in Europe.'

She leaned in.

'Listen carefully, Captain. In Europe a war is coming. We all know it. But the last thing *we* need is for the US to be neutral. Worse, to get in bed with the Germans – which is what we believe to be the ulterior motive of the American National Party. There's a growing German–American antipathy towards the Entente Cordiale, and it's that blasted party that's stoking it.'

She opened her handbag and lay a black-and-white photograph on the table. It was of a square-faced, stern-looking man, craggy of features, with slicked-back dark hair.

'Senator Abel Schultz,' she said. 'The National Party's leader, a man with big political ambitions. It is in Britain's interest – our *allies'* interest… the American *establishment's* interest – for his movement to be taken down. The best way to do *that* is to cut the head off the snake…'

She waved the photograph before tucking it away again.

'*This* snake.'

Finch spluttered incredulity.

'You mean by bumping him off?'

'Please, a little sophistication. That would be too obvious. Plus the last thing we want on our hands is a martyr. It would be counterproductive. No, the surest trick is by embarrassing him… by pulling the rug from underneath. And the best way to do *that* is by exposing any illegitimate funding that may be flowing into Schultz's coffers.'

She smiled to herself.

'If there's one thing Americans care about, it's money.'

'The way you're talking, I'm sensing an urgency.'

She exhaled smoke.

'Very perceptive, Captain. Senator Schultz – that ambition of his I mentioned? It's no secret he sees himself one day with his feet under the desk in the Oval Office.'

Finch pulled a face.

'He couldn't win a Presidential election. *Could* he?'

'Probably not, not *yet*. He simply doesn't have the numbers. The Democrats and Republicans should have Capitol Hill locked for the foreseeable future. At least we're *hoping* they do. Though politics is anything but predictable. Third parties have upset the apple cart in recent memory.'

'Plus, the next election's still *way* off. What, three years?'

'Quite, Captain. Conventional analysis had always suggested Schultz would show his hand next spring. And, even then, popping up only as a sideshow.'

'So what's changed?'

She sighed.

'Word is he could declare himself as soon as next week, a surprise announcement. Ridiculously early as you suggest, but with a chance to steal a march on the opposition, well before the mainstream party machinery clicks into gear... You know, grab the spotlight for himself.'

'But if he stands no chance of winning...?'

'Think about it, Captain. A prolonged election campaign – hustings, primaries, mid-terms; conventions, caucuses, town hall meetings... National publicity for his cause, months and months of public discussion on America's priorities and sympathies? It can still do us *enormous* political damage. We simply can't let this man carry on.'

There came a wry smile.

'Which is where *you* come in, Captain Finch.'

'Me?'

'America can't have its security services snooping around, sabotaging its own. Toppling Schultz needs an outsider, a spy – *you*.'

'How on earth am I—?'

'I can tell you no more. All will become clear. Plus, you *owe* us...'

She studied him, her tone cold again.

'And, as an interloper—'

She didn't need to spell it out but did so anyway.

'—you're completely expendable.'

The silence hung. She removed her cigarette from its holder and ground it out in the ashtray.

'If anything goes wrong, you will be disavowed. Here...'

It was a small stack of business cards. On them were printed the name 'Bradley Collins' and a company, 'British Nitrate'.

'My apologies, we should have got them to you sooner. But you did well at dinner.'

He tucked them inside his jacket.

'And you'll need this.'

It was a small red book, cloth-bound, not much bigger than a cigarette packet.

'A pocket Bible?'

'In a manner of speaking.'

43

He flipped through. It was full of columns of numbers and letters, like a schoolboy's logarithm tables.

'A codebook?'

She nodded.

'The instructions within are self-explanatory. You are to cable your movements to an office in Washington DC within each 24-hour period. The office is located inside the British Embassy, staffed by Military Operations, Section 3.'

She raised her spectacles and looked him in the eye.

'I remind you, it is to *us* you are responsible, MO3 – *not* the National Bureau of Criminal Identification, *their* chief security agency – though the Americans will do the best they can for you and brief you further on arrival.'

Beyond the doors there was a sudden excited shout, a commotion.

'You are to use a different telegraph office each time and *never* a telephone. Operators listen in. Fail to do so and you will be assumed dead. Do you understand?'

He indicated that he did. She drained her glass and beamed. The old Lady Brunswick had returned.

'Thank you, Mr Collins.'

She extended her hand for him to ease her up.

'An iceberg,' one of the women was yelping. 'See! Come quick!'

Finch helped Lady Brunswick on with her sable coat. She took his arm and he escorted her outside. The others were already leaning on the rail, glasses still in hand. From second class and steerage, the lower observation decks were filling too, passengers craning excitedly for a glimpse at this natural marvel.

From the bridge, someone swung a spotlight. There, in the distance, shone a great big hunk of white.

Finch took his place next to Captain Smith.

'New York, Mr Collins,' he said. 'You'll like it. It's a great city.'

Chapter 5

The red Ford Model B cruised past the Bohemian and Polish tracts which, just like the Old World, fringed the greater German territory. The car skirted the imposing Germania Bank building, then turned onto Second Avenue, past the Ottendorfer Library and the *Deutsche Poliklinik*, down Avenue B, the 'German Broadway', with its part-covered sidewalk – past the workshops and the stores; past the beer halls and the oyster saloons and the lazy drift of daytime pianola.

In Tompkins Square the car pulled over. The huge Amerindian unfolded himself from behind the wheel and stepped down to open the door for his master.

A cry went up.

'Mr Muller! Look, it's Mr Muller!'

Manfred Muller smoothed down his grey silk suit and straightened his tie. He smiled and waved. He was late 30s, of average height, but in good physical shape, with a tanned face, bright blue eyes and a scar running down his left cheek – 'handsome enough for respectability,' as a female reporter from the *Evening Post* had written (in a clipping framed in his office), 'rugged enough to convey menace.'

It was the local youths who recognized him – the clean-cut, vigorous types you found in the shooting club gymnasium. Not the grime-faced urchins and ragged ne'er-do-wells of the other ethnic quarters. Then others stopped – ordinary folk going about their daily business – shopping, walking, talking.

An excited, middle-aged woman bustled out from Maier's grocery store, a basket of carrots and spring greenery dangling from her elbow.

'Mr Muller,' she cooed. 'Thank you so much, Mr Muller...'

A friend joined her.

'...for all that you've done for us.'

Muller palmed away their salutations with a gesture of modesty, shot his gold cufflinks and reflexively touched the strap on his Cartier watch.

Behind him, his lawyer, Bernie Krank, climbed awkwardly out of the vehicle, his pink baby face accentuated by Muller's contrasting virility. He answered on his boss's behalf, and with a certain camp snideness to go with it.

'Mr Muller is happy to do all he can to help,' he boomed, his plummy round vowels operatically resonant.

Muller stepped over to a florist's wagon and purchased the biggest bunch of gladioli available, generously overpaying in the process, then walked through the gate into the park. There were barely any young children on the rows of swings, he noted... barely any children at all. No mothers, no nannies.

At the milk house, the men waiting for their daily fresh ration stopped queuing and drifted over. Some, noticeably, but not *all*.

Krank huffed and puffed to keep up. He dabbed his brow with a silk handkerchief.

'The League youths will take their names,' he assured his master, nodding to the loyal corner-boys.

There were 20... 30 men now, removing their baggy caps in respect. One of them shuffled up, nervously, not sure if he was at liberty to speak.

'Just wanna say, Mr Muller, sir, me an' the boys... We wanna thank you... Y'know, for lookin' out for us.'

Muller smiled and shook his hand, calfskin glove still in place.

'Well, we're hoping for some good news very soon.'

A roughly hewn stone had been laid in the middle of the park, a memorial to those who had died on the *General Slocum*. It was temporary, Krank reminded onlookers, at such volume that no one might miss it. A permanent marker was being carved, thanks again to the generosity of Mr Muller. They laid the flowers and bowed their heads.

'Who'd-a thunk? Nine months already,' sighed an older man. 'God bless 'em all. God bless *you*, sir. *Gott mit uns*.'

The black-framed portraits in the windows watched on.

'*Gott mit uns*,' repeated Muller.

As Muller returned to the sidewalk, more well-wishers appeared, some wishing their wellness (though none would admit it) with a hint of fear. A mother pressed a toddler into Muller's arms – all golden curls and whirling arms – which he kissed on the forehead and handed back strategically, before the long string of drool touched his sleeve. All the while the Amerindian loitered by the car, not willing to let his perceived freakishness cause alarm.

'Please come, Herr Muller,' urged a waistcoated café owner in a thick Swabian accent, as he stepped out of his shop in a crisp white apron, clips on his sleeves. He had pomaded hair, a lush moustache and bowed in deference, gesturing to his shop door.

He tugged at Muller's forearm with too much familiarity, at which Krank gave a nod and members of the St Mark's Youth League closed in. Muller stayed them. The man simply wanted him to come inside.

'It will be my pleasure, Herr Egeler,' he said.

Krank pointed to his watch, but Muller nodded for them to follow regardless. The door jangled. The patrons put down their drinks, their newspapers, and stood, awestruck. Muller doffed his homburg.

Egeler ushered Muller and Krank into the back room where a private table was set with a red-and-white check tablecloth. He bade a waiter fetch Mr Muller a steaming hot *schwarzer Kaffee*, 'just the way Herr Muller likes it'. He then pressed a thick envelope into Muller's hand.

Like an Atlantic City croupier, Muller indicated that he never touched the money personally. He would rather it be proffered to his lawyer.

'Herr Muller... the *problem*,' the man said, lowering his voice. 'The one with, you know... the *other* gentleman.'

He looked sideways furtively.

'It has...' he whispered, '*gone away*.'

Krank hissed a catty laugh.

'I think it's fair to say the *other gentleman* has gone away.'

There was a sudden, panicked expression on Egeler's face, as if he only now fully comprehended the enormity of the transaction; the Faustian pact that had been struck.

'Business is doing very well. I thank you,' he added, suddenly hollow.

The coffee arrived. Muller sipped politely. The envelope disappeared inside Krank's jacket.

'A pleasure doing business with *you*.'

The waiter returned with a cake box done up in pink wrapping paper and a big red bow.

'Please... for your *lady friend*,' said Egeler and presented it to Muller.

Muller passed it theatrically to Krank. The café owner instantly regretted his use of words... the *implication*. He flustered.

'Sorry, Herr Muller, what I meant was...'

Muller smiled.

'It's okay, Herman. I know what you meant. I'll see that *she* gets it.'

There was an American National Party poster in the shop window. On his way out, Muller noticed it. He turned.

'Senator Schultz will appreciate your support.'

Outside on the sidewalk, a small boy, no more than about eight, approached, offering to 'watch Mr Muller's car'. Muller burst out laughing. He ruffled the kid's hair, then peeled off a $10 bill from his money clip.

'For your mother. You hear?'

'That's more than his family earn in a week,' breathed Krank.

'A family now in *our* pocket.'

Krank led him across the square, towards Schwab's Bier Hall, and they went on in.

The saloon was typical of the neighbourhood – dark, deep brown wood. The bar itself hosted a row of ceramic pumps for its Bavarian beers, on the wall a blackboard boasting snacks of pork and herring, with pickled cucumbers, cabbage and sauerkraut.

Save for three men sitting at a table, their frothing steins of lager half drunk, the place was empty. Muller nodded at the barman and he came out to bolt the door shut.

Two men rose. Their evident leader, meanwhile, remained seated.

'Good day, Manny,' he said.

He was a bald, heavyset man with a sweat-stained collar.

Muller bristled at the familiarity.

'Good day, Councillor Donaghue.'

Donaghue returned to reading a huge menu card. He nibbled on some peanuts.

'They say the food here's terrible,' he said. 'And yet, I just counted, there's over 200 items on the menu...'

He gave a sardonic snort.

'You Krauts – I thought you were a pragmatic people.'

He waved vague introductions at his colleagues.

'Mr Wozniak from the City Planning Department; Mr Bertolini from Finance.'

A square-faced man nodded hello, as did a short, darker man with a centre parting and a swish blue suit.

Muller turned to the barman.

'Franz. Some more drinks for our esteemed guests.'

'Really, it's okay,' said Wozniak, fidgeting.

'Please, gentlemen...' said Muller. 'Sit.'

Donaghue looked over to the bar and prodded at his menu.

'Think I'll try the veal schnitzel,' he yelled. Then to his colleagues, 'Guess that's pretty difficult to fuck up.'

Muller and Krank sat down. Slowly and theatrically, Muller removed and folded away his calfskin gloves.

'So what can I do for you, Councillor Donaghue?'

Donaghue smacked off the salt from his hands. He laughed to himself.

'Gotta hand it to you, Manny. You got a nerve. Union boss hasn't got the stones for a sit-down, so he goes cryin' to Mama. Like *you're* gonna give me something new.'

'Then what do you suggest?'

'What do I *suggest*? I suggest that with your German labour force out of work now for nearly three weeks, you've come crawlin' back to the table to accept our terms.'

'And what terms might *they* be, Mr Donaghue?'

Donaghue sighed with exasperation.

'Don't get cute, Manny. Like I told the union last time – *they* get back to work... only at a dime off the dollar 'cause of all the hold-ups. That ways *they* can put food in some bellies and *I* can get the goddamn Manhattan Bridge finished and according to schedule.'

He sniffed.

'Yeah, I seen them at the milk stand over there, the bread line at Fleischmann's. They can only hold out for so long.'

Wozniak interrupted. He attempted to put it more diplomatically. Donaghue curbed him.

'Then we can walk away from this thing all nicey-nicey. I'm a reasonable man, Manny. I don't hold grudges... Only against shitty food.'

He laughed. His colleagues only pretended to.

Franz the barman came over with the schnitzel and set it before Donaghue who liberally peppered it, carved it with the edge of his fork, and took a bite. He raised his eyebrows in approval.

'Not too bad. I guess when you set your expectations that low...'

Muller watched Donaghue eat for a minute, barely chewing each mouthful before gulping it down, lest it hold up the next one. With his napkin tucked into his collar and the tomato sauce round his mouth, he was the epitome of a slob, a boorish *Untermensch*.

'Okay, if that's the way you see it then that's food for thought,' said Muller. 'A man is entitled to his opinions. But let me tell *you* something, Councillor…'

He waited as Donaghue popped another large piece of veal in his mouth, watched for the Adam's apple to move in a swallowing motion, then brought his palm down hard – *smack!* – on the table. The glasses jumped in the air, beer sloshed everywhere and Donaghue's two stooges recoiled. Donaghue, meanwhile, was stuck still – gagging for air, flapping his arms, with a piece of veal lodged in his throat.

'Yes, let me tell *you* something, you fat fuck. German labour built this city. German labour built the Brooklyn Bridge and the Williamsburg – and it sure as hell *is* going to complete the Manhattan. And on time…'

Donahue wheezed and clutched at his windpipe, ripping at his tie.

'My lawyer here…'

He gestured to Krank.

'…has examined the agreement you have with your contractors – that *you* signed on behalf of the Mayor – the budgets, the deadlines and the penalties for overruns… So the only one doing any "needing" round here is *you*.'

Donaghue's face was turning crimson, his eyes beginning to bulge.

'Please!' urged Wozniak.

Muller raised a palm to stop him. Casually he took out a small cigarillo, wet it between his lips, lit it, then exhaled a cloud of blueish smoke in his adversary's direction.

'And you forgot something else, Councillor. It's called the Chinese Exclusion Act. No coolies for hire. Not any more. Where else you going to find a thousand skilled men, experienced men? And at such short notice? You gonna trust that sort of work to Micks like yourself?'

He blew out more smoke and a note of sarcasm.

'Yeah, sure, the chiefs at Tammany Hall are going to give you an easy ride on *that* one! Not without a substantial kickback. I'd like to see you break *that* news to Big Tim Sullivan.'

Donaghue was making a pained whining sound.

'You gonna trust it to the Polaks...?'

He gestured at Wozniak. Then to Bertolini.

'...to the Wops...?'

He gave an ironic snort.

'...ha. To the *negroes*?'

Donaghue was turning purple.

'So here's what we're gonna do, Councillor. And I want you to listen good. First of all you take my guys back, every single one of them – and you backdate their pay for the three weeks they missed.'

'Water!' screamed Bertolini. 'He needs some water!'

'Then you're going to *double* their rate for the rest of the job. Think of it as a favour.'

'Favour?' floundered Wozniak.

Muller pointed at Donaghue.

'Me saving *his* miserable life.'

'Help!' pleaded Bertolini.

'We got a deal, Councillor? A *deal*?'

'Help, he needs help!'

'What he needs is to *agree*.'

Muller shoved his face right into Donaghue's.

'Do we have an agreement, Councillor?'

Donaghue nodded his head.

Then, Muller went round behind him, delivered a hard kick between the shoulder blades and a piece of veal shot across the table. Donaghue slumped forward, clutching, panting, dribbling.

Muller threw him Krank's silk handkerchief.

'Clean yourself up.'

Added Krank: 'Always a pleasure, gentlemen.'

They stopped by the door. Muller nodded back.

'Sorry, Franz. Looks like our food disagrees with him after all.'

He peeled off several large dollar bills.

'For their lunch... and for *your* inconvenience.'

'Yes sir, Mr Muller, 'ppreciate it.'

The pair emerged into the afternoon sun, all smiles.

Back at the car, the Indian was furtively handing the St Mark's Youth League youths small paper wraps – rectangular folds, no bigger than a cigarette paper. He discussed where to sell them and the price they should charge. They were able, at current manpower, assured one of the youths, to cover the main corners of Greenwich Village. The bohemians were eager customers. They had already figured out where business was brisk.

As Muller approached, the Indian waved the youths away.

To bid farewell, Muller stood on the running board, raising himself up.

'Thank you for your kind words and hospitality,' he told the assembled throng. 'I know you have suffered hard times. But... a piece of good news. I can inform you that a resolution has just been reached with regard to the ongoing labour dispute on the Manhattan Bridge Project. The City has been most generous with its settlement.'

There was a cheer. He waved and turned to get in the vehicle.

'Mr Muller, sir... Mr Muller... There's someone wishes to speak with you.'

There, being helped through, was an old woman hobbling on a stick – stooped, her grey hair matted. Muller swivelled back. As she got close he noticed the cataracts clouding her eyes.

'This is Frau Seherin,' the man escorting her explained. 'She's ninety-four years old.'

Muller stepped down again, bowed and kissed her hand theatrically.

Her voice was so weak, he had to lean in close. She clasped his hand in hers.

'I came to the United States when I was 10 years old – the year 1821,' she told him. 'There have been many changes.'

'I'm sure there have,' said Muller.

'Back then, this had been marshland, drained for a farm... Peter Stuyvesant's old farm. I used to play in the fields right here...'

She pointed across the square. Muller smiled.

'I ran along the Bowery when it was a muddy track... Can you believe that? I watched our *Kleindeutschland* grow—'

She broke off to cough.

'I had two sons fought in the War. My eldest, God rest his soul, he died at Antietam.'

'I'm sorry, ma'am. You have my deepest respect.'

'My other boy, dead now too. 67. An old man by anyone else's measure. Up in Boston. Two years ago. The smallpox epidemic...'

She sighed.

'A parent should never outlive their children.'

'True words, ma'am. True words.'

'And my husband? Gone so long ago I can barely remember his face. Long before photographs. Way back when New York was… Hell, I don't really know *what* it was.'

Muller smiled and patted her forearm.

'You have served our community with duty and sacrifice, Frau Seherin. I thank you. We *all* thank you.'

There was a smattering of polite applause.

'But I can tell you something else, Herr Muller,' she went on. 'I may be blind, but I can *see*.'

She pulled him in close, her trailing voice barely a whisper.

'And I see a man who's gone astray…'

Her hands gripped him tightly.

'*Der Germanenorden*… The Order of Teutons… The ancient ways…' she rasped. 'Do not dishonour the gods.'

Chapter 6

Finch limped along Central Park South, past the incomplete Plaza Hotel, the New York Athletic Club and the Gainsborough Studios artists' building. He thought about a drink and promised himself a reward at the earliest opportunity.

In the street, curiously, steam seeped from the edges of the manholes. He had never seen anything like it. A double-decker motor bus of the Fifth Avenue Coach Company rattled past. On the sidewalks, gentlemen strolled in blazers and boaters, the ladies in long dresses and wide-brimmed hats tied down with chiffon. It was a bright, clear afternoon.

Columbus Circle was just ahead, at the south-western corner of the park, marking the busy intersection between Eighth Avenue and Broadway. It was, essentially, a traffic roundabout, in the midst of which stood a pristine statue of Christopher Columbus set atop a granite column. It had been raised in 1892 to mark the 400th anniversary of the discovery of the New World.

Finch wondered whether 'discovery' was apposite. According to a theory purported by a Danish historian, Vikings had set foot on the North American mainland half a millennium before that. He wondered what the Native Americans made of it all. Hadn't they 'discovered' America when they crossed the Bering Strait?

Around the Columbus statue, the traffic whizzed at breakneck speed – horses and carts, wagons, sportier traps, trolley buses and motor cars. Though a couple of people had made it across the road to the monument, it seemed a perilous undertaking. Instead, Finch chose to sit on a bench on the park side of the street, planting himself next to a man reading a newspaper. He had been sure to synchronize his watch with what the clerk at the front desk assured was spot-on Eastern Standard Time.

He threw a furtive glance at the man's *New York Times*, the 'Gray Lady' of renown. News of Russia was evident – ongoing Tsarist oppression in the wake of a 'Bloody Sunday'. There was something about the island of Crete. Alarm bells were ringing over its self-proclaimed union with Greece. He didn't recognize the names of the belligerents, but evidently New York was not immune to political turmoil either, the greater part of the front page taken up with details of factional political bickering and labour disputes. He would try and learn more.

But there, in bold type, above all, was a headline.

WILL SCHULTZ DECLARE ASSAULT ON HILL?

The dismissively militaristic tone meant the *Times* didn't approve. But for the firebrand Senator from Ohio, *that*, in its own way, was an endorsement.

He waited for the seconds to count down to 1.52. Given the precision, he wondered whether meeting at Columbus Circle meant *literally*, not on the periphery. He decided that he should perhaps try and make it through the traffic. He stood up and moved to the edge of the sidewalk.

'You're taking your life in your hands there, buddy,' came a voice from behind him.

The man had put down his newspaper.

'Mr Collins?'

'Yes.'

He got up and offered his hand.

'Freddie Delgado, NBI.'

'NBI... What happened to the "C"... for "Criminal"?'

He smiled.

'Too much of a mouthful. We prefer "NBI" or just plain old "Bureau".'

Finch shook the hand in greeting.

A car came flying round, its offside tyres clear off the road, the driver gripping the steering wheel for dear life.

'You know, not too long ago it was a free-for-all. Could go round Columbus any way you wanted. The City restored some order by dictating you had to travel in a counter-clockwise direction. But watch...'

The Broadway streetcar clanged along the tracks and proceeded to cut across the circle in a straight line, right through the swirl of traffic. Car brakes screeched, horns blasted, horses bucked, the air was full of invective.

'Guess there's still some figuring out to do.'

Delgado was in his 30s, had a smart blue suit, the clear, darkish skin of someone of Latin descent, and mischievous dark eyes. Finch smiled. He seemed several degrees more genial than the previous agent.

'Can I ask, why 1.52?' Finch asked.

'Well, *one* – my bosses got this notion in their heads that specific timings convey an air of professionalism.'

Finch laughed.

'But *two* – 'cause we really *do* got business to attend to, Mr Collins.'

Delgado dropped his newspaper in a waste bin and turned on his heel.

'Come on.'

He was a brisk walker and Finch struggled to keep up. They proceeded north up Broadway as it cut a diagonal across the street grid till they ended up at the arterial junction with Amsterdam Avenue and 72nd Street, lined with small shops and dime stores.

At the crossroads, Delgado motioned for Finch to halt. On the far corner was a hardware purveyor, pots and pans hanging outside the window. Its side wall had a chimney breast protruding. He told Finch to go over and shield himself behind it.

'What for?'

'You'll see.'

Finch's knee felt like it had a dagger thrust into it. But he complied with Delgado's order and made his actions appear inconspicuous, casually crossing, acting like he was just minding his own business.

Crossing was easy, for the junction had something he had never seen before – traffic signals; four of them mounted on the corners, on poles, a bit like lamp posts. Each had a semaphore sign sticking out of it, currently a green 'go' for the up-down traffic and a red 'stop' for the cross street.

He watched the signals change through several cycles and was amazed, for all the city's apparent chaos, that they were strictly observed. As he waited, he noticed several policemen around the junction, with other men loitering, looking in shop windows or standing around smoking. He had learned enough on his adventures to know that these were plain-clothes officers.

Nods were exchanged between the lawmen. Something was afoot. Finch watched as a policeman opened the maintenance box on one of the traffic signals and, at a given sign, turned all the traffic semaphores to 'stop'. Travelling south on Amsterdam Avenue, a green Mack motor van came to a halt at the head of the queue.

In the blink of an eye, uniformed police officers had surrounded the vehicle, their long Colt revolvers drawn. Along the sidewalk, the plain-clothes officers also pulled weapons and assumed shooting stances.

The driver and front passenger were yanked from their seats, hands raised, and spreadeagled on the tarmac. But that was not the end of it. An officer banged long and hard on the rear door. When no one came out, a colleague shot the lock off.

What happened next took place so quickly that Finch, from his vantage point, could barely compute it all, but in a sudden whirl several men had burst forth from the rear doors, guns blazing. There was an infernal racket. Bullets sprayed everywhere. The grocer's store window shattered, as did others.

While Finch ducked back behind the chimney breast, lead slugs rattled a high-pitched tattoo on the metalware hanging from the shop's awning and puffs of brick dust exploded around him. He pulled himself in even tighter.

And then silence...

For a few seconds the smoke and smell of cordite wafted... and then, too, the unmistakeable aroma of whisky. There were shouts. He heard the word 'clear'. Poking his head out he saw bodies lying on the ground, the miscreants all dead, save the driver and companion who were dragged off and bundled away. All around lay smashed crates and bottles of Scotch, the van's cargo. The smell of liquor was stoking fires within him.

An officer had been hit in the arm and was clutching his bicep, but he was the only apparent casualty on the police side. Finch's old battlefield instincts were to the fore and he felt the urge to step to the man's aid. But there was already an officer on hand with a red cross medical bag who seemed to know what he was doing.

Delgado was now striding over towards Finch. He motioned that they should leave the scene.

'I just wanted you to see that,' he said, 'so you know what's going on in this city.'

'Who were they?'

'The "Cosa Nostra". Italians – *Sicilians* more to the point. Bootleggers and gunrunners. Some call them the "Mafia", a name they hate. They're starting to become a real problem.'

The hardware store owner emerged, shouting like a madman and waving his arms, protesting that the police were reckless and could have got innocent bystanders killed – and who the hell was going to pay for all the damage?

They walked two blocks east to Central Park, over-looked by the lone, massive Dakota Building with its high sharp gables. Once inside the park they found a bench to sit on. Cyclists whizzed past on the path at a furious pace – young, athletic-looking men in sporting sweaters and caps – as if the pedestrian walkways were all part of an enormous velodrome.

'You take your life in your hands in this city, Mr Collins,' he quipped. 'Even in a public park. D'ya cycle at all?'

Finch thought for a moment about his country bicycling back home with Maude, the lady friend he had treated most shabbily. He had not been a gentleman.

'Not much,' he said.

'Lucky.'

'Why?'

'No – *Lucky* – Lucky Strike?'

He was offering Finch a cigarette.

'You want one?'

'Thank you,' said Finch.

Delgado lit them up.

'That's a strange name… for a cigarette.'

Delgado laughed.

'Some say it's 'cause there's marijuana hidden randomly in some of the packs. Which is a crock of horseshit. Officially they're named after the Gold Rush. You know, prospectors hitting the motherlode.'

'I see,' said Finch.

They sat and smoked for a minute. To Finch the cigarette tasted more burnt, more toasted than a Navy Cut, but was not unpleasant. He marvelled at this huge slab of green, right in the middle of the city, with its beech and elm and hornbeams, not to mention its lakes.

'So, Mr Collins, whaddya know?'

Finch exhaled.

'What do I *know*?'

'About your mission? Why you're here?'

'I know what I *need* to know,' said Finch.

Delgado smiled.

'That's a good answer, Mr Collins. You need to be on your guard. Trust no one. Not even me.'

He paused.

'Okay then, let me ask you… How much do you know about the National Bureau of *Criminal* Identification?'

Finch shrugged.

'Then allow me to tell you a thing or two – give you a bit of context – a "heads-up" as we call it here.'

Delgado dragged on his cigarette.

'The Bureau was set up by Teddy Roosevelt in the wake of President McKinley's assassination back in 'o1. Only Roosevelt is no run-of-the-mill Commander-in-Chief. Way before his elevation as a military hero – you know, the cavalryman of Cuba, the famous "rough rider" – Roosevelt was New York's Commissioner of Police, lest we forget.'

He tapped the side of his nose.

'Knows a thing or two about the "Dark Arts", if you get my drift. How the police need to be *policed*…'

He laughed to himself.

'Hell, how politics needs to be *politicized*.'

He leaned back, crossed his right foot onto his left thigh, and exhaled a lungful of smoke skyward.

'You've read the news, Mr Collins, you can see what a mess we're in – the Democrats and Republicans have internal splits; there's either pride or unease, depending on where you sit, on American territorial expansion, our empire-building. The Philippines… Cuba… the incorporation of Hawaii. Congress is already eyeing up Alaska… And who's to stop us?'

Finch nodded along.

'To top it all, we now have the damned American National Party to deal with. We got the same bunch of jerks as you do in London trying to rain on the parade – anarchists… revolutionaries… enemies within… It was an anarchist's bullet that did for McKinley. But *this* lot want to bring the house down wearing suits.'

He turned to look Finch in the eye.

'I heard about what happened with the Russians in London, Mr Collins – the assassination attempt on their ambassador. I don't know what part you played in preventing it specifically. Hell, I don't even know what your real name is – and don't *want* to know either – but I *do* know from my chiefs that you come highly recommended. Sweet as a Georgia peach.'

Delgado looked around.

'And which is why you and I should be careful about being seen together out in the open for too long.'

He stood up and motioned for Finch to do the same, at which two muscular men stepped out behind them. Delgado saw Finch stiffen.

'Our backup, Mr Collins. Been shadowing us the whole time.'

He turned to them.

'You can stand down, boys. Mr Collins and I are going to take a ride Downtown.'

They walked back to the kerb on Central Park West. There was a Ford motor cab waiting at the stand and Delgado commandeered it.

'C'mon. I'll brief you further en route.'

The pair got in behind a burly cabbie, who pulled the vehicle out into the southbound traffic. As they drove, Delgado continued, explaining how the NBI had embellished Collins's cover story, setting up some bogus business venture, assuring certain details should he need to refer to them for legitimacy.

'You're operating outside the jurisdiction of the US Security apparatus,' he reminded him. 'We can advise but can't intervene. I'm really just here to show you the ropes, get you started.'

He repeated what Lady Brunswick had told Finch, that he should answer directly to MO3 via the British Embassy in Washington DC.

'It keeps our hands clean. But it's a reciprocal arrangement that works well – Britain and America sharing intelligence and covering for each other.'

Finch nodded at the driver.

'I thought you told me to be circumspect. You're telling me all this in earshot of a cabbie.'

The man turned. He had a round bearded face and was chewing on a toothpick. He broke out a smile.

'Don't worry,' assured Delgado. 'He's one of ours.'

'Where are we going?' asked Finch.

'You'll see.'

Chapter 7

The cab pulled up on the cobbles of the Meatpacking District. The air was rank with the stench of flesh and death. Amid the shouts of the butchers and the meatpackers, you could hear the squeals of terrorized cattle coming from the slaughterhouses. Finch's mind drifted back to South Africa and the horrors of the field hospitals.

A uniformed police officer stood outside a roll-down warehouse shutter. Delgado flashed him a badge and he opened the door next to it. From the look on the policeman's face, the advent of a suit from the Bureau was not a welcome prospect.

Inside, the floor ran with sluiced blood. But *this* place was empty, as if everyone had been sent home. Delgado led Finch across the sawdust, past the vacant cattle pens and up a wooden staircase. The upstairs meat hall was hung with serried rows of skinned, gutted cow carcasses – pale, greasy and pungent. At the far end was a man in a gabardine overcoat and a trilby. He was in conversation with a police sergeant, fussing over one carcass in particular.

As they closed in, Finch saw that it wasn't a cow but a man. He was hanging upside down in his grubby undergarments, a meat hook clean through his calf muscles. The man's throat bore a deep, dark slit, and he had bled white, the blood having run down his extended arms to congeal in a pool on the floor. His face, hair and arms were caked in it. A drip still hung on a fingertip.

'What we got here, Angus?'

The man in the trilby looked up and nodded a hello. He wore a pair of horn-rim glasses.

'Didn't say his prayers.'

Delgado looked the corpse over.

'Short Tail?'

The man nodded.

'Morello's handiwork.'

Delgado introduced: 'Mr Bradley Collins... the gentleman I was telling you about.'

He turned to Finch.

'This is Deputy Inspector Angus MacLeish.'

'Pleased to meet you, Mr Collins.'

'Likewise, Detective.'

MacLeish asked the sergeant to give them a moment and the cop trudged off towards a delivery chute at the far side of the hall.

'Sorry, Mr Collins. Didn't check first whether you had the stomach for somethin' like this.'

Finch was about to say that he'd been a battlefield surgeon, but stayed himself.

'Think nothing of it.'

The dead man had a strange leer, like his executioner had just told him one hell of a joke.

'Short Tail?' asked Finch.

'Short Tail Gang – Irish,' Delgado explained. 'Lower East Side. Plunder cargo from ships and piers on the East River...'

'Wear these waist-length coats, hence the name,' added MacLeish.

'...'cept this one's a little underdressed.'

That the man was still wearing black socks and elastic suspenders seemed a curious comic signature.

'Morello?' asked Finch.

'Those Sicilians I was talkin' about.'

'From up in East Harlem,' said MacLeish. 'Comin' down here to do this on the Short Tails' doorstep? That's a bold move.'

He sighed.

'Goin' to be trouble. A lot *more* trouble.'

'And *this* Joe?' queried Delgado.

He squatted down for a close-up.

'One of O'Malley's deputies,' said MacLeish.

Delgado stood again and MacLeish pulled hard on a chain. The dead man, socks and all, squeaked along the metal rail to the sergeant across the way, a string of dead cows Pied-Pipering behind.

'Get him to the morgue quick, Sergeant. Before Riis shows up!'

'Who?' asked Finch.

'Jacob Riis. Photographer. Tight with Roosevelt,' said Delgado. 'On a one-man mission to show the world what a shitty, fucked-up city we live in.'

Quipped MacLeish: 'Like nobody had ever noticed.'

The police detective led them back down outside to breathe fresh air. They moved away from the shrieking cattle and the shouting butchers and stood at the end of the street facing the Hudson – not far, Finch recognized, from where his ship had docked only this morning. He could see New Jersey across the water.

'I'm warnin' you, Freddie, this is all off the books,' said MacLeish. 'You understand? NYPD? NBI? Ours is a turf war to put the others in the shade.'

'Wouldn't be calling in a favour if I didn't need it, Angus.'

Finch passed around his cigarettes. Delgado got out his lighter. The men lit up. MacLeish began spluttering.

'Jesus Christ. What the…?'

'Navy Cut,' said Finch. 'English.'

Delgado was struggling too.

'No wonder we gave King George the bum's rush.'

'Bastard Sassenachs…' added MacLeish.

He smiled.

'My own people hail from Scotland, in case you hadn't guessed.'

'You notice how he didn't flash his *own* smokes?' Delgado wisecracked.

'The Highland Clearances… Isle of Skye… My grand-parents.'

Finch assumed the guilt for his forebears. He exhaled a lungful.

'You ever been there?' he asked. 'Scotland?'

'We can't all afford White Star, Mr Collins.'

The remark threw Finch. MacLeish clearly knew more about him than he thought. But if Delgado trusted him…

'So, gentlemen. Why am I here?'

MacLeish glanced at the pocket watch chained to his waistcoat. He mulled over where to begin.

'You know enough by now about Senator Schultz and the American National Party, I take it?'

Finch nodded.

'Maintaining a well-oiled political machine, running a party, it's an expensive business, a huge undertaking, especially when you have to mount a campaign. It requires a lot of funding.'

So far it was all along the lines of Lady Brunswick's briefing.

Said Delgado: 'Officially, Schultz's money comes from legitimate donors – East Coast and Midwestern industrialists mainly, most with German roots. It's all for Congressional show. Keep up the appearance that he's clean. All legit.'

'But the numbers don't add up,' said MacLeish. 'The National Party have gone from a fringe special-interest group to serious political players in less than three years. No party can rise *that* quickly without their funds receiving – how shall we put it? – a bit of a top-up.'

Delgado tapped the side of his nose again, conspiratorially.

'A *big* top-up.'

'You mean *dirty* money.'

The two men nodded.

Said Delgado: 'That way to discredit Schultz? To bring him down? Sure, we go after the money. But that's too broad, too vague. *We* think we've hit upon something specific. Although we've got to act fast – especially, if rumours are true, that Schultz is on the verge of a tilt at the White House.'

MacLeish spoke slowly, choosing his words.

'Look, Mr Collins. I don't know what your part is in all this. And frankly I don't *want* to know. Neither do I care too much about the political angle. That's one for Freddie. I'm a cop. *My* interest lies with organized crime. And I'm fed up to the back teeth. That little pop-gun ambush you just witnessed with Freddie on the Upper West Side? That was nothing. *This* little throat slicing…?'

He shrugged.

'All I can tell you is that it's getting worse – *far* worse. The Irish, the Italians, the Jews… We got Russian gangs, Chinese gangs, too… We got Black gangs, Hispanic gangs. And now…'

'The Germans,' said Delgado.

MacLeish dropped the cigarette and ground it out with his shoe.

'And they're smart, far more organized, more discreet. And the real worry is that it's not just crime for crime's sake or economic gain, for local power or plain old cultural dick-swinging – all the traditional motives – but that it's being channelled into this political movement, just like Freddie says.'

'Chief culprit is a character named Manfred Muller – *Manny* Muller,' Delgado continued. 'Runs an organized crime syndicate out of Little Germany. Muller is a smooth operator, a typical gangster, who presents as a legit businessman, but he's a mean SOB with a real hold over the German–American community.'

MacLeish rubbed the back of his neck.

'And they're particularly vulnerable at the moment.'

'Vulnerable?'

MacLeish chewed over his words.

'You hear of the *Slocum* Disaster?'

'I think so,' said Finch. 'Boating accident…? Lot of people killed. I remember reading something in the papers in England.'

'Too right a lot of people killed,' said Delgado. '1,021 to be precise.'

Finch exhaled a whistle. MacLeish carried on.

'Last June, a pleasure cruise. Mainly women and kids. Off for a day on the water. School's out. Here comes the summer… You know the sort of thing.'

'Only the ship was a death trap,' added Delgado. 'Catches fire. No emergency facilities. Captain's a shit-for-brains. You get the picture...'

'We were pulling bodies out of the East River for a week.'

'Pretty much ripped the heart out of the German community – Little Germany... *Kleindeutschland*. Tight ethnic quarter they'd created round Tompkins Square Park.'

'400 city blocks at its peak,' said MacLeish. 'though much reduced today.'

'Only the ensuing inquiry does them no favours either,' Delgado went on. 'They get no recompense. No real sympathy from City Hall – just a bunch of rivals muscling in to take over businesses and vacant properties. Quite ruthless.'

'So what you got is a community under siege,' said MacLeish. 'Bereaved people, backs to the wall – and with a grievance.'

'I see,' said Finch.

Said Delgado: 'That's where the likes of Muller and Schultz come in. You know, classic power vacuum... Moving in to fill it.'

'Muller, we suspect, is laundering money into Schultz's coffers through a sophisticated illegal operation. So anything someone can do to take *him* down in the process will be much appreciated by me and my department.'

MacLeish reached in his pocket.

'Here...'

He placed a small waxed-paper packet in Finch's hand. He unfolded it. It contained about half a teaspoon's-worth of an off-white powder.

'Last year Congress banned the sale or use of opium. Publisher William Randolph Hearst whipped up the public with his "Yellow Peril" scare and got it taken off the market. Instead we've got *this* to contend with, a new illegal drug – *heroin*. Mix this opiate with liquid acetyl and you can inject it, amongst other methods of consumption. And it's highly addictive. Chloral hydrate? Cannabis indica? Laudanum? Knocks them all into a cocked hat.'

Finch licked his little finger, dabbed it, took a small taste. It was not unlike battlefield morphine.

'Simple law of economics – drive any commodity underground, increase its scarcity and you inflate its value,' said MacLeish. 'And heroin is no different. It's an easily portable, easily disguised product. And, once it's used, it's gone.'

'Plus, with its users hooked and craving for more,' Delgado mused. 'Kinda like what you Brits did in China... the Opium Wars. What you call a captive market.'

He put the packet away.

'No need for truckloads of booze or guns like the other mobs deal in. We're talking about something near invisible. The wealth from the heroin trafficking is then being ploughed into all sorts of legitimate enterprises—'

'Property, foodstuffs, machinery...'

'Heroin's already started showing up in bohemian circles. And, inevitably, the Tenderloin.'

'Tenderloin?'

'The name we use for our red-light district. Just a few blocks north of here. Ladies of the night turning tricks to fuel their drug habit. A vicious cycle.'

Delgado remembered something.

'Tell him about the police lab.'

MacLeish removed his spectacles and gave them a polish.

'Results confirm that the latest batch comes from a strain of opium harvested in the Pacific region, more specifically from Samoa.'

'Which is now a German colony,' Finch acknowledged. 'You mean there could be *wider* implications? Foreign involvement?'

They nodded.

'A narcotics conviction would bring down Muller and, by association, "Honest" Abel,' said Delgado. 'A win for the NYPD, for the NBI – a win for the United States.'

'*And* for any other interested party,' said MacLeish, knowingly. 'Like, for example, speaking purely hypothetically… British MO3.'

MacLeish looked at his watch again. He nodded that he had to get back. They walked with him.

'Our problem,' he said, 'is that we can't figure out how the heroin is being smuggled in. We got the port of New York under intense scrutiny. Yet, every time we raid a consignment of cargo even *remotely* connected with Muller, we turn up nothing. Once into the city, the heroin is being trafficked through middlemen and then dealers, who sell it on the street.'

'How do you *know* the heroin's connected to Muller?'

'Because we employed a little chicanery of our own,' expounded Delgado. 'Some of the dollar bills used in a high-level exchange were marked. They were introduced by an NBI undercover agent called Kimmel who'd worked his way in with Muller's racketeers. It was all the proof we needed. Unfortunately…'

Their heads hung. They didn't have to say it. Kimmel was dead.

'He was a good friend,' related MacLeish, wistfully. 'Ex-NYPD. Worked vice together for many years before he transferred to the Bureau.'

Finch rubbed his chin.

'So this is *personal*?'

MacLeish bristled. He stopped. He looked Finch right in the eye.

'No, Mr Collins. But "personal" is the cherry on top.'

Delgado jumped in.

'We know that Kimmel was onto something else, too, but he never got the chance to reveal it.'

MacLeish turned to go back into the meat hall. Finch extended his hand.

'I'm sorry,' he said. 'That was insensitive of me.'

MacLeish took it.

'Don't mention it. Whatever you're involved in here, you got a tough job on your hands. I wish you luck. Sincerely... And *safety*.'

Their cab arrived. They climbed in behind the NBI driver. Soon the Meatpacking District was behind them.

'It's another reason our service requested the Brits,' said Delgado as they turned through Greenwich Village. 'It's far too delicate for our government to go poking around in German–American affairs. We need an outside agency to prove that the Germans are up to no good on our behalf. To do our dirty work for us. We're even happy to let the Royal Navy swoop in and cut off the contraband.'

Mere blocks from the slaughterhouses, there were streets of elegant town houses and polished lamp posts. It could have been somewhere in Mayfair or Kensington, thought Finch. His mind drifted back to his MO3 masters. On the one hand, all that he had been told today pretty much concurred with what he had been briefed. On the other, it was a proposal without a plan. He felt extraordinarily out of his depth. That horrible word echoed in his head, and not for the first time – that he was 'expendable'.

He changed the subject.

'How do you two know each other, you and MacLeish?'

'Before I got into this game I worked for the Pinkerton Detective Agency. Our "Rogue's Gallery" was the envy of police departments everywhere.'

'Rogue's Gallery?'

'Collection of files – mug shots, case histories… even fingerprints… blood tests. A pioneering detective archive. Let's just say I helped Angus out on occasion. Still scratch each other's backs, time to time. He's a good guy… well liked.'

They passed a toy store. He pointed.

'If not quite as popular as *some*.'

It had the latest line in the window – soft, stuffed bears… 'Teddy Bears.'

'Named after the President. Imagine that, kids are even cuddlin' him. Tell you what, he's got a hell of a team workin' on his so-called "public relations".'

He gestured again.

'Got *these* fellas in his pocket.'

To the south, the towers of 'Newspaper Row' rose up, the tail end of Manhattan dominated by the domed edifice of the Pulitzer Building and the colossal Park Row skyscraper. Ahead lay the latter's vertical rival, the curious triangular Flatiron Building. The landmarks were already aiding Finch's orientation.

As they passed the Flatiron at 23rd Street, the wind whipped in hard, funnelled by the building's aerodynamic shape. There were youths loitering expectantly on the corner. Delgado nodded at them.

'Call it the "'23 Skidoo".'

'The what?'

'Watch.'

Two young women crossed in front of the building. As they did so they gave a spontaneous yelp, suddenly forced to wrestle their skirts down against the updraught. The watching lads wolf-whistled. A copper yelled at the voyeurs to 'skidoo' – to 'beat it'.

Delgado laughed.

'Never short of entertainment in this city, Mr Collins… Speaking of which, you like the fights?'

He registered the blank look.

'*Boxing*… Got tickets to see Jack Johnson tonight. Madison Square Garden. You know, the great negro heavyweight.'

Finch had heard of Johnson all right. There had been great excitement in the press back home about the possibility of him crossing the Atlantic to challenge some of the European champions. His expression had already said 'yes'.

'Then it's all sealed,' said Delgado.

They pulled up outside Finch's hotel.

'Pick you up at eight o'clock.'

'That's a more rounded time.'

Delgado smiled.

'You got a tux?'

'A tux?'

'A tuxedo – a dinner suit?'

Finch had been so sick of being trussed up like a penguin, he'd deliberately left his behind on board the *Baltic*. He shook his head.

'Don't worry, we got your size. We'll send one over.'

Finch waited till Delgado's cab was out of sight, then walked a couple of blocks till he found the Western Union office he had been told about by the bellboy. It was a frustrating exercise but, after a few attempts with the codebook, he managed to send a seemingly gobbledygook message to MO3 in Washington, informing them of his movements and of the new heroin connection.

Then he did something else. He went to a gentlemen's outfitters, bought an off-the-peg jacket, a pair of trousers, a couple of shirts, underwear, socks and a leather Gladstone bag. After stuffing the clothes into it, along with some spare cash, he limped east to Grand Central Station and hired a left-luggage locker, number 774. There he stashed the bag and tucked the key into his wallet. If experience had taught him anything, it was to have an exit strategy.

Back at the hotel, the clerk on the front desk alerted him to a telegram. He stepped aside and read it. It assured him '*your grandmother is well*' – meaning that MO3 were happy with his progress. It was time for his room... for that drinks cabinet.

Up in his suite on the 17th floor, a parcel was waiting – a smart white cardboard tailor's box addressed to '*Mr Bradley Collins, British Nitrate*'. It was the tuxedo. He set it on the table in the living room and pulled the string on the bow, only for the air to be pierced by the shrill ring of the telephone in the bedroom.

He walked back through to answer it.

As he did so he was stunned by an ear-splitting crack and flung to the floor amid a cloud of smoke and dust.

Chapter 8

Finch was slumped in the bedroom chair. A man with a stethoscope had opened his shirt and was listening to his chest. He was holding an index finger upright in front of Finch's eyes and asking him to follow its movement.

'Just dazed,' the man said to someone over his shoulder. 'He's had a shock to the system but he'll be fine. It'll pass.'

'Thanks, Doctor,' came a voice.

'What?' said Finch.

'Guess he's still rattled.'

Finch realized that the 'doctor' was not himself. That was another life. He needed to remember that in order to maintain his cover.

His self-diagnosis told him only this – that his ears were ringing; his vision was a little blurred; he could smell nothing but explosives; and he felt like he had a colossal hangover, which was the cruellest trick of all.

'Here...'

Something was pressed to his lips – a lit cigarette.

'Delgado?'

'Lucky Strike. Figured one of your own would finish you off.'

'What I need is a drink.'

MacLeish was calling from the other room.

'Got here as soon as we heard. You were lucky.'

Finch glanced down. He was dusted black with soot. It had streaked across the bedroom through the doorway from the living room. There was still smoke hanging beneath the ceiling.

Delgado attended to the drinks cabinet. He poured Finch a Scotch.

'Soda?'

'Jesus, *no*.'

Delgado pointed.

'You were face down on the floor right there. Looks like you got out of the way just in time.'

'I remember... the phone...'

It hung off its hook.

MacLeish was hunched over the table, prodding at something. The damage was worse in there.

'The hotel put a call out to the police,' said Delgado, 'but we've managed to keep it off the NYPD record – and ward off the Fire Department – for the *moment*. They're just finding you another room. Will seal this one off. You get a Bureau guard posted from now on.'

'I thought the NBI said I had nothing to worry about?'

'Sorry,' said Delgado. 'Threw us a curveball.'

'A what?'

'Never mind.'

Finch sipped. It was a 'whiskey', with an 'e', a sour mash bourbon. He'd tried some on the boat. Different but not unpleasant. He downed it in a couple of gulps.

'So what the hell *happened*?'

The official doctor was packing away his medical kit. They didn't want to speak in front of him. He took the hint and nodded goodbye.

'You, my friend, were the victim of a bombing,' said MacLeish.

Finch set his glass down, put his hands on the armrests and eased himself to his feet. He wobbled a bit but waved away help. He re-buttoned his shirt.

'More precisely a *crackerjack bomb*,' Delgado continued. 'Small but deadly, relatively quiet, too – a piece of gear designed to cause damage in a limited, confined area. Didn't even blow the windows out, see...'

He gestured. There were cracks in the panes but no breakage.

'It was in a tailor's box.'

Delgado refilled Finch's glass. He picked it up and walked back through. There was a charred mound on the occasional table, some remnants of the box – made of crisp white card – still visible underneath. There was a clear line of blast.

'I pulled the string... the phone rang... I...'

MacLeish indicated that some of the mechanism was still intact.

'The string was the trigger.' He repeated it: 'You were *lucky*.'

The detective had been busy. Some blackened brass remnants were laid out on the dresser – bits of mangled springs and levers. He poked at them with a long pair of tweezers.

'You think this was Muller's people?' asked Finch.

Delgado poured more drinks. It was having the required restorative effect.

'There's a distinct possibility, but even if it *was*, they'll see that it gets blamed on others, whipping up further unrest – another reason we're keeping this under wraps.'

MacLeish held up a cog, bent out of shape, about the size of a silver dollar.

'The thing is, Mr Collins, I've seen a device like this before… Any fool can make a bomb – explosives, a fuse – but this is sophisticated. To engineer something with such *precision*…?'

He arched his eyebrows, bestowing a sort of grudging respect.

Delgado handed MacLeish a drink and raised his own in a 'cheers'. Finch and MacLeish did likewise.

'This is the work of a craftsman, a *professional* bomb-maker. And these fragments here are what you might call a signature. If we can get a handle on the artist…'

'Then we may,' enthused Delgado, 'be able to deter-mine the artist's *patron*.'

He said it with a mock French accent.

MacLeish scooped the pieces into a brown envelope.

'We've done the prelims, Mr Collins. According to the bellboy, the box was delivered to your room around about half past five. Evidently, you were out.'

'Where were you, by the way?' asked Delgado.

'Just wandering. I needed a few bits and pieces…'

He over-embellished, unnecessarily.

'…toiletries and things… Got so used to all the complimentaries on the *Baltic*.'

'They would have watched you come and go,' nodded MacLeish. 'Seized their opportunity… Anyway, the bellboy brought it up, let himself in with the pass key, left it on the table. All regular behaviour. It had been dropped off in reception about ten minutes before that. The desk clerk took it from a courier.'

'You have a description of him?' asked Finch.

'Unfortunately there was quite a bit of activity around then,' sighed Delgado, 'some guests checking in with a lot of luggage all at the same time.'

'I do remember, the lobby was busy.'

'A party from Philadelphia, in town to see a show. An ideal distraction.'

Explained MacLeish: 'The tailor's box was just left on the desk, with the person who put it there already on his way out before the clerk had had a chance to look up. A dark coat is all he can recall.'

'No receipt? No bill?'

'No, but that's not unusual,' said Delgado. 'Not everything is signed for.'

'What we do know is *this*,' said MacLeish. 'Whoever sent it clearly knew that you were expecting a delivery of a tuxedo at around that time. If we rule out the possibility that it was a tailor with a grievance...'

'Although you should never take anything for granted in this town,' quipped Delgado.

Finch managed a laugh.

'...then whoever sent it must have known that it had been ordered on your behalf. We're talking *inside intelligence*.'

'You mean someone from the NBI?'

The two lawmen exchanged a look.

'Not necessarily,' Delgado continued. 'Sure, the NBI set the wheels in motion – just bureaucratic procedure – but the actual order to procure a tux and get it delivered was organized through the NYPD. We're checking backwards now through the sequence of command.'

'It pretty much confirms what we've suspected,' echoed MacLeish, 'that the various mobs have got cops on the payroll.'

'Trust *no one*,' intoned Delgado.

'Maybe they *were* tipped off by someone at the tailor's?' Finch suggested. 'Or the delivery company?'

'We'll look at everything, far-fetched or otherwise. But on previous experience, and given the timeline, my hunch… *our* hunch…'

MacLeish nodded in agreement.

'…it's a cop.'

The detective cleared his throat.

'That said, this bomb is possibly good news.'

'*Good* news?'

'Because, if we can pin this on Muller's crew or find a link in *any* fashion, it also connects Schultz, by association, to terrorist violence. Along with the drugs money there's more than enough there for a Federal prosecutor. We just have to prove it, is all. We've taken statements from the hotel staff, by the way, and will get one from you too, Mr Collins. This will all be recorded. The NBI have just requested that we sit on it for a day or two, till they've smoked out their man.'

'See, you have your uses, pal,' said Delgado, clapping him on the shoulder. 'Which is why I still need to borrow you this evening.'

'In the meantime… regards the bomb-maker…' said MacLeish, patting the envelope. 'There's someone I'd like to ask a few questions of.'

'Who?'

'Guy named Chang – Jimmy Chang.'

There was a knock on the door, the bellboy.

'Package for Mr Collins.'

It was a tailor's box.

'They say lightning never strikes twice,' Delgado jested.

'I'll let you test that theory,' said Finch.

He downed his bourbon and left the room.

Delgado called after him.

'See you at eight.'

MacLeish slipped the boatman his fare before he climbed up onto the jetty. It was a generous incentive but a necessary one, for the detective knew he was operating outside his official remit. He promised the second of the two dollars if the boatman waited to row him back across the East River.

In the moonlight, with its curtain walls and fake battlements, the state penitentiary looked like a medieval castle or a Gothic ruin, some haunted palace out of Edgar Allan Poe. With no road to connect it, Blackwell's Island was an offshore repository for the city's filth – not just the prison but the lunatic asylum, with its hexagonal tower, standing right next door; not to mention the smallpox hospital down on the southern tip. At the north end, a lighthouse winked for attention, like a man desperate to be rescued.

Even Blackwell's Island could not resist the city's unstoppable onward march, enveloping everything in its path. Looming right over the island were the skeletal girders of yet another bridge under construction, which would extend from Manhattan's 59th Street to Queensborough on the other bank. The moonlight flickered through the latticework.

Prisons had a sound and MacLeish was all too familiar with them as his shoes crunched across the gravel to the entrance. At night, after lights out, came the tribal cries – threats of violence… threats of sexual violence – and the chorus was now warming up. But Blackwell's could outdo even that. The smallpox hospital added distant wails and sobs. But eclipsing all came the asylum, with its screams of hysteria and unbridled banshee shrieks. If the inmates weren't genuinely mad on admission, thought MacLeish, then they very soon would be – in whatever establishment they had ended up in on this sorry holm.

By using his NYPD badge there were no questions asked when he entered. He just made sure to distract and avoid signing the visitors' book. He had called on Jimmy Chang enough times over recent years to know exactly where to find him and headed to cell block B.

MacLeish was soon clanging along an upper walkway, accompanied by a guard. The prison was of the penitentiary design with cells like stacked cages – battery-farmed criminals. It was a human zoo... and smelled liked one. The detective stopped, dismissed his escort, waited till he had gone, then shone his flashlight into the gloom. There was a grunt from behind the bars and a hand shielding eyes.

'Hey, man. What the fuck...?'

'Hello, Jimmy.'

There was a rustle and a creak as the man sat up on his bunk.

'MacLeish?'

'Long time no.'

Jimmy Chang's voice came whispered but with force. Even in the coarse American vernacular, his Chinese accent and phrasing were still strong.

'Fuck you. You come here like *this*? The others... they peg me for snitch.'

'Then I'll keep it brief.'

Chang looked worse than the last time he'd seen him. He was gaunt, his skin sallow – even by flashlight – and with dark rings around his eyes. And he'd had his head shaved. Lice.

Chang stood and came towards the bars.

'Here,' said MacLeish, and held out the cog he had retrieved from the bomb mechanism in Finch's room.

The prisoner extended his right hand to take it. He had the third and little fingers missing, gone right down to the knuckle, the flesh a parchment of burn scar tissue.

'What is it?'

MacLeish exhaled and shook his head.

'Jimmy, please... Don't play me for a fool.'

'I lock up here, last two year. You no put this on me.'

'I didn't say I would.'

He pointed at the cog.

'It's from a parcel bomb,' added MacLeish. 'Just like one you knocked up for those bourgeois anarchists you used to hang out with.'

Jimmy Chang turned the cog over a couple of times, feeling its edge.

'I tell you. It nothing to do with me.'

'I know it wasn't *you* who made it, Jimmy. I'm not daft. You've been too busy enjoying yourself in here. But with *this* design? It's a racing cert you know who *did*.'

In the thin beam of light, MacLeish saw the beads of sweat forming on Chang's forehead. Not because of nerves, but from something else.

'You either got a protégé out there, Jimmy... or an admirer. Someone who's seen you working up close. You know what they say, imitation is the sincerest form of flattery.'

'That it, huh? You pump me for information...?'

'C'mon, Jimmy, as popular as you were, that's still a pretty exclusive fan club.'

Chang was getting angry now.

'Fuck you, MacLeish. I no owe you. Way I see it, you owe *me*. Not just you, whole shitty country. America orphan me, Mr MacLeish. Boxer Rebellion. I come here start new life. Coolie on railroads. But America, she treat me like dog. Then I learn something – dynamite, how to blast through rock. So now I got skill. That skill worth somethin'. See, I learn how be good capitalist. Live American Dream.'

He ground out a mocking cackle through stubs of blackened teeth.

'Yeah,' said MacLeish. 'Well, I got somethin's worth somethin' too.'

He pulled out of his pocket the small fold of wax-paper with the heroin in it. He extended his hand. Though when Chang snatched at it, he pulled it back, like a parent taunting a child.

'Usually, you guys in here, it's a case of singin' like a canary... after bartering for a more lenient sentence, a better cell, maybe protection from someone who just pummelled his ass in the washrooms. But you, Jimmy? What I like about you? Your needs are always a little more bespoke. So, we got a deal? You gonna tell me?'

This time, when Chang reached out, MacLeish placed the small fold into his palm.

'Sure. I tell you.'

The mocking cackle came again.

''Cause if you don't, Jimmy... You hear *that*...?'

In the distance through the small window up high, came the screams and wails from the asylum.

'...I will arrange for an immediate transfer next door. I promise.'

Chapter 9

The giant searchlights sweeping the air caused Finch to stop. For a moment he was back on the South African veld, attempting to relieve the siege of Kimberley.

'C'mon,' said Delgado, taking him by the arm.

They proceeded along East 26th Street.

'I know I'm not supposed to ask,' said Delgado. 'But am I wrong in supposing you are army or *ex*-army?'

'Why?'

'Just somethin' about the way a man carries himself – a certain detachment, an economy with movement… with words.'

'Then you'll forgive me if I apply extreme economy to my answer.'

Delgado laughed.

The further they progressed, the more people there were – turning out of every side street, every streetcar, every new subway station, all heading in the same direction. There were the cries of street-corner hawkers, selling peanuts, pretzels, frankfurter sausages in bread buns…'hot dogs'.

Finch was starving. He hadn't eaten since breakfast on the ship. Hunger was an unusual sensation given the gluttony of the past few days. He sated it with a three-cent hot dog which he slathered in a garish yellow mustard and a tomato 'catsup' sauce.

There were glances cast – a 'gent', a tuxedo, chowing down on fare meant for the baggy caps and bowlers.

'Watch the shirt,' warned Delgado as a dollop of sauce dripped.

The NBI man purchased a programme and studied it while Finch ate.

'And you?' Finch asked between mouthfuls. 'Military service?'

'Yes, as it happens. Did my bit for Uncle Sam. From Pinkerton's I was co-opted into the Signals Corps – military intelligence, the Spanish–American War. Like I was sayin' before, of all the Presidents, Teddy Roosevelt's the first one to truly appreciate the value of a secret service. So, afterwards, when he acceded to the White House...'

Half of the sausage had slithered out onto the sidewalk. Finch wiped his face and hands with a napkin. The thing was messy.

'You went with him?'

'Me and a few hundred others. With the McKinley assassination, Pinkerton's turned over its archive to Washington... that Rogue's Gallery I was talkin' about. Resources were pooled under the Department of Justice. Such was the fear of anarchists – a threat which can be ratcheted up or down according to political need, by the way – that the Bureau was born.'

Finch screwed up the paper wrapper and threw it in a trash can.

Said Delgado: 'Course you know why they call it a hot dog, right?'

Finch didn't. Delgado grinned.

''Cause it often has mashed–up canine in it.'

When they turned the corner, the building rose like some transplanted version of the Alhambra palace, grand

and ornate, complete with soaring minaret – an incongruously exquisite venue for two men trying to bash each other's brains in.

And there was the source of those spotlights, being yanked round by their operators, burning into the sky, heralding the impending 'Big Event'. On the concourse, people swelled around the entrance gates. There was a fevered buzz of anticipation.

Back home, Madison Square Garden had become synonymous with the shows of Barnum & Bailey. But, once inside, it was evident that *this* was no less of a circus. The round auditorium was festooned in red, white and blue. Around the perimeter a college marching band strode, blasting out the latest stirring offering from Sousa. And there, in the centre of a baying bear pit of a standing crowd was the circus 'ring' itself – albeit rectangular – 400 square feet of canvas stretched across a raised platform.

In Britain, sport and showbusiness were entirely separate disciplines. In America, they were one. Finch had heard of 'razzamatazz' before, a concept somewhat abstract. *Now* he got it.

'Not every day you get to sit in a private box,' enthused Delgado, surveying the scene like a satisfied Caesar. 'I guess the Bureau's not all bad.'

The box was for four. They even had seats to spare.

Amid the throng of drab day-suits down below, a tuxedo was jostling its way through. It was a struggle. Minders were trying to beat a path for its wearer.

'Actually, there's a good reason the Bureau procured us a box – *three* good reasons. One, we're up here out of harm's way and with a damned good view to boot. Two, we get to use *these* without suspicion...'

He unclipped a pair of opera glasses from beneath the velvet balcony rail and motioned for Finch to do the same, easing back into the shadows to make it less obvious.

'And three?' asked Finch.

'*There*,' said Delgado. 'Lower tier. Five boxes along.'

He followed the line of Delgado's arm. It took a moment to pull focus.

'The man in the grey suit?'

He was middle-aged, fit-looking and tanned with slick dark hair.

'Uh-huh,' went Finch.

When he moved to his left you could see a deep scar on his cheek.

'Allow me to introduce Mr Manfred Muller.'

He was laughing and joking with a pudgy-looking male colleague and an attractive blonde-haired woman.

'Never misses the big fights. Likes to be seen... *and* run an illegal book. The biggest purse tonight? Won't be Johnson's, I can tell you.'

Down below, the sporter of the lone tuxedo hoisted himself up and eased himself between the ropes, blinking into the spotlight. He was handed a megaphone, at which he proceeded to make an inaudible announcement – something about public safety. It elicited a round of jeers. There was already blood on the canvas, Finch noted, courtesy of the undercard.

In their box there had been a courtesy bottle of Tennessee whisky waiting for them – a straight bourbon, Jack Daniel's Old No.7. Delgado poured two glasses. As they toasted each other's health there was a commotion to one side of the auditorium. And then Finch saw it: Johnson's opponent, Jim Jeffords, entering the arena.

'Ya dumb palooka!' taunted Delgado, a man now in his element.

With his trainer and team, Jeffords followed the same path to the ring that the MC had trodden. As entrances went, it was inauspicious. When he neared the centre, there came a cacophony of boos and abuse.

'From California,' asided Delgado. 'Used to fight bare-knuckle.'

A crewman parted the ropes for Jeffords. Someone threw a drink at him and missed. While his team went to their corner and set up the stool, Jeffords, a pasty man in blue trunks, went through some shadow moves – feints and jabs.

And then it went completely dark. The full dramatic entrance had been reserved for another. As a single spot-light picked out the tunnel, all eyes turned.

Jack Johnson was an impressive physical specimen – a shaven-headed black man in a black silk robe, over six feet tall with arms that seemed just as long and hands the size of shovels. At the sight of him, the arena erupted.

'Look at 'im, the magnificent bastard!' yelped Delgado.

He was on his feet, whooping and clapping as much as anybody else.

The spotlights spun and swivelled for effect, turning the great hovering fug of cigarette smoke into a flashing thundercloud. The marching band struck up another tune, though you could barely hear it.

Where Jeffords looked on edge, Johnson exuded a quiet determination. He had a bigger entourage, that was for sure. They ploughed enough space for him to conduct *his* shadow boxing all the way through the crowd and into the ring. Once in, ropes stretched apart for him, the robe was removed to reveal an oiled, muscular torso glinting in the spotlight above his jet-black trunks.

The referee, in shirt sleeves and waistcoat, went through the ritual of the rules and nodded to the ringside judges. To a volley of wolf-whistles, a young woman, in a skirt and tunic fashioned from the Stars and Stripes, walked around the ring carrying a sign saying 'Round 1'.

And, with her exit, the two boxers were touching gloves. If there was a bell, no one but those up close heard it. The next thing you knew, the pugilists were skipping around, testing each other out – a few jabs, a few pokes – both of them experienced enough not to try anything silly this early.

'You know they locked him up once in Texas,' said Delgado.

'Muller?'

'No, *Johnson*…! Galveston, his home town. Prize-fightin's illegal there, see. And of course, they don't take too kindly down there to a negro whuppin' the ass of a white. That said, he'd just been KO-ed by Joe Choynski, who was a big deal at the time, but past his prime… one of his last bouts. So anyway, they throw 'em in a cell together – 28 days – and what does Choynski do… old "Chrysanthemum Joe"? Teaches Johnson everything he knows, that's what. Master and student. And now…? Look at him, the beautiful sonofabitch!'

As if to sign off the opening round, the beautiful sono-fabitch threw Jeffords a sharp left hook to the side of the temple.

'Ha, somethin' to think about!' Delgado mocked. 'Stumblebum!'

As the boxers took their corners, the cheering and hollering transitioned to the buzz of discussion.

'Delgado!'

Someone was calling the NBI agent's name.

'Mr Delgado. I *thought* that was you.'

'Shit.'

In the gradual rake of the auditorium, the shout came from the tier below, a few boxes along, slightly forward. It was a man in his 50s, balding but with a lustrous, thick moustache.

'I say, Mr Delgado!'

'Who is he?' asked Finch.

'Name's Stanford White,' said Delgado. 'Pain in the goddamn ass.'

Delgado winced out a smile and an insincere return.

'Mr White. What a pleasure!'

White made some gesture, about having a drink together… about coming up.

'Shit,' went Delgado again. 'Last thing I wanted is my name bandied about.'

In the ring, the trainers set to work with their buckets and sponges.

'How do you know him?'

'The Pinkerton days. Did some work for him while he was building *this* place.'

Delgado registered the look of confusion.

'*This*… Madison Square Garden… Technically it's his home. Keeps an apartment up on the roof – the penthouse. Designed the Washington Square Arch, too, amongst others. Damnit, Mr Collins… Stanford White… he's the most famous architect in all of the Americas.'

Finch had glimpsed the arch earlier when traversing Fifth Avenue, a great triumphant marble portal – part Parisian, part Ancient Rome… part Hyde Park. It fit with

America's new imperial ambitions. Though he felt stupid for not knowing who White was.

The boxers were out of their corners again.

'Spent most of my time getting *dirt* on White's rivals, *love* rivals, for his interminable lawsuits.'

He touched the side of his nose conspiratorially.

'Let's just say Mr White has a problem keeping it in his pants.'

He pointed.

'See, down there…'

Next to White sat a teenage girl, quite pretty, with long brown ringlets, in a revealing turquoise dress.

'His daughter?'

'His goddamn *lady friend*.'

'Oh.'

'Name's Evelyn Nesbit. Chorus girl, actress, photographer's model… you get the picture.'

'I see.'

'Only it gets worse. She's actually somebody else's *wife*. Some other crazed millionaire. Short fuse. I don't know why White flaunts her so brazenly. Only one way it can possibly go.'

Johnson was at Jeffords again, affording his opponent the courtesy of some body blows, but always nudging him back into the target zone, there to drop him when required.

Finch panned his binoculars over to Muller's box. He seemed of a piece with Stanford White – the bon vivant, enjoying his company, quaffing champagne. Only this time there was someone new – a tall, thin man who, though wearing a dinner suit, had dark skin and long braided hair.

Delgado noted the surprise.

'You just seen the redskin, huh?'

'*Who?*'

The second round was into its third minute. Johnson signed off this time with a sharp jab to the gut, which had Jeffords doubling over.

'Name's Teetonka. A warrior brave. Blackfoot Sioux. Plains Indians. One of the few survivors of Wounded Knee, or so they say. What you might call the strong silent type. Works for Muller as a valet, his muscle, henchman… call it what you will.'

There was a knock on the door. It was Stanford White.

Delgado shook his hand and introduced Finch. The man was drunk to the verge of slurring his words. Delgado sat him down in one of the rear chairs. He clearly needed Delgado's assistance with some private matter he wished to discuss. To Finch's embarrassment – and Delgado's extreme irritation – he entered into a whispered conversation, from which Finch could merely discern Delgado's protest that he 'wasn't in that line of work any more'.

Poor Delgado, thought Finch. All he wanted to do was watch the fight. He was like a kid at Christmas. He tried to save his host by distracting White with a remark about the beauty of the building.

'I say, you're from England,' White garbled. 'New in town?'

'Arrived today.'

'Then, dearest fellow, you'll have come in on the *Baltic*…'

The third round was about to begin. This time it was Delgado who jumped in.

'Really, Stanford, can't you just let our guest enjoy the show?'

Back in the ring, Johnson clearly had the measure of his opponent but wanted, or felt obliged, to put on a performance. He let Jeffords push him back on the ropes and took a defensive stance, gloves over face, forearms over ribs, letting the other man pummel away at his midriff, burning himself out in the process.

'Jesus Christ, Stanford. Not here!'

Finch spun round. To Delgado's exasperation, White had rolled up his sleeve. On his lap was a leather wallet which he had opened to reveal a syringe and a vial of liquid.

'Sorry, old friend. I thought, you know... us boys up here together.'

'Damnit! What the hell in tarnation...?!'

There was a spot of blood on White's forearm, a strap around his bicep. It was too late. He slumped back into his own personal bliss.

Finch's medical instincts got the better of him. He checked his pupils, his pulse.

'He's in the equivalent of a heavily sedated state. Best thing is to just make him comfortable.'

He loosened White's bow tie, the upper studs of the shirt, and eased some room in the cummerbund. Delgado zipped up the syringe and vial in the leather wallet and stowed it in his own pocket.

'Hopefully they'll just think he's drunk,' he said.

Delgado, clearly irked at having his evening's enjoyment compromised, made up for lost ground by turning back and bellowing some boxing combinations – not that Johnson's corner could hear, or would be remotely interested in following them.

Meanwhile Johnson did his own thing and placed his left fist on Jefford's forehead, keeping him at arm's length, causing his adversary to swing away wildly. As he did so, Johnson whirled his right arm like a windmill, signalling that he had complete control, sending the crowd into rapture.

Finch went back to scanning with his binoculars, keen for another look at the strange and exotic Teetonka. He panned along and found him again...

Only this time, Teetonka was staring through binoculars right back at him.

As their gazes locked, he felt a visceral chill.

'Delgado, I think we should...'

There was another knock at the door – an usher in a braided uniform, bearing an envelope, a crisp vellum. Delgado tipped the man, screening White as best he could, and he left.

He opened it. There was a card inside. Finch stood over his shoulder while they read...

> *Dear Gentlemen,*
>   *It is with revulsion that I learn of the unfortunate incident today at the New Netherland Hotel.*
>   *By way of consolation, it would be my pleasure to host your joint company at my establishment, the Bierkeller, following the conclusion of tonight's entertainment. A driver is at your disposal.*
>   *Yours sincerely,*
>   *Manfred Muller*

The boxers came out for round four. They turned back to watch. There was a steely determination on Johnson's face now, like he'd put on enough of a show.

'Muller's got some *cojones*, I'll give him that,' growled Delgado.

Finch lit himself a Navy Cut.

'We can't possibly go along, *can* we?'

'It's a smart place, an after-hours club,' said Delgado. 'Over in Yorkville – actually not far from where the *Slocum* went down. There's a new German quarter springing up there. Sort of like a place of pilgrimage. A lot of the bodies were never recovered… Right across from the Hell Gate.'

'Hell Gate?'

'Look out on the East River and it's as calm as can be, like you could skim a stone to the opposite shore. But there's a confluence of tides and currents swirling underneath – the Atlantic, Long Island Sound and the Harlem River all beatin' the crap out of each other, like these fellas here… A great big whirlpool just waiting to suck the innocent down. I can think of no better metaphor for this crazy, goddamned city.'

Johnson was straight into Jeffords now. It was like the first three rounds counted for nothing.

'You think we should go then… to Muller's club?'

'I mean, why not?' Delgado added. 'Getting up close and personal with the opposition could score some prize intelligence.'

He quoted Sun Tzu, *The Art of War*: 'Know your enemy.'

Finch shrugged. He was unsure.

'And I'm betting you already got sanction from MO3 to go where the night takes you, right?'

Finch didn't need to answer.

'Plus,' he assured, 'I got my guys shadowing us. We'll be safe.'

The crowd roared. Johnson was like lightning. *Left-right, left-right, left-right*… Jeffords wobbled, his legs buckled and he was on the canvas. The referee over-exaggeratedly waved the count down. But there was no getting up. The place went wild.

Delgado clapped Finch on the back.

'Things, my friend, have just taken an interesting turn.'

As they got up to leave there was a faint moan – Stanford White.

'Fuck 'im,' said Delgado. 'They'll find him soon enough.'

As they stepped round White, an arm reached up, caught Finch's lapel and pulled him in close.

'The occult,' White groaned. 'Beware the occult.'

Delgado prised off his hand. He rolled his eyes.

White slumped back.

'Goodnight, Stanford.'

Chapter 10

They were met by the maître d' who ushered them personally to a private booth near the dance floor.

'You know, Mr Collins, I gotta hang out with you more often,' Delgado jested.

The band, a collection of black musicians in purple sequinned tail coats, played with fury and passion, the piano leading the brass through the quickstep of the fashionable new ragtime repertoire.

'It's all the rage,' Delgado explained. 'Comes out of New Orleans originally. Sheet music's flying out of Tin Pan Alley. "Jass", they're calling it.'

The Bierkeller was dark and smoky, illuminated by the dim red lamps on the cabaret tables. It was also crammed, not just with post-fight partygoers, but the cream, apparently, of the social scene, puffing furiously on cigars and chugging back flutes of champagne or with their noses in brandy bowls.

There had been a box of *Romeo y Julieta* waiting for them on their table. Delgado clipped them both a pungent Corona, then lit up.

'Gotta be some perks to running Cuba, right?'

The taste was strong, the exhalation yielding big blue clouds. If you did so without sufficient thrust, Finch discovered, the smoke crawled up and made your eyes water.

Delgado picked out a few of the 'nobs' and 'swells' for Finch's delectation. Some Finch had heard of. There were others – Billy Murray, the singer, or Honus Wagner, the baseball player – over whom Delgado enthused, but their names meant nothing to him.

'Okay, then try this guy for size,' said Delgado.

He singled from the sea of tuxedos and moustaches a man in his sixties being feted and glad-handed.

'Clubber Williams.'

'Who?'

'Formerly Inspector Alexander Williams of the NYPD. The "Tsar of the Tenderloin", as some called him – and some still *do*. Made it his personal beat... a bit *too* personal.'

'Why "Clubber"?'

'You know what he said, when he was accused of using excessive force against perpetrators one time...?'

He affected a preaching tone.

'"There is more law at the end of a policeman's night-stick than in a decision of the Supreme Court..."'

Finch laughed.

'Name kinda stuck... Actually, he did some good, clamped right down on the gangs, the Gas House Gang in particular – mean bastards – but got rumbled in a corruption scandal, as they nearly always do...'

He sighed to himself.

'Temptation, she's a lady who's hard to resist.'

There was a man with a beard leaning over Williams, simultaneously summoning a waitress for more drinks.

'Who's that bending his ear?'

Delgado snorted a certain amount of disdain.

'Name's Trump – Frederick Trump. Bavarian by origin. Supposedly made all his dough in the Klondike Gold Rush. Or so he says. Others claim it was through the brothels he ran there. More money than sense. And I'm talking very little sense indeed.'

Finch's cigar went out. He relit it.

'You see what we're up against, Mr Collins. We got senior police officials here, members of the Mayor's staff, influential dignitaries – all in the pocket of organized crime, no matter how much they may kid themselves that they're not.'

Delgado blew out a big fat smoke ring and watched it rise.

'You see *him*,' he nodded, discreetly. 'Him too... and him over there, the one with the red hair... at the bar?'

Finch nodded.

'More famous names?'

He shook his head.

'*My* guys. NBI. There if we need 'em.'

Finch understood. He drank it all in. The musicians, behind their stands, were working up a head of steam. Some women had dragged their reluctant menfolk onto the dance floor. None seemed versed in the art of dancing to this sort of music, instinctively clinging to their partners when the beat suggested they would be better off letting go.

'And Stanford White. Is he part of this scene?'

'Absolutely,' said Delgado. 'When he can *stand*. The man likes a party, all right. Likes to err on the side of decadence, shall we put it?'

Delgado leaned in.

'You know, at his house, it's claimed, he has some kind of "love dungeon". Has this red velvet swing suspended from the ceiling that his lady friends are pushed back and forth in... without their undergarments... All sorts of erotic "paraphernalia", if you get the picture.'

He elbowed Finch knowingly.

'Mind you, I think he likes to start those rumours himself.'

He waved at someone across the way, trying to attract attention.

'What he said as we left...' asked Finch. 'What did he mean by "the occult"?'

'Search me,' said Delgado. 'Lotta mumbo jumbo. For a smart fellow, he can be apt to spout nonsense. Don't get me wrong, this guy's the *smartest*... Off the scale – I mean, Thomas Edison, George Westinghouse, Nikola Tesla smart. But he's gonna self-destruct, I tell you. Heroin's only one part of it. And you can bet your bottom dollar that if people like him are partaking of that shit then we got something on our hands, a drug that doesn't discriminate... rich... poor. And taking down rich folks is a hell of a lot more difficult, let me tell you. Makes it a lot harder to wage war on it altogether.'

A woman in an evening dress sashayed over. It was silver in colour but dark, like aged metal. She was bearing an ice bucket of champagne. Finch looked up and caught her eye. She was tall, slender, had deep blue eyes beneath well-defined brows and hair that was a shade short of full-on blonde. It was done up in a chignon with a peacock feather sprouting from it, her swan-like neck adorned with more silver. A cluster of diamonds hung from each ear. Below a slender nose was a Cupid's bow of an upper lip, rouged to a deep blackcurrant red.

She set the bucket down, her hands clad in elbow-length velvet gloves. The champagne came in a golden bottle, Cristal.

'Compliments of Mr Muller,' she said, with the slightest of German accents, though without conveying much expression.

Finch knew her right away. She had been the woman in Muller's box at Madison Square Garden, part of his entourage. Indeed, when he looked back over he could see Muller now in a booth on the far side. The man was raising a glass in their direction.

'Tell Mr Muller we are both most appreciative and eager to make his acquaintance,' said Delgado, trying to strike the balance between gratitude and professional scepticism.

She gave the sense that she would convey the remark without saying so, then popped the cork and poured two glasses. Delgado lifted his to Muller in return in a perfunctory fashion. Muller nodded and turned back to his company.

Finch, meanwhile, couldn't tear his gaze from the woman and felt embarrassed when her eyes caught his.

She said it pertinently.

'Will that be all?'

'Yes,' he flustered. 'Thank you.'

'The menu,' she added. 'Anything you want. It's on the house.'

Then she slunk away with Finch's eyes glued to the light dusting of freckles on her shoulders before drifting south.

Delgado chuckled and clapped him on the back.

'See sumpin' you like, buddy?'

'I'm sorry. I just… It's been…'

'A long day…? Or a long *while*…?'

Finch smiled. They clinked glasses. Finch was not normally one for champagne. He felt it was a drink you *ought* to partake of without necessarily enjoying – oft served too warm, and usually at some occasion you'd rather not be at. But this, he could tell, was of excellent quality. Ironic, he thought, that Cristal should have been created for Alexander II, the old Russian Tsar – an assassinated Tsar – one blown up with a bomb.

'You married, Mr Collins?'

'No.'

'You *ever* been married?'

'"No" to that too.'

Delgado gave him a light mock punch to the shoulder.

'Listen, I can tell by that puppy-dog look you were admiring the lady, not her dress. Not that there's anything wrong with that. This is the 1900s. Some of the best spies bat for the away team, if you get my drift.'

'They also have a habit of being compromised, Mr Delgado.'

'True.'

The band leader introduced the next song, '*Maple Leaf Rag*', by a new composer, Scott Joplin. The piano player cracked his knuckles and took a turn in the spotlight.

'And you?' asked Finch.

'Me?'

'Married?'

Delgado laughed again.

'So my wife likes to remind me.'

He nodded at the woman, disappearing now into the crowd.

'Well, I guess you already figured...'

'Muller's girl?'

'Yep. And strictly *verboten*... Name's Katia. Beautiful, no doubt. But a real ice maiden. She and Muller been together now two, three years. There's a fair bet she knows where all the bodies are buried.'

Finch wrinkled his brow.

'Figure of speech, Mr Collins. Though, in Muller's case, probably a little more literal than for most.'

The ivory-tinkler was whipping up a hell of a storm. He seemed to have an extra set of fingers. But he was cut off in his prime, drowned out by a sudden cheer that began at the back of the room and swelled forward.

Heads were turning. There, at the entrance, stood Jack Johnson himself. The spotlight swung over. Even in his civilian clothes he cut an impressive figure. He was huge, broad... and, save for a piece of surgical plaster over his left eye, looked like he'd done nothing more energetic than ingest a late breakfast.

He strode in like royalty with an expensive-looking fur coat draped over his shoulder, a flash of gold on his fingers and teeth, and – Finch imagined for outrage as much as theatrics – a scantily clad white woman on each arm.

'You know, I want to ask you something, Mr Delgado.'

The NBI man was on *his* feet too, clapping away.

He sat back down.

'Please, *Freddie*...'

'Okay, Freddie... The Germans... German–Americans. I'm curious. Ever since unification, since Bismarck, a huge part of their nationalist tendency, fostered by the Prussian elite, has been founded on the notion of a racial purity – "Aryanism" for want of a better word... You must have heard the expression.'

'I have.'

Finch waved an arm around, indicating all that was before them.

'And yet here we are, at Muller's behest, communing to laud a coloured fighter... and with a black orchestra over there keeping the party stoked. I don't understand.'

Delgado sighed.

'You want me to get into racial politics? It's complicated enough in these here United States without adding an international dimension. It's only 40 years since we did away with slavery, Mr Collins – a blink of an eye. You got to remember that. The South's still run by segregationists. You know, the Jim Crow Laws... They got the Klan on the loose, lynchin' black folk from trees with impunity...'

He sipped his drink.

'And even here in the North... Yeah, we pat ourselves on the back for our supposed enlightened thinking, but we still self-partition, even if it's not decreed by statute. You go to Harlem – Hell, you go to Brooklyn, the Bronx, Little Italy, Chinatown, *Spanish* Harlem – *whole* o' damned New York's compartmentalized... Split up into fiefdoms – negroes, guineas, chinks, spicks, micks, not my choice of words, just using the vernacular. It's why the mobs are so strong, fostering the tensions, offering protection, encouraging a partisan loyalty.'

Finch recalled his time in the Cape and its absurd racial codifications – of the blacks there who had been the biggest casualties of all in that strange white man's war. He remembered the extraordinary bushmen he'd encountered who'd trekked across the desert. He thought of Mbutu, the Basuto, whose heroism matched that of any Tommy with a medal – not, he conceded, that he'd appreciated it at the time.

'But to address your point,' Delgado continued, 'your average white supremacist is not averse to a black man at all, or a brown man or a yellow one or a sky-blue goddamn pink 'un, just so long as he doesn't get ideas above his station. For a black man that means cook, clean, toil in a field. Or be part of the house entertainment – the minstrel… singin'… dancin'… *boxing*. A Chinaman…? As long as he's doin' your laundry… For them it's all about upholding a so-called "natural order"…'

He shook his head in frustration.

'Bunch o' fuckin' assholes is all it says to me.'

'Then how about Teetonka? Where does *he* fit in?'

'That, my friend, is an interesting question. Funny thing is, the German purists venerate the Native Americans. They consider them honorary Aryan, especially the Sioux. The "noble savage". Uncorrupted. The very *essence* of man.'

He puffed on his cigar and shrugged his shoulders.

'Personally, I think it's just horseshit. Politics is about expediency, it's about control. You know, promise the Injuns their land back, get 'em onside. That's a powerful political card to have up your sleeve… For the *American National Party* to have up its sleeve.'

'Where is he…? Teetonka. I don't see him.'

'And you won't at things like this.'

'Why?'

'Coupla reasons. *One*: See that fella over there…?'

There was a happy-looking man in round spectacles with the inevitable full moustache.

'L. Frank Baum, the author.'

'*Really?*'

'Uh-huh. In town from Chicago. His show version of *The Wizard of Oz* has been a big hit here on Broadway. All nicey-nicey with your Scarecrow and your Tin Woodman and your little fuckin' Dorothy. 'Cept cuddly Uncle Frank is also the author of an infamous newspaper editorial advocating the wholesale extermination of the American Indian.'

'I had no idea.'

'Yup, you'd have to keep our Injun brave off a-scalpin' him right there – something which might have put a crimp in the evening's proceedings.'

'And two? The second reason?'

'Sad fact is, Redskins and liquor just don't get along. Situation like this? Not good at the best of times. Tends to skip out. But in light of the above…'

'I see.'

He issued a sardonic grin.

'Funny thing.'

'What?'

'For all that you've said, you're overlooking something.'

Finch didn't get it.

'Muller… He isn't actually German at all.'

'He *isn't?*'

'No, sir – a colonial. Hails from Windhoek, from a family of settlers in what is now German South West Africa.'

'So, he has a chip on his shoulder?'

'Possibly… I mean, he wouldn't be the first. There's a long tradition of nationalists coming from someplace else, wanting to demonstrate they should be a few more rungs up the ladder. Alexander the Great wasn't Greek but Macedonian. And Napoleon? He was from Corsica – the island was only ceded to France in the year of his birth. Ethnically he was Italian – minor nobility – Napoleone di Buonaparte.'

Finch topped up their glasses.

'George Washington was a British citizen,' he reminded Delgado.

The NBI man winked.

'At *first*.'

They clinked again and swigged.

'Not to put this sonofabitch in the same category but to give you the brief history – Muller came to the States in his teens, got involved in the local rackets and swiftly progressed through the ranks to become a high-end operator. Which is code for "thinks nothing of eliminating opponents". Though of course we can't ever pin anything on him.'

'That agent you mentioned before... Kimmel?'

Delgado downed his drink in one. The nerve was still raw.

'Don't be taken in by anything you see here tonight. This is all for show. Kimmel's corpse was dismembered and wound up as a series of appetisers in the lion cage at the Bronx Zoo. They had to sew him back together before they could bury him in Green-Wood Cemetery.'

'Jesus.'

Delgado nodded.

'I know... Wife and two kids.'

He poured himself another.

'Muller fronts his criminal activity with public good works,' he continued, 'in this case a charitable foundation for city boys called the St Mark's Youth League... Actually a bunch of "street Arabs" as they call 'em – waifs, strays, orphans, shoeshine boys – all now living in a nice new lodging house he had built. Our Good Samaritan ended up going on some sponsored philanthropic mission to Europe where he disappeared for a few months, came back an ardent German nationalist... *and*, we think, a spy, acting for *Nachrichten-Abteilung*, the intelligence branch of the German Imperial Navy.'

'Navy?'

'The *N-Abteilung*'s arguably superior to their Army's *Sektion IIIb* espionage operation. Currently, anyway...'

He gave another wry smile.

'One thing in our favour is that Germany's military High Commands spend as much time trying to outdo each other as actually gathering intelligence.'

'Why can't you just arrest Muller? Even on suspicion.'

'It's a powder-keg situation, Mr Collins. We're talking possible race riots and a political stand-off. Tompkins Square's seen its share of revolt in the past. The German population is too big, too sensitive after the *Slocum* Disaster.'

Delgado waved across the room again, trying to catch Katia's eye.

'Anyway,' he said. 'Down to business...'

She worked her way back towards them, conveying a certain sense of irritation at being hailed like a common waitress. Finch made sure to keep his eyes lowered.

'About that audience,' said Delgado, nodding towards Muller. 'Your fellow over there said something about setting the record straight. It's why we're here.'

Finch wondered if he wasn't being too blunt.

She turned back to give a signal. Muller checked his watch and nodded, then stood.

'He'll be here in a moment. People to attend to. In the meantime, please, make yourselves comfortable.'

She reached up. They hadn't noticed but the booth had a velvet curtain on a rail that could be drawn around it for privacy.

It was then, out of the corner of his eye, that Finch saw it. The red-headed man at the bar, the NBI minder. He was being carried out unconscious by a pair of bouncers.

And the others…

Finch went to warn Delgado but it was too late. His lips moved but the words wouldn't come. He tried to stand but his legs were numb.

The curtain came round.

'Collins… Mr Collins,' he heard Delgado groan.

In their isolated velvet pod, everything was now swirling.

Chapter 11

Finch felt a dryness in his mouth… a bitter taste… a grogginess. It was dark but there was a smell… of pine… and smoke.

He was in woods somewhere – a forest – deep in the dark of night.

But no, it couldn't be. The ground was hard… cold… *boards*.

And the darkness… the constriction… the condensation of his own breath…

He blinked as the sack was pulled off his head.

He was lying on a floor. There were people… pinpricks of light… They swirled as he tried to find a point of convergence.

'Stand.'

The voice was deep, resonant, commanding. It was close. And it echoed.

Shaky but conscious, Finch tried to reel his thoughts back into the realm of the logical. He knew from bitter experience that remaining calm, assessing his environment, was his surest means of staying alive.

There was no pain in his body, other than the dull habitual one in his knee. He had not been physically injured. Although he was encumbered in some fashion. Yes, his hands were tied. But in front of him, not behind – that was always preferable.

The medical man within him tried to figure out what the drug might have been. It was wearing off quickly and its after-effects were not crippling, which meant it was not excessive in dosage – a knockout drop to incapacitate him for, at most, two, maybe three hours. A sedative – diphenhydramine? An opiate?

He tried hard to remember – the Bierkeller Club... the *champagne*... Yes, it was in the champagne. And Delgado...

Delgado, where are you?

The voice came again, stronger.

'Stand!'

Finch slowly manoeuvred himself. His wrists were bound with twine – no, not twine... some kind of fibre... a *vine*. He managed to press down with the heels of his hands and edge himself onto all fours.

There was a murmur, a whispering as he did so. From how many voices, he couldn't tell. But there were several. Again, they echoed, meaning the space was large. But there were no windows he could see. They must be underground. A basement.

'Silence...!' boomed the man for a third time and those same voices became still.

His knee hurt too much from the effort, making the last thrust to his feet beyond him. It didn't matter. Suddenly there was a figure either side, hoisting him upright. As his focus became clearer, the lights, winking through the smoke, became candles. And the woodland smell...?

Around the room was foliage, the hue by candlelight a dark green. There were cloaks, hoods, robes... What the hell?

Beware the occult.

The voice came again. It was addressing the room... announcing.

'It is our purpose to uncover the intentions of the *"Ausländer"*.'

Ausländer... foreigner...

The men about him stood in a circle, in a closed rank. They kept their heads bowed, covered, like monks, so as not to reveal their faces. On the left breast of each robe was a symbol, in gold – like a cross, but with each arm bent perpendicular at midway. It reminded him, curiously, of a Catherine wheel, pinned to a post, that had just burnt out...

He had seen the emblem and tried to recall where. Indian troops in South Africa had carried good-luck charms bearing something similar. Hindu... Something from ancient mythology.

The man giving the orders was sitting in a huge chair – a throne – fashioned from wood. He behaved in the manner of a high priest... like some kind of Druid elder. In his hand was a huge staff carved in the style of vines creeping up a gnarled branch; around his neck a laurel-leaf garland, the ongoing theme pagan, elemental.

He banged the staff three times on the floor – a resounding, ominous thud.

'Declare yourself, *Ausländer*.'

'Declare myself?'

'DECLARE YOURSELF!'

'I rather think it's you who should declare *yourself*.'

There came a hard blow to the backs of the thighs and Finch's legs buckled. He just managed to break his fall. He was jerked to his feet again.

'I say again, declare yourself.'

'I'll do no such thing... And where the hell is Delgado?'

There was no preamble, no drama, the action was swift.

The man nodded. Two men swept Finch up and dumped him on a large wooden slab behind him. He hadn't noticed it.

An altar?

His bound wrists were wrenched up and over his head leaving his midriff utterly exposed. There was no point in struggling. It was a waste of energy. It would also concede to them the psychology of victory – that they had broken him. Something bad was about to happen but he had to *think* his way out of it, not fight.

Another robed figure strode over from beside the throne and grabbed Finch's left hand. While the first two held him down, the third came behind him, took his little finger and, with a consummate ease, as nonchalantly as pulling a wishbone, yanked it back as hard as possible.

CRACK!

Jesus fucking Christ!

The pain was like an electric jolt that ran from Finch's hand, up his arm to his brain. He fought to control it, to contain it, to keep it within. It took a minute for the white-hot stab of agony to recede to mere excruciation.

Then the damned voice rang out again.

'I am hoping that we now have your full attention, Mr Collins. Think of it as an education, an experience from which you will have learned something. Your discomfort will serve as a reminder of the consequences of failing to treat our enquiry as a concern of the utmost gravity.'

He felt his torturer grab the next finger, the ring finger... not that he'd ever worn one.

'I must stress that the truth is something that will ultimately be elicited regardless of any attempt on your part to play this out as some sort of game. Of that you can rest assured.'

Finch looked upwards to his hands. He had seen enough battlefield carnage in his time – injuries to turn the hardiest of stomachs and to which he had built up a solid professional immunity. The sight of his *own* little finger jutting outwards at ninety degrees at the first knuckle was another matter. It looked curiously like the arm of the cross they wore on their robes. His head began to spin.

Focus, damnit. Focus!

And then he saw... the hand of his torturer was female... just the shape of it, the nails, its softness, its poise, if not its strength. He couldn't see within the hood, even with his upward vantage – she had been careful not to betray that.

The two assailants held him tight while the torturer gripped the next finger, ready to continue her handiwork.

He looked forward to his interrogator again. This time he yelled out, not in pain but defiance.

'Delgado... Release him... He's done nothing wrong. Let Delgado go and you can address everything to me!'

The voice was eerie in its calm.

'Mr Collins, the fate of Mr Delgado is none of your concern. But the fact that this gentleman is a known operative of the National Bureau of Criminal Identification marks him out as someone hostile. This, coupled with the detail that you are a British subject, newly arrived on our shores, as well as being in league with him, leads us inexorably to the conclusion that you are working for

an intelligence organization, most likely "Military Operations 3".'

Finch wasn't going to let them have the satisfaction.

'Well, that would be news to my employer, British
Nitrate.'

'You were observed in the company of Mr Delgado
and a detective of the New York Police Department at a
warehouse in the Meatpacking District this very morning.'

'Like I say, my company is in the business of nitrates –
meat preservatives, animal foodstuffs. You are welcome to
check my credentials if—'

The voice cut across him – admonishing, domineering.

'Need I tell you that the presence of an outside
espionage agency, especially one with such a nefarious
agenda, is injurious to the cause of our people.'

'Your people? The local fancy-dress association?'

SNAP!

The next finger went too. He blacked out. A hard slap
to the face brought him back – stunned, stinging and, for
a moment, diverting from the agony. He panted hard.

'I would caution you a second time, Mr Collins, that
this is no time for jest. It is in your interest to divulge
everything about your mission on our continent. *Everything.*'

Give them nothing. Give them absolutely bloody nothing.

'I've told you all you need to know.'

'Very well…'

The man nodded a signal.

'…if physical persuasion has no effect, then maybe *this*
will concentrate your mind.'

The men restraining Finch released their grip. He was
prodded back to his feet and lowered his bound hands.
The blood rushed to them in a flood of pain.

His torturer came back round to resume her place by the throne. The height, the movement... there was no doubting who it was. This time there was the briefest glimpse of a soft chin.

The high priest nodded to a lieutenant who made a summoning gesture. From behind the wall of cloaks, a further group of four or five bodies squeezed their way through. They were dressed the same as the others but seemed younger to Finch – adolescent in their movement, gangly, cocky, eager to please. One of them, with both hands, was cradling a green velvet bag tied with a drawstring. It contained something weighty, round... a ball, a spherical object of some sort.

On a further nod, a second youth untied it and the first one tipped its content across the floor. It thudded towards Finch, rolling asymmetrically, till it came to a halt at his feet.

It wasn't a ball... It was a head... a human head.

MacLeish's head.

The dead eyes and the open mouth leered up at Finch. As if in some twisted joke, they had put his spectacles back on.

Finch's own head swam. The scene was so surreal, the act so utterly barbaric, that it defied any sense of rational opposition. He felt his own vision go, his legs collapse under him.

He was picked up again, another slap delivered.

'The fool had been insinuating himself into matters of which he had no concern,' came the high priest's voice, the decapitation as casual as the swatting of an irritating fly.

There was no logic for Finch any more. In not even 24 hours he had been removed from a pampered VIP existence and plunged into a world which no longer conveyed any civilized meaning.

'WHAT THE HELL HAVE YOU DONE? YOU SAVAGES!'

The words being fired back at him meant nothing – drivel about harmony in nature and of purity and impurity and his own unreasonableness. The man was quoting Friedrich Nietzsche, something about 'beautiful surfaces' betraying a 'terrible depth'. But Finch could think only of something else Nietzsche had said.

God is dead.

There were German sons and daughters being sacrificed, a persecution, the man was now lecturing. There was a debt of blood owed in return.

Finch was willing himself to be present, but his legs were buckling again.

The others began to chant in unison… *what* he did not know. But it was resonant, visceral, disturbing… issued at a low frequency that seemed to unsettle his guts.

'We can only conclude by your presence amongst us that you mean harm,' the man was ranting over the top. 'The English and the Germans share Anglo-Saxon blood – so did the Americans until their mongrelization. Fortunately, the ruling classes maintain their purity.'

'Are you insane?!' yelled Finch.

But his words were lost.

Finch felt himself hoisted back onto the altar. Hands ripped open his shirt. The high priest banged his staff three times again. The room fell silent once more.

With a soft slow shuffle of feet, a big man ambled forward. Tall… ridiculously tall, his robes barely concealing him. He came to a stop before the altar and, with an ominous metallic hiss – and a palpable thrill from those looking on – slid a great knife from its scabbard.

'We should be seeking common purpose,' bellowed the high priest. 'It is a betrayal of that bloodline for the British to be in opposition…'

The tall man raised the knife to the room, the candle-light glinting on the curve of the steel.

'It will be a huge feather in our cap to have claimed a British agent at large in the United States.'

There were markings etched into the blade… runes…

A signal was given. The chanting resumed, rising to fever pitch. The tall man turned to the throne and the head nodded. The knife was raised high, poised…

God is dead!

But then the staff pounded again.

Silence.

'Which is why we will not kill you… *yet.*'

The knife was lowered, sheathed. It was offered aside, into the care of accomplices.

'Take him away!' boomed the voice. 'We will deal with the *Ausländer* later.'

The huge hands jerked Finch to his feet again. He was dragged out of the circle. Next thing he knew he was being bustled by the tall man along a narrow under-ground passageway lined with flaming torches. This time he felt the barrel of a gun being pressed into the small of his back.

There were screams of pain – male – coming from somewhere.

'Delgado?!'

The gun was rammed in harder and he was hastened on his way.

There could be no doubt as to who this was too – Teetonka. Finch understood that suggestion-without-revelation would be part of the terror mounted against him – utterly unprovable, and with hints at his own insanity, should he ever be free to recount his experience of tonight.

The underground corridor was long. At the end of it, a door opened into the night. As they got closer he could see two henchmen waiting, a car behind them. He could hear its engine running. They were going to take him away somewhere.

He was too numb – too tired, too pained, too utterly shocked – to even calculate the odds of success, but he noted one thing and hoped that it could be used to his advantage. Even though he was positioned behind him, he could tell that Teetonka was struggling with his ill-fitting robe – too restricting for comfortable movement and with an impractical hood and baggy sleeves that were frustrating its wearer, constantly having to be tugged back.

Finch's problematic knee was the least of his worries, but his limping was a given and, when he stopped to bend and rub his leg, he seized his moment. As Teetonka thrust the gun at him again, he twisted and, from a low point of attack, using the combined strength of his bound wrists, pushed the man's right arm, his gun arm, back.

BANG!

The shot echoed. There was a shout. It took a second. But as soon as he had righted himself, Finch realized that one of the henchmen at the end was now writhing on the ground, clutching his belly. The other man was rushing towards them.

The pistol had gone flying across the floor. It was an automatic, a Luger. Finch dived for it and, aiming from a prone position, with what seemed like an explosion of red paint, shot the oncoming second man in the head.

With the physical fury of a man possessed, Teetonka was upon him and flipped him onto his back, pinning him rigid. He grabbed the gun from him and, using its handle as a club, was about to rain it down, raising it high to bludgeon with maximum impact.

But… the sleeve… It arced towards a flaming torch, the cloth wafting right through.

Teetonka – his arm – it was on fire.

Finch stumbled to his feet then staggered forward, bumping off the walls. Another shot rang out, but it missed. He fell again and caught a glimpse behind him. Teetonka was rolling, engulfed in flames.

Finch darted for the exit, stepping over the first henchman, still squealing, hands clamped to his guts. There seemed no one else ahead of him. He was on his own. Though he could hear a commotion swelling behind.

The car's engine was running. He gulped the night air and climbed behind the wheel. He barely knew how to drive but, in an instant, found himself haring out of an alleyway, suddenly barrelling along a New York street.

Chapter 12

Finch lurched from the cobbles onto what seemed a wider
arterial road, which he figured aligned north–south. But
he saw the moonlight shimmer on the water up ahead
and knew soon enough that he had got it wrong. From
the silhouettes of the mighty suspension bridges, it was
obviously the East River. There were huge cables slung
between the towers of one still under construction, the
Manhattan Bridge, nestled up against the instantly recog-
nizable arches of the Brooklyn.

He was Downtown, on the Lower East Side somewhere. He reorientated himself and headed north. He
cursed himself for not making a proper note of the location whence he had just come, not even the street name.
His instinct for survival – his instinct for flight – had
come at the expense of being an effective spy. There were
German names… on shops, on restaurants, on bars. He
would remember that.

But Delgado…

His prime motive now was to save his poor comrade
and to get him out from their clutches before it was too
late, wherever the hell that might be. But who could he
inform? Who could he trust? The police? No. He'd had
evidence enough that there was a deeply corrupt element
amongst them. The NBI? He didn't even know how to
make contact.

The only rational option was to communicate the details of the past hours to the MO3 office in Washington. He would need to find a telegraph office right away. Maybe there was one open at a railway station?

As best he could, with his bound hands, he patted his breast pocket. But then – the cold shock of realization – the codebook was no longer there. It had either fallen out during his abduction or been taken from his person… along with his wallet and passport. He was meant to guard it with his life.

In his mind, he retraced his steps of the past few hours. And then he thanked himself for his own carelessness. His room… the bomb… the tuxedo… the general daze… In all that had happened, he had left the codebook behind. On transfer to a new hotel suite, he had wedged it under the edge of the mattress while he got changed, meaning to put it back in his pocket.

He must head to the New Netherland immediately, retrieve it and get the hell out as soon as possible. They would surely have the place marked.

With his hands spliced together, Finch made heavy weather of steering the vehicle. But with the streets empty, he thanked heaven for small mercies. He had had a few token turns behind the wheel of an automobile; having once railed against the advent of these accursed noisy contraptions, he had since thrown in the towel and fancied that he might like to purchase one.

Bamboozled by the stream-of-consciousness babble on the parts of several automobile salesmen, who were fast acquiring a reputation for turning their profession into a high art of misinformation, he had yet to follow through on any deal.

According to the emblem on the dashboard, the car was a Packard, the model a Roadster. It had a shorter wheel base but was more powerful, more sporty, than the Ford he had tried out back home – with just a single bench seat meant for three abreast. The layout was the same with three pedals – brake, reverse and clutch, which went through a first, second and high gear when depressed – and a hand throttle tucked behind the steering wheel.

It was only now that he returned to the issue of his broken fingers. The adrenaline had done its utmost to mask the pain, but the third and little digits of his left hand were a bruised, limp mess and he would have to tend to them at the first opportunity.

The gears ground and the car lurched. There was no one on his tail that he could see. But he would need to zigzag and he remembered his time on the battlefield, dodging Boer bullets across the veld.

He turned west, across the Bowery and its canopy of 'El' train rails, then up via the Cooper Union and Astor Place, taking Broadway past Union Square and onto Fifth Avenue. He came out right under the great triangular edifice of the Flatiron Building and thought, for a second, of his brief acquaintance with his fellow traveller on the *Baltic*, then those lecherous lads on the street corner.

He was right back where he had been earlier that night. Ahead lay Madison Square Garden. In the other direction, at the southern end of Fifth Avenue, was the triumphal arch of Washington Square – both Stanford White creations.

There was pink on the horizon. Dawn was breaking. He could see the light and space of Central Park in the distance. He slammed the throttle to maximum and belted north up the wide open boulevard.

But he was not alone. Along with the milk carts and the delivery wagons now bringing the city to life he noticed the other car in his rear-view mirror, maybe three or four blocks back, revving along at breakneck speed. Even though he was careening along at a flat-out 40mph, it was gaining on him.

An early-morning streetcar trundled across a junction and, using it as cover, he threw the steering wheel over and made the Packard screech into a sharp series of left-right-lefts. It was not effective. The other car was close enough now for him to see four men in it.

Crossing Sixth Avenue, he braked to a sharp halt and used the reverse pedal to back into an alleyway in the ice-cold lee of a massive building – somewhere, judging by the grey slush, that the sun never shone.

Reversing was not his forte and the Packard jerked too quickly. With a crunch of metal, the rear bumper scattered some dustbins before the whole back end went thudding into a wall. Trying to ease forward, the car whined and grunted but got no traction. It was jammed solid.

Knowing how complicated it was to get a car restarted, he kept the engine running but yanked down the throttle to a gentle tick-over while he assessed his options.

He heard the engine of the other car dip. It had slowed, obviously searching for his hiding place. Finch fumbled for the switch and killed the Packard's headlamps. Strategically he had made an error. He had gone from the safety of a wide-open space to a dead end… quite possibly literally. He cursed himself for not having the presence of mind to have at least picked up a gun on his escape. Maybe they didn't know that?

Within mere yards, the pursuing vehicle passed the end of the alley. A face in the rear seemed to be staring right at him. He held his breath. But the darkness had saved him. It travelled on. Finch waited as it picked up speed again, listening then for the noise of the engine to recede into the distance.

He climbed out and walked to the main road. He saw the framed posters on the wall – the New York Philharmonic performing Wagner's *Flying Dutchman* and Lizst's *Faust Symphony* – and realized he was behind Carnegie Hall. Save for a lone distant milk cart clopping over the cobbles, there was no one about.

He had a brainwave. The Packard's engine was still running. He popped open a sprung panel on the hood and took the binding on his hands to the fan blades. Careful not to make an errant move, he held firm while they sliced right through. Hands free, he examined his left one. The third finger was not jutting out like the little one and seemed more of a straightforward dislocation, but he needed to fix them as best he could.

He grimaced, reset them and, using a fountain pen as a splint, strapped them tightly with his handkerchief. Christ, he needed a drink. Instead he lit a Navy Cut.

He was taking a big gamble in going back to the hotel but it was the only way. Sure that he was no longer being followed, he limped along 57th Street and up round the rear of the building site of the Plaza. He found the back entrance to the New Netherland and went in through the kitchen, now a hive of hissing and sizzling as it came alive for the breakfast shift.

Dressed in a crumpled tux, ripped shirt and looking a little rough, he got a knowing wink from a cook frying up a pan of bacon and eggs – just another gent sneaking in after a good night out. As he made his way through there was an empty office and a pegboard of pass keys. He grabbed his – room #1921 – rather than go via the front desk.

He hopped into the service elevator, alongside a waiter wheeling in a room-service trolley that smelled suddenly tempting, and got out with him at the 21st floor, walking back down two flights of stairs.

From the stairwell he pushed open the door an inch and peered into the corridor. He recalled that Delgado had said the Bureau would post a guard on the new room and he wondered for a moment whether this might be a better person to approach for help.

But there was no one there. Maybe they were elsewhere? Taking a quick break? And then it dawned – they could have been eliminated.

He must hurry.

Finch crept to the room and put the key in the lock. His heart pounded as he turned the knob and eased it open. In the dim light, it appeared exactly as he had left it, as if nothing extraordinary at all had passed that night. He determined not to turn on the light lest anybody be watching from the street.

But… he sensed movement.

The curtain at the far window was flapping. Someone had just climbed out. There was a clang of motion on the fire escape and he rushed to look out. It was still too dark to see properly. That side of the building was still in shade. But there, scuttling down, was someone.

He ducked across the windowsill ready to head after them but, in his condition, with his knee and his general state of fatigue, he knew it was pointless. He returned to the bed, slid his good hand under the mattress to the place where he had hidden the codebook, and faced the inevitable.

It was gone.

His mind raced. There was only one thing for it, the last resort – the locker at Grand Central Station. He would leave the hotel by the same back route and go there right now. He would take his bag and get out of Manhattan. By a circuitous route he would make his way to the embassy in Washington. That, too, still meant taking a chance.

If anything goes wrong, you will be disavowed.

No... British territory. He would head for Canada.

There was a sudden, loud rap at the door. He kept still... very still.

The volley of knocks came again, more forcefully, only this time with a voice.

'Open up! Police!'

Finch rushed to the fire escape, but it was too late.

There was a rattle at the lock as they let themselves in, a bellboy on hand with a pass key. Several constables were upon him, guns drawn.

'Freeze!'

Finch put his hands in the air.

A man in a gabardine coat moved to the fore.

'Bradley Collins, you are under arrest!'

Chapter 13

Finch sat in the interview room with his hands bound again, this time handcuffed to a metal bar running across the table. His left one hurt like hell.

The state-of-the-art NYPD headquarters on Centre Street – the brand new Downtown home of 'New York's finest' – had been constructed as part of Roosevelt's reforms. But, when it came to interrogation rooms, it boasted all the usual trimmings – or lack of them – windowless, airless, spartan. Beneath the pale electric bulb there were already the scuffs, the marks, the scars of those who had passed within its walls.

Finch didn't know whether to use this opportunity to sleep, or if the act of doing so might raise the ire of his interrogators. He suspected they would rush in and wake him up. Inevitably there was a long horizontal mirror built in to one wall – he was being observed. They had removed his watch as well as his tie, braces and shoelaces. How long he had been sitting there he didn't know. But it must have been for the best part of an hour.

Just as he was about to throw in the towel and put his head down, the door was opened and the detective who had arrested him was ushered in by a constable. Finch had been told nothing of any charge against him and so had been left to writhe on the hook, knowing that there were multiple permutations as to the cause of his detention.

The detective sat opposite him, his constable at the end of the table, pencil and notebook in hand, ready to document proceedings. He wore an anonymous suit and tie and had slicked-back greying hair, the obligatory stress creases around his tired eyes.

He introduced himself as 'Detective Copeland, NYPD' and was as purposeful as any other investigator Finch had met in the line of duty, going all the way back to Harry Brookman, the venerable Cape Town gumshoe, who, now he thought about it, was indirectly responsible for every scrape he'd been in ever since and whose voice still echoed in his head.

Assumption is our enemy, Captain Finch.

Copeland also had the standard detective's prop before him – the folder containing the charge sheet and other information, which he flipped open and rifled through, there to suggest that he knew more about events than Finch did and, by virtue, had the upper hand.

Finch had been in this environment enough times to know how it worked and to understand the basic psychology. They would turn every statement on its head and throw it back to you as a question. He was desperate for someone to get out there and find poor Delgado but he also knew that the police couldn't necessarily be trusted… *yet.* The man sitting before him might very well be in Muller's pocket. The way to proceed was to stick to the facts and to treat it as an exercise in extracting as much information for himself – in effect, to interview his interviewer.

'Detective, if it's not too much trouble, I'd like to know why I've been arrested.'

The detective turned in mock exasperation to look at the policeman – a little bit of theatre.

'You mean other than shoot two men dead at an address near Tompkins Square and send another to New York Presbyterian with third-degree burns?'

This detail was good, thought Finch. They knew the location. If they had searched the premises, they might already have found Delgado. If they hadn't bothered – or hadn't *tried* – then they were possibly in cahoots with Muller. Or just plain slack.

Finch decided to keep Delgado's name out of it for the moment.

'I don't deny it,' said Finch, 'although, if I may correct you, at the time of leaving the scene, only *one* of the two gunshot victims was dead. I killed him, yes. The other man was shot accidentally by the man who got burnt… Goes by the name of Teetonka—'

'Teetonka?'

'First Nation… Red Indian… Very tall… But you already know that.'

The lawmen exchanged a glance.

Yes, they knew it.

'Incidentally, I can't take credit for that either. It was an accident. He was about to stave my brains in when he got his clothing entangled in a flaming torch. Went up like a Roman candle.'

The specifics of Finch's answer had clearly thrown them. Too much detail for a fumbling bullshitter, and certainly not a story that was hastily improvised. The detective closed the folder.

'*Why* did you kill him? The first man?'

'Sorry, you mean the second man. I'm not being funny, just want to be clear. The *first* man was the one with the wound to the gut. He'd already gone down at the time of me seizing the gun – a German Luger by the way – and shooting dead the second man... a head shot.'

'You're not answering my question.'

'*Why?* Because I was effecting my escape from a perilous situation, Detective. I had been drugged, kidnapped, tortured...'

He nodded to his fingers.

'I never knew anyone die from a broken finger,' huffed the detective.

'True, but that was just the start... I believed my life was in serious danger... Kill or be killed. Plus I'd just borne witness to the unpleasant aftermath of *another* murder... the horrendous slaughter of a police officer.'

'A police officer?'

There was more urgency to the detective now. Finch knew this would change the dynamic.

'Deputy Inspector Angus MacLeish.'

At the name, the detective froze, the blood drained. He got up abruptly, beckoned his constable, and they headed for the door. Finch was on his own again.

Five minutes later they re-entered and resumed their positions. Detective Copeland was clearly trying to keep a lid now on simmering feelings.

'How do you know about MacLeish's death, Mr Collins?'

'Because someone presented me with his severed head.'

There was another glance.

'MacLeish's headless corpse was found dumped in City Hall Park just over two hours ago,' the detective revealed.

'Then surely that proves...'

'Mr Collins,' he barked, patience now slipped, 'be under no illusion as to the seriousness of your situation. We have several officers who can place you in MacLeish's company yesterday afternoon on two separate occasions – one in the Meatpacking District where he was investigating another crime and a second time when he was apparently driven to your hotel, the New Netherland.'

And then he lost it completely. He leaned across. Spit splashed on Finch's face.

'Moreover – *I want to know what the fuck you are doing in this country?!*'

He got up and began pacing about, the constable scribbling furiously as he did so. He threw a glance to the mirror.

Coolness was being perceived as nonchalance, Finch knew. His accent wouldn't have helped. He would sound aloof to them, superior. He tried to affect a more cooperative tone.

'As I told you on my arrest, I am an employee of a company called British Nitrate. I have full credentials – bona fides, as you say. If you need...'

'You can cut out the smarmy Limey bullshit, Collins...' *He had been right.*

'Yeah, we checked it out, British Nitrate. The card in your pocket. The company exists, all right. But it just doesn't stack up. You swan into town like some big-shot businessman – a swanky hotel, Madison Square Garden, the Bierkeller – yet, somehow, within hours, you're leaving a trail of bodies.'

It sounded hollow but he said it anyway.

'I was in the Meatpacking District on official business.'

The detective came back and slammed his fist down hard. There was a fury, as if he'd known MacLeish personally. He probably did. It suggested he was a good cop.

'That's a crock of horseshit, Collins. And you know it!'

Finch mulled over his options. He could only play out the increasingly lame British Nitrate angle for so long, and it would *not* save Delgado. Conceding anything to do with his true mission, however, would place him as a spy. Lady Brunswick's voice came again...

If anything goes wrong, you will be disavowed.

'MacLeish seemed a decent man,' Finch said, doing his best at empathy. 'He was bent on clamping down on the gangs... drugs, I understand. Told me how his forebears had immigrated from Scotland. He came to my hotel, came to my personal *aid*, because I had been the victim of an attack – a bomb. It went off in my hotel suite on the 17th floor.'

'A *bomb?*'

'A crackerjack bomb. MacLeish said it was of an unusual design, a precision weapon.'

'Hold on, hold on...!'

He began pacing again, rubbing the back of his neck. This was all new information.

'Why the hell would anyone want to bomb you, Collins?'

'I wish I knew myself.'

'And, more pertinently, why the hell is there no record of this incident? A bomb goes off in my city, I *hear* about it.'

'Because the NBI asked MacLeish to sit on it... To buy time.'

'*What?*'

'MacLeish said he thought he knew the bomb-maker – or someone who could shed light on who had made it... He had gone off to investigate.'

'Where? Where'd he go?'

'I don't know. But there was a name – Chang.'

'*Jimmy* Chang?'

Finch shrugged. Detective Copeland nodded to the constable, who hurried out of the room again.

'Listen, do you have a cigarette?' asked Finch.

'Why the fuck should I give you a cigarette?'

'Because,' said Finch, 'I'm telling you the truth. I'm trying to help you. Please, I think you know it.'

There was something in the detective's sigh and reach for his pocket that suggested to Finch he had given them pause to believe his version of events... if not the bit about his official cover.

Detective Copeland sat back down, tapped out two cigarettes from a blue-and-white pack – Chesterfields. He placed one in Finch's mouth, lit it, then did the same for himself. They sat in silence for a moment. Then the constable returned, came over, and whispered in the detective's ear. Copeland waved him back to his seat.

'Jimmy Chang is a bomb-maker, Mr Collins, as you say. Was a mine demolition expert. Tooled around out West before he pitched up here. Was convicted as an accessory-after-the-fact in the assassination of Frank Steunenberg.'

'Who?'

'Guess I can't expect you to know *that*. Governor of Idaho. A strike-breaker. Blown up outside his house near Boise by a bomb rigged to his garden gate. Perp was a disgruntled mine union member. But it was Chang told him how to do it. He was already in New York by that point – his services were suddenly in demand by the various anarchist groups we got here. Currently serving a twelve-year sentence in the penitentiary on Blackwell's Island.'

'So you think MacLeish visited him there?'

'It's a possibility. He'd been doing some liaison work with our new Bomb Squad, after all. Fenians... *Clan na Gael*... anarchists... revolutionaries... Suddenly everybody's sweet on explosives. He'd consulted Chang before.'

'Well, if he *did*, then...'

'We just telephoned. There is no record of MacLeish having visited in the past 24 hours. Maybe he never even got there.'

Finch slumped back, hoping that they would register his disappointment.

'Okay, I'm going to give you a name,' Finch said. 'Freddie Delgado.'

'Freddie Delgado?'

'An NBI agent.'

'I never heard of him.'

'Please don't ask me to explain,' said Finch. 'I was holding back for good reason but he was with me yesterday. I was in his company when members of your police department staged an ambush on a mob truck somewhere west of Central Park... Don't ask me where precisely, I couldn't tell you, though I do remember Amsterdam Avenue. About the only street round there that wasn't a number.'

'You were there?'

'Yes, and it was shortly after that that Delgado introduced me to MacLeish, in the Meatpacking District as you say. Took me down there. MacLeish was examining a body, throat slit, a "Short Tail". Then there was the business at my hotel as I've described – Delgado and MacLeish again. Last night Delgado took me to the Johnson fight on the Bureau's dollar – and with witnesses to back me up on just about everything I've said here. We were then invited on to the Bierkeller Club by Manfred Muller himself, a personal invitation. Muller arranged for our ride there...'

The two men exchanged yet another look.

'It was his girl, Katia, by the way, who played chopsticks with my fingers. Some weird pagan ritual they've got there – a lot of smoke, gowns and some big-voiced fellow bashing a big stick.'

There was no response.

'Delgado was drugged alongside myself – a sedative in the champagne. I heard him being brutalized somewhere else in the building. I got out, exactly as I said, and I was hoping you'd tell me Delgado did too. But, if he *didn't*, he may still be in there somewhere.'

The response was cold, blunt. Detective Copeland had changed.

'Like I told you, I never heard of Freddie Delgado, Mr Collins, nor any of this fantasy bullcrap for that matter. But what I do want to know *now* is why a businessman from England is poking around my backyard in the company of the NBI?'

'It's complicated. If you give me time I can explain. But, please, the address in Tompkins Square, you need to go there and find him.'

'There was no "place" specifically. The bodies were dumped in an alley. The burn victim was taken separately to the hospital by an anonymous Good Samaritan... the same person who gave up your name as the culprit. To which end, Collins, you've already sung like a canary.'

The detective stood up. It was over. The constable gave a supercilious smirk. Broken fingers or not, Finch felt like delivering him a left hook.

'You know what else MacLeish did?' growled the detective. 'Investigate anarchist groups. Is that why you bumped him off?'

Finch was flustering now.

'Kimmel… There was someone in the past named Kimmel!'

He had hit a raw nerve again.

'Are you an anarchist, Mr Collins?' raged the detective. 'Some kind of enemy agent maybe?'

'Please, I can explain.'

The detective made a signal to the two-way mirror.

In a flash there were policemen in the room, bundling him off to a cell.

Chapter 14

American jail cells were not like British ones, Finch discovered. Back home they had four walls and a solid door. Here they were like cages – bars wall-to-ceiling, no place to hide, the prisoner utterly exposed. He stared out, waiting for something to happen.

In this part of the basement there were two of them, effectively holding pens. The neighbouring one was occupied by four young men, all steaming drunk, clearly of violent means, their coarse clothing filthy dirty. Their main grievance came not at a lack of food, water or want of a fresh slop bucket, but at the fact that Finch had a whole cell all to himself. Their howls of abuse were met periodically with a constable's nightstick rapped on the bars, which only seemed to increase their sense of injustice.

In the end, unable to get a rise out of Finch, they turned on each other, yelling in their native tongue – Russian, Ukrainian, Polish... Finch couldn't tell. The smallest of them, the runt of the litter, bore the brunt of it in the shape of a few blows to the head. Eventually they all fell asleep on the benches, leaning on each other, snoring loudly.

Finch had absolutely no idea of the time of day and assumed it must be mid-morning. Way beyond the pull of slumber, he sat and waited and turned over the events of the past few hours in his mind.

Eventually there was a click of heels down the corridor. Heralded by a rattle of keys on the part of a policeman, Detective Copeland was shown in. He beckoned in a colleague, a small, bald man. He was a police surgeon. Copeland gestured for him to tend to Finch's broken fingers. As he examined them, he had to keep pushing back thick glasses which were intent on sliding down his nose.

'Whoever set these did a good job,' he purred, admiring Finch's handiwork.

He applied two wooden splints.

'Popsicle sticks,' he explained. 'Some wiseguy figured you could freeze flavoured soda water and sell it on a street corner. Little did he know he also revolutionized the medical industry. *There…*'

He bound them with a clean white bandage.

'Can take up to five weeks to heal properly. Got to keep them immobilized. You hear?'

Finch nodded. The man left.

Copeland thrust at Finch a brown paper bag. It contained his tie, braces, shoelaces, his cigarettes, his lighter and his watch, which he duly strapped on.

Another man appeared behind them. He had a square, close-shaven face, dark eyes and a turned-up nose. He wore a sharp black suit. Copeland threw a glance towards him.

'Your lucky day, Mr Collins,' came his parting, sarcastic shot. He turned on his heel and exited. The two men did not speak.

The new man flashed his badge discreetly – NBI. He jabbed a thumb back towards Copeland, beating his retreat.

'They don't take too kindly to the Bureau around here.'

Pointedly, the cell door remained open. He was free.

'Agent North...' the man added, extending his hand.

He whispered the next bit: '...a colleague of Freddie Delgado's.'

Agent North cast his eye at the slumbering drunks next door, one of whom had soiled his trousers, then looked around to check that there wasn't a guard within earshot. He leaned in and spoke to Finch's ear.

'You're not safe here.'

He added with urgency: 'Some of the people in this building may even have been complicit in MacLeish's death.'

He pointed at the next cell.

'Even *these* guys may be plants.'

Finch threaded his laces as quickly as he could with the fingers that still worked. North leaned in again.

'We have to leave casually, like it's all a matter of routine. Understood?'

'Yes.'

'You got your things?'

Finch nodded.

'And the codebook?'

'No, it was stolen.'

The look of desperation flashed across the NBI man's face.

'*Shit!*'

He scooped up Finch's paper bag for him.

'C'mon, we've got no time to lose.'

Outside, grey clouds were gathering. On the kerb beneath the spanking new Police HQ, which looked like some baroque European palace, a motor cab was waiting. It was the same one which had picked them up at Central Park yesterday. It was driven by the same beefy, toothpick-chewing driver who nodded a sombre hello.

'I'll get straight to the point,' said North as they climbed in. 'We're just as concerned for Freddie's safety as you are. I read the police interview notes from your interrogation. Poor MacLeish... *Jeez*...'

He shook his head.

'And as for Freddie – we've had agents scouring the Lower East Side... Germantown. We're beginning to fear for the worst.'

Finch cursed himself.

'The location... I should have paid more attention.'

'No, Mr Collins, you were in our care. We had men shadowing you. It was *our* responsibility. It was a miracle you managed to get the hell out of there, wherever that hell may be.'

'How did you find me?'

'MO3. When they got wind of what had happened – your arrest – they asked us to pull you out right away.'

Finch dug out his cigarettes and offered one to North, who declined. He lit one up for himself.

'That said, you need to be fully debriefed, Mr Collins. This pagan *ritual*, this occult thing you talked about? I mean... Christ. We need to go through every detail of what happened at the Bierkeller and all points beyond. I'm guessing you were prudent enough not to spill all to the NYPD?'

He nodded.

'I've had my fair share of corrupt cops.'

'Then that's good, at least.'

They passed the great tiered wedding-cake edifice of the City Hall Post Office, which retreated behind them as the car crossed Canal Street. There were suddenly awnings and signs written in Chinese characters, like they'd crossed a border.

'Where are we going?'

'A safe house. There's no way you can go back to your hotel. We need somewhere to hide you while we figure this thing out. And the codebook… find out who took it. Then we need to get you out of the city.'

'Is the codebook really of such importance?'

North exhaled, like the parent of a disappointing child.

'I'm afraid it is. It's a standard book for British agents in the field – people like yourself. Sure, MO3 swap their codes, but only every week. The code-setters try and shake it up each time, switch things around, but the thing is they're predictable. A codebook gets in the wrong hands, it's a big heads-up to our mutual enemies. Shows them our line of thinking. MO3 can mitigate against it – rip it all up and start again – but for the moment, till they do, every agent out there is exposed.'

'Why are the NBI so concerned?'

'Because we all operate out of the same playbook. We share a *lot* of intelligence. The American Secret Service uses a pretty similar signals arrangement. Same goes too for the Canadians, the South Africans and our friends down in Australia and New Zealand.'

By the time they hit Mott Street, they were in the centre of a full-on Oriental enclave. Finch thought of the Chinatown in London – the original one in Limehouse, by the docks, more than the commercialized variant that had sprung up in Soho.

There were restaurants and shops adorned with traditional red and gold, paper lanterns swinging, street carts packed with brightly coloured produce. Plump glazed ducks hung in the windows, everything caressed by the heady waft of spices and sizzling woks.

Finch realized how hungry he was.

There were barely any women, he noticed too, just men going about their business in their adopted Western jackets and bowler hats, living the American Dream, yet wheeling carts, or toting huge stacks of baskets while children played around their feet as if field hands in the days of the Ming dynasty.

They pulled up outside a restaurant called Mee King Lun. Finch went to step down.

'No, wait here,' said North.

He gave a sign and a mule cart appeared, driven by an elderly man. It pulled up alongside. It had a flat wagon with its goods in the back under cover. The man had long white wispy hair and a long beard but no front teeth. He wore a tatty pinstripe jacket over a grubby traditional changshan shirt that came down to his ankles, with sandals over gnarled bare feet.

He bowed his head to North.

'Okay, Mr Collins,' said the agent. 'Your next ride.'

Finch went to sit alongside the old man but North pointed to the rear.

'Under the tarp, I'm afraid.'

Finch did as he was told and climbed over the tailboard. North pulled the covering back over him. With his bad knee and patched-up hand he made heavy weather of it and lay prone in the dark. He heard the car drive off, then felt the hooves scrape and clop. The cart rattled as the mule ambled away across the cobbles.

It was hard to breathe in there. The tarpaulin was musty and damp, but it was the smell it had corralled within that was the killer. It was near retch-inducing. From amongst the sacks of rice he had glimpsed on entry came the unmistakeable whiff of raw meat... meat that was already beginning to turn.

And Finch was not alone. There was a scuffling and scratching – live produce of some sort. Finch felt for his lighter to get a better look. There were dead, skinned chickens and, catching him by surprise as he turned, right up against his head, jars of pickled snakes.

Then he realized the reason for the darkness. There, by his feet, was a wooden cage crammed full of... rats? He felt a wave of revulsion. No... not rats... *bats* – not the little flitting pipistrelles of home but huge creatures, brutalized and immobile, squashed in like sardines, their ugly pug faces seeming suddenly forlorn. He had heard how they were boiled up for soup. Meanwhile, their pungent, nervous excreta had squirted all over the floor and all over the raw chicken.

Finch could only contain the gagging for so long. He soon threw up – only there was so little in his stomach left to heave that, after the remnants of the hot dog, all that was released was a stream of gastric slime.

The cart came to a halt, the old man banged on the sideboard and Finch bashed down the tailboard and scrambled out, sucking in the fresh air. The driver pointed across the street, to the corner – a news-stand. It was where he was meant to go. Finch closed the tailgate and the cart clip-clopped off.

Finch bent and spat the residual bile into the gutter, taking a moment to recover his senses. The sky was a charcoal colour now. He felt the first spots of rain.

He crossed the street. At the rack, he stood under the awning and examined the newspapers. From the headlines – *the Washington Post, the Sun, New York World* – he hadn't missed much in his absence, although *the Post* was waxing over the delights of some performing elephants at Coney Island. But he had barely been gone for twelve hours, still only in New York for just over a day.

Some street urchins pointed at him and laughed. He checked his reflection in the shop window. He saw a man in a scuffed, stained tuxedo buttoned over a ripped shirt, only now with vomit and guano all over him.

'*Pssssssst!*'

A man in work overalls was beckoning him.

He followed him across Mulberry Street where, Finch had read, on its notorious 'Bend', before recent demolition, stood the slums and rookeries, the gangland of the infamous Five Points.

Within yards they had gone from the Orient to the Mediterranean. They were now in Little Italy, its sights, sounds and smells as authentic as if one had taken a stroll through Old Naples. Brightly striped awnings covered the storefronts; there was red, white and green bunting strung.

Up high, laundry hung between the buildings; bedding aired on the fire escapes, de facto balconies. On the street, grocery stores and fruit emporia stood next to tailors, shoemakers, wine merchants, apothecaries, musical instrument purveyors.

The street was packed, lively, noisy, the crowds artfully picking their way round the horse dung, either perusing the market stalls and street carts piled with brightly coloured olives, fennel, fat sausages and *zeppole* pastries; or heading to St Patrick's Basilica for the festival of a saint – which one, he wasn't sure.

The man moved with purpose as he weaved in and out, Finch struggling to keep up. He turned onto a new block, gesturing to a waiting Studebaker, its canvas roof up.

'Get in,' called the driver. 'Duck down in the back.'

A light drizzle increased to hard rain as they turned west again. There were umbrellas being hoisted hastily by pedestrians, others darting into doorways as they crossed Sixth Avenue into the maze of Greenwich Village, whose roads ran off diagonally from the standard street grid before descending into a random, organic pattern.

He'd skirted the area yesterday. It was wealthy, clean, bohemian. The elegant rowhouses, of Hanoverian vintage, had been built in colonial times, when New York, gained from the Dutch, was starting to boom as a British port city. It had expanded to envelope 'Groenwijk', the once-rural settlement beyond the landward palisade now marked by Wall Street.

Finch didn't get a good look at his driver, just the back of his head. By checking off the street names, Finch understood that the man was circling, doubling back on himself for extra precaution. They entered Christopher Street for a second time.

'Here.'

The driver pulled over and cranked on the handbrake. They were outside a glossy red door with brass fittings. The rain lashed hard on the panes of the Georgian windows.

'Shave and a haircut, two bits,' he said.

'*What?*'

'The knock... on the door: *rat-ta-ta-tat-tat... tat-tat.*'

Finch got out and the cab drove off. He was now soaked as well as filthy. He rapped the brass knocker in the pattern described. The door opened. It was North who answered.

'Inside, quick,' he commanded. 'Jeez, you're a mess.'

He stood, dripping onto the welcome mat.

The house was sumptuous but not too 'lived in', like a very rich person's pied-à-terre – silk wallpaper and uphol-stery, a thick Turkish rug over polished boards, tasteful portraits and ornaments on the baby grand piano, the woodwork of the skirting and door frames glossed white.

North threw him a towel and showed him up the stairs.

'You need to meet my superior,' he explained. 'Someone who can make sense of everything that's been happening.'

Finch went first, marvelling at how, perhaps only in New York, you could cross not just continents but the chasm of a class divide within the space of a few blocks.

'The first door on the left,' said North, as he ascended past a green Tiffany lamp, an ornate Venetian gondola carved from ivory, and photos of various well-heeled types with guns posing with dead mountain lions in the Amer-ican West.

'In there,' hastened North, and Finch pushed the door. But...

The cross.

Just fleetingly, for a mere second, he glimpsed it, reflected in the landing mirror from a room across the way. It was carved in dark wood and mounted on the wall, above a chaise longue. It was only small but its shape was unmistakeable – four limbs crooked halfway at a perpendicular angle.

It was too late. With a sharp shove from behind he found himself thrust into a study – with a leather settee, a desk, a chair and bookshelves.

…and Muller's mistress, Katia, facing him.

She locked him with her icy gaze. Though it was the sleek black Luger in her right hand which was grabbing Finch's attention.

The gun had a long cylindrical silencer screwed to the barrel. She gave it an upwards flick. He instinctively raised his hands. Pathetic drips of rainwater fell to the floor.

'Please don't make this any more unpleasant than it needs to be,' she said.

The muted shot seemed so innocuous, the thud of the bullet so trivial, that it took a moment to register what had happened… Agent North hung motionless, a neat crimson hole now carved between quizzical eyes, before he crumpled forward onto the carpet.

She turned to Finch and trained the gun again.

'Now you are in *my* care!'

Chapter 15

Finch stared down at North. He had landed on his knees, forehead to the ground, with his arms flung out before him like a Mohammedan praying to Mecca. A deep red stain was expanding across the pale green carpet, soaking into the thick pile.

He turned back to Katia, with her cold, emotionless expression.

'I want you to listen and listen good,' she intoned. 'If you want to get out of here alive, you'll do *exactly* as I say.'

His eyes flitted down again. She had extinguished North without a second thought – the same consummate ease with which she had broken his own fingers.

'No, not at him… Look at *me*,' she barked.

Finch went to protest. She raised a palm.

'You will keep your mouth shut and do as I tell you. Understand?'

She waggled the gun.

'*Understand?!*'

He nodded.

'Now, in case you hadn't figured it out, this is Muller's house…'

He hadn't known it was Muller's specifically, but understood that he was, without any doubt, deep in hostile territory.

In the sudden eerie silence, you could hear the carriage clock ticking away on the mantelpiece. She had half an eye on it. It was almost three o'clock.

'And we've got precisely two minutes to get out of here.'

She went to the window and looked out furtively, keeping the Luger on Finch all the while.

'If Muller is anything, it's ridiculously punctual, even by German standards. Every day he arrives home at three o'clock, alongside his lawyer, to attend to his business affairs—'

She turned back.

'—only today there is an extra item of business to add to the agenda – the execution of Mr Bradley Collins.'

'Me?'

'It's why you were brought here. He's none too fond of that little stunt you pulled – escaping, shooting two of his men…'

'Actually it was just one.'

'He now wants to kill you himself – *slowly*. That's the new plan.'

Right on cue there was the noise of a car engine. She beckoned him to the window.

'See?'

She was no dilettante. Everything about her – the way she held the weapon, her stance, the barrier of defensive distance – spoke of someone trained in the art of dispensing lethal violence.

Down in the street, a red Ford was purring towards the house. It was about 50 yards away. Its roof was up against the rain. You couldn't see inside.

'Quick.'

She hustled Finch towards the door, nudging the silencer between his shoulder blades for good measure. He had to step over poor North's body. He hesitated.

'He was no more NBI than you or I,' she uttered and prodded Finch again.

She stooped to retrieve something from North's pocket, then hastened him down the stairs, along the hall and into a passage that went past the kitchen. Evidently there was no one else in the house. The passage opened into a small, largely paved, back garden, with high walls against its neighbours, a dug border, a small rockery and some garden furniture still covered over from the winter.

The wooden gate in the back wall was stiff. Its hinges and latch had rusted, showing little sign of usage. She gestured for Finch to help her yank it open, which he did his best at one-handed. A plank of wood splintered off. She lost patience and, with a high-laced boot, kicked it off its lock. It jammed, leaving a narrow gap.

They heard the front door open. Behind them, there were hurried footsteps into the hallway, raised voices. Muller already knew something was wrong. It was the smell of cordite, guessed Finch, evidence of a discharged weapon. Someone was scuttling up the stairs.

'Go, go, go!' Katia urged and squeezed Finch through. He ripped his jacket.

There were noises inside, a shout from the first floor. A face appeared at the study window.

'After them!' came the command.

Finch and Katia were already ploughing into the lashing rain, splashing up the alley. She ran like an athlete, Finch observed – long purposeful strides, even in an ankle-length dress, arms swinging like pendulums. He did his best to keep up, but his knee hurt like hell.

At the street they paused. He calculated his odds at bolting away from her. But she had second-guessed him. She grabbed him. He felt the power of her free hand on his bicep. She snarled right into his face.

'Don't even *think* about going it alone. Your life depends on me. You *hear*?'

'Who *are* you?'

There were shouts from behind. Two men in the alley were rushing towards them.

'Muller's henchmen. Butchers. Come on.'

A streetcar clanged by. It was headed Uptown. Rain beat hard on the cobbles, throwing up a curtain of spray. They sloshed through the wet and heaved themselves up onto the tailboard. As it pulled away, the two men were now in the middle of the road, sprinting after them for all they were worth.

'We're on Hudson Street,' she said. 'We get off in four blocks.'

They eased their way among the passengers standing in the gangway. Finch was conscious of his appearance… and his smell.

Then, agonizingly, the streetcar began to slow. The conductor had seen the men and told the driver to show mercy. The two henchmen caught up.

'Easy, fellas, where's the fire?' he quipped, genial as could be. He even extended a hand to help them up. They nodded polite thanks. They wore long coats. There was no doubting that underneath them were weapons.

Finch and Katia moved deep into the throng, hanging on the rail. They elicited tuts and harrumphs with their forcefulness. Muller's men doffed their dripping fedoras and followed. They were now but feet away.

Outside, in the torrential rain, there were barely any pedestrians, little traffic. They had scant cover out there, they both knew. But the streetcar would only protect them for so long. If the men got closer…

They were already squeezing their way along towards them.

Katia motioned to the front exit. Their best hope lay in a sudden, explosive break-out through the door at the front. Finch flicked his eyes to the horizontal wire above them which rang the stop bell. She gave an almost imperceptible nod.

He took a deep breath, reached up and tugged it.

The second the streetcar slowed, Katia burst to the front, scattering people – old, young, it didn't matter – Finch in her wake. Amid volleys of abuse they were pounding through puddles again.

'Hey, you!' yelled the conductor.

And now the two men bounded out, 10 yards behind, guns drawn.

'The corner,' she yelled.

At a mailbox they threw a sharp left. Immediately after it, Katia yanked Finch into an alley. She clearly knew her terrain. It was premeditated. The two men hurtled past.

The alley was a tight, foul-smelling cul-de-sac full of all the usual city garbage. A drainpipe, that had been snapped halfway up, cascaded water down. They crouched behind a dumpster listening to the rattle of their pursuers' footfalls fade in the rain.

They had not gone far when they stopped. Then the slap of footsteps resumed, getting louder. The men had turned. They were coming back.

A few seconds later they appeared at the alley entrance. Having seemingly trapped their quarry, they bore the smug countenance of those about to have fun with an easy kill.

Katia got up and eased out before them. Finch didn't know what she was up to.

'Thank God you're here,' she said. 'He let me go. Ran off.'

They let down their guard.

'Which way'd he go?' asked one of them.

It was too late. They had made their fatal error. With two swift thuds, Katia made tidy work with her silenced Luger. It had been hidden in the fold of her skirts.

One fell dead, the other lay flapping like a trout landed on a riverbank, only squealing. She walked over and put another bullet in his head.

Finch thanked God there was no one around.

The first man's gun had skittered across the cobbles, a Colt revolver – long-barrelled, double-action, he knew... quick-fire should he need it. It was mere feet away. Finch edged towards it.

She kicked it away and spun round to train her Luger back on him.

'Don't even think about it.'

She collected both men's guns. There was a drain cover. She ordered Finch to prise up the lid. He scraped it to one side, then she dropped them in. It took a second or two for the splash.

'In here,' she said and motioned to the dumpster... meaning the bodies.

It was hard work, but with Finch's hands under the armpits and Katia taking the legs, they dragged each man and heaved him up and over into the trash, then slammed the lid shut.

'Come on,' she said.

'Where now?'

'Jersey City… the Pennsylvania Railroad.'

They were out on the street again.

'Walk naturally,' she said and took his arm. 'We'll have to fix you up. You look like shit.'

'Thank you.'

He could still feel the hot barrel poking into his ribs.

At the end of the street they were back on the shoreline again, the Hudson Piers. There, along the quays to the north, almost beckoning him to step aboard, was the good old *Baltic*, cranes over it, loading provisions. He had taken its luxury for granted.

They were soaking wet, without coats. There was a wooden booth nearby, unattended, the clerk in huddled conversation with one of the drivers queuing to get his wagon onto a ferry. In it hung some black oilskins. Without breaking stride, she whipped two off the peg.

'Hurry, before they see.'

They weaved in and out of the carts, wagons and pedestrians with luggage destined for the Jersey shore. They took shelter behind a stack of packing crates and shrugged on the coats.

'Here,' she said.

It was his wallet and passport. She had retrieved them from North.

'Go to the kiosk. Buy a ticket to the Penn Station. The next ferry.'

'And if I don't?'

'Then *you* must be terminated too.'

'Is that what you said to Freddie Delgado?'

Her hand came hard and flat across his cheek. It stunned him.

'You can walk away any time you like, Mr Collins. But *now*...? After what's just happened? As far as Muller's concerned, on top of everything else, you just killed a trusted lieutenant and abducted his mistress... in his own house. Not to mention those two extra bodies that'll turn up in the trash. You'll be hunted down. You won't last an hour. Who are you going to run to... the *police*?'

'There are other places I can go.'

'Like DC, the British Embassy?' she mocked. 'You think they won't have *that* staked out?'

'What makes you think I...?'

She cut him off.

'And don't assume Canada's any safer.'

Up close, he could feel the gun against him, but she stepped back. She showed both hands. He was not a captive. He was free if he chose.

'I'll do as you say on one condition,' he said. 'That you explain to me what the hell's going on.'

He thought he detected the faintest flicker of a smile. Almost imperceptible.

'You really are in no position to negotiate,' she scoffed. 'One signal from me and you're done for.'

She turned to go.

'Track 28. The Missouri Express. Bound for St Louis... There is a reservation for you in the name of Travers.'

And she was gone.

He went after her but she had merged into the ticket queues. Just another figure in black, hunched against the driving rain. He was on his own.

Finch stood and thought. This was his moment. If he could make it to Grand Central Station and his precious locker...

He mulled over alternative escape routes beyond the obvious… of forest trails into Canada and a steamship out of Halifax; of a way out via a Southern port – Charleston, Savannah, Mobile, New Orleans; to the British Bahamas via Florida; maybe even through Mexico… on to the West Indies.

But something compelled him to do as she bade.

The Hudson's southern quays were for the ferries to the railway terminals lined up next to each other on the opposite shore – the Jersey Railroad at Communipaw; the Erie Railroad at Pavonia; the Delaware, Lackawanna & Western at Hoboken. Between them stood the dominant station, Exchange Place, home of the Pennsylvania Railroad, the 'Pennsy' as the ticket seller called it.

It seemed strange that, for a city the size and importance of New York, it had no direct rail service to the rest of the country, other than north up into New England via the Hudson Valley. But such were the restrictions of being an island.

The ferry was large and reasonably busy. Though it was covered, he stayed on the open deck for the short crossing. He wondered what Katia had meant by her 'kidnapping'. She had got him out of a jam, all right, through this pretence, but altruism was never a motive in this game. She was using him for something.

The Hudson was grey and choppy, different to yesterday. As the towers of Manhattan retreated, shrouded in murk, so the Jersey shore loomed. The ferries ran straight into the station complex, which sat next to the giant works of the Colgate company. He recognized the name. Their dental cream came in a tube. There had been some in his cabin on the ship – 'toothpaste'.

Catching a train to the West was a well-executed routine. The ferry pulled in next to a covered walkway, which channelled passengers all the way up to the kiosk windows and platforms.

He did as she had asked and picked up his ticket.

A cheery black porter appeared, dressed in a maroon suit and cap, though he abandoned his luggage trolley when he realized that Finch, unusually, carried none.

'Gen'man's travellin' light today,' he mused. 'This way, Mr Travers…'

Having had one alias already, Finch was now going to have to get used to answering to another.

Exchange Place was as busy as any station in London and with the usual hubbub of activity – the whistles, the hisses of steam, baggage everywhere, the thrill of excitement or the numbness of boredom, depending on the familiarity. There were cafés, stores, a bookshop, newspaper stands and enough shoeshine boys to keep New York commuters polished till Doomsday.

He was limping, he realized. The adrenaline had masked the pain, but now his knee was up to its usual tricks. He was tired, aching and, above all else, hungry.

This was the point, he realized, where the continent truly began, as if New York were just a way station, a halfway house between Old World and New. There were trains for destinations he was yet to discover, deep in the heart of the Middle West – locomotives to Ohio, Indiana, Illinois, Michigan; to Cleveland, Indianapolis, Chicago, Detroit. And, on Track 28, sat the great steaming behemoth of the Missouri Express, bound for St Louis.

The carriages were sleek and silver, unlike anything back home, and the platform was low, such that one had to mount steps to climb aboard, lending a sense of size and power that one normally didn't appreciate.

There was a blast of compressed air and a hiss of steam. She was primed and ready.

They moved up the corridor. The porter showed him the way.

'Sleeper's right up here, sir. Yo' wife's already on board.'

'My wife?'

He knocked the door for Finch. He turned the handle.

'Yessir.'

And there she was.

Chapter 16

She was sitting on the bunk. When she saw him, she rose and brushed his cheek with her lips.

'Hello, darling. I was getting worried.'

She pulled him in close. She smelled not of perfume, just clean – soap, a hint of cedarwood. But he felt the Luger silencer again, just below the ribs, just out of sight.

The porter gave a knowing smile at the apparent display of affection.

'Gotta be goin'. You folks have a good trip.'

Finch rooted in his pocket for some change and, with a 'thank you', but without breaking the embrace, pressed some coins into the man's hand.

'My pleasure, Mr Travers. If you folks kin be waitin' a few minutes, one of my colleagues gon' be here with the dinner menus.'

As the porter departed, Finch resisted, but she jammed the barrel in hard.

'I'm going to tell you for the last time. If you want to live, you'll do as I say.'

Outside, there came the cry of 'All aboard!' and the vibrations of a powerful locomotive ready to take the strain of its carriages. Soon there was a conductor's whistle and a great hiss of steam.

'Do you understand me?'

He nodded.

'I'm serious.'

'Yes… I understand.'

Katia eased off, but only a fraction. He felt her move the gun to one side as a safety measure – his 'accidental' killing, he figured, not part of her plan. The chains clanked and the wheels began to creak. Then came a judder as the great Missouri Express began to pull away.

The staccato jolt was Finch's moment. With the unexpected lurch, he took a chance and struck a blow to her wrist. To his surprise, he smacked the weapon clean out of her hand.

For a second the gun lay on the bed, incongruous on the gold satin quilt. Thrown off balance, caught off guard, she failed to right herself in time. Finch scooped it up, turned and shoved it straight back at her.

'Okay,' he said. 'Now I'd like some answers.'

The stare came back at its most resolutely steely, as if this were only a minor setback in the greater struggle. She threw a contemptuous look down to the gun. Finch snarled back.

'I don't know what the hell you're up to but, the way I see things, you're nothing but a sadistic killer. Last night, for Christ's sake, you were torturing *me*! And don't even get me started on that crazed fancy-dress ritual you were part of. I think I deserve an explanation for what the hell's going on!'

She issued a snort of derision.

'You call that *torture*? You haven't been in this line of work very long.'

'You broke two fingers. And rather professionally, might I add.'

He waved the bandaged hand for effect.

'It was the least damage I could get away with,' she said. 'And your left hand at that. It had to look convincing. I even let you get a glimpse of me, remember?'

Finch felt his blood rise.

'You tell me what I need to know right now or I swear to God…!'

He jabbed the gun at her again and, for a fleeting moment, he thought she looked scared, something he hadn't yet witnessed.

'…I mean, you go from being my tormentor one minute to my helper the next… my saviour? *Why?*'

She let out a sigh.

'Because I need something from you.'

'*Need* something?'

He could see her brow wrinkle slightly as she assembled her thoughts.

'For one there's the codebook,' she said.

'The codebook…?'

He issued a wry smile.

'Not that again… I'd half imagined it was *you* who took it.'

His response confirmed something for her. She spat out a name and cursed it to herself.

'Delgado.'

'And where the hell *is* he… Delgado? What have you done with him? Poor bastard. I assume he's being held by Muller… if he's not dead by now?'

'You assume a lot of things—'

Assumption is our enemy.

'—Captain Ingo Finch.'

His own name. It threw him.

'How do you…?'

'I'll come to that in a bit… And as for Freddie Delgado? Rule number one, Finch. Trust no one.'

'I don't get it.'

She gestured to the bunk. It was a pull-down double bed, a narrow one.

'Look, do you mind if I sit?'

'Keep your hands where I can see them.'

She kept her palms up and facing him as she perched on the edge of the mattress.

'You should sit too,' she said.

'I'm fine.'

As the train picked up speed, it began to rock. He braced himself against the wall. He kept sufficient distance in case she was hoping to seize an opportunity and reverse the balance of power – a sudden swing of the leg perhaps.

The cabin was cramped, not unlike that of second-class ship accommodation, from what he'd witnessed on a mooch around the lower decks at sea. It had all that you needed in miniature – a small en-suite bathroom, shelves, a tiny dresser. There was nothing visible that could be used as a weapon immediately, though he didn't doubt her ingenuity.

He tried to read her but she was as yielding as a statue. That she had placed herself in a seated position seemed a deliberate act of submission… perceived or otherwise.

Through the window, the sun was setting and it bathed the room in an orange glow. They were rumbling out across the New Jersey flats and its meandering creeks, past the silhouettes of Newark.

'I suppose you're going to tell me that Delgado planted the bomb, too?'

'Actually he *did*… plant the bomb… It was me who telephoned you – got you away from the blast.'

'*What?*'

He rubbed the back of his neck, incredulous.

'Then how about you killing North? Whatever the circumstances, that was a sheer cold-blooded execution.'

She issued a hiss of disdain.

'The least he deserved. He was Muller's factotum, with more than enough blood on his hands, including the torture and dismemberment of Agent Kimmel.'

'Kimmel?'

'I'm guessing you've heard his name.'

He nodded.

'Why was Kimmel murdered?'

'Because he was close to something. And so was MacLeish. And it's why they'll try and kill you too.'

'So where does Delgado fit in?'

'Unlike North, Delgado *is* NBI. But he's on Muller's payroll. You didn't know it, but you were in Muller's pocket the minute you stepped off the boat. Delgado led you right to him – the fly to the spider – after he failed to have you blown up, that is… Your death was to be pinned on the Cosa Nostra, the Irish or Chinese gangs, anarchists, or whoever else they found expedient. I wouldn't get too beat up about Delgado either. Once he'd drugged your drink he went home to a warm feather bed. Possibly even his own.'

'I don't believe you.'

'That's too bad.'

'And you?'

'What about me?'

'You've still got a lot of explaining to do.'

There was a knock at the door. Finch cracked it open, keeping the gun trained on Katia the whole time. It was a steward with the menus. Finch took them and shut the door again.

'When was the last time you ate?' she asked him.

The question threw him.

'I can't remember,' she added.

'Aside from a mouthful of three-cent hot dog… me neither,' said Finch.

'The key to this is to keep up appearances,' she told him. 'We don't know *who's* on this train.'

She nodded to the gun in his hand.

'The dining car. I promise. I'll tell you there.'

They were shown to a table in the restaurant wagon. It was busy but not full. With his free hand, Finch had done his best to sponge off his jacket. He held his left arm down to conceal the rip in the seam that proceeded south from his armpit. The waiter went off to fetch their cocktails: a gin and tonic for him, a whisky and vermouth concoction for her – a 'Manhattan'.

Finch kept his right hand inside his jacket on the Luger. Outside, lights drifted by in the twilight as the Missouri Express dipped south-west now to Philadelphia, the first major stop on the route, before the track turned west again across Pennsylvania, on to Harrisburg, then Pittsburgh.

There was force in her whisper.

'Are you really going to shoot me right here, Captain Finch?' she taunted.

He had the gun, but there was no doubting who was still in charge.

'How do you know my name?'

'All in good time.'

He offered her a cigarette. She took it. He lit hers then his.

'But you should really do something about that lighter,' she said.

Its monogrammed initials were there for all to see – 'I.F.' He really was an amateur he knew, a lamb to the slaughter.

You're completely expendable.

'Okay,' he said, and, out of the view of others, lay the pistol down, covering it with a crisp white napkin, close enough to hand should he need it. It was a peace gesture. At the very least it gave a pretence of conviviality, their cover of man and wife.

The drinks arrived – hers reddish brown with a black olive, his with too much ice. All drinks in America came with too much ice, in his opinion.

She toasted him.

'Chin-chin, darling.'

He clinked his glass against hers.

'Cheers…' And then sarcastically: '…*darling.*'

The waiter asked if they'd had a chance to look at the menus. They hadn't, but were hungry enough to choose on the spot – steak and fries as the main.

'Look,' said Finch, 'can we at least reach some truce where we're honest with each other – within the bounds of reason?'

She sipped her drink.

'That would be acceptable.'

'You said there were two things you wanted from me,' he continued. 'One was the codebook… So, what was *two*?'

He could see her thinking how to couch her answer. She could clearly only reveal so much. She put her glass down.

'Look… Five years ago, in the South African War, the Boer War as you British call it, you got yourself involved, inadvertently, in – shall we say – a case of espionage.'

'How do you…?'

She raised a finger to her lips.

'Please… I need you to listen.'

He nodded his understanding but didn't like her knowledge of his affairs any the less.

'During the process of this – "adventure" – you came across some classified information, documents. Those documents pertained to the evident use, testing, by British authorities of a new weapon, poison gas… gas to be used in a battlefield scenario should – *when* – another war comes. Am I right so far?'

'I'm forbidden to comment.'

'Then I shall continue… Acting in a freelance capacity you and an accomplice—'

Annie. He'd been trying not to think about her.

'—chose to ignore any semblance of military protocol and mounted your own independent mission to expose this, successful as it turned out… a *qualified* success at any rate.'

'I do not regret anything that may or may not have happened.'

Way up ahead, the train's whistle gave a series of blasts.

'At a critical juncture, you outsmarted your adversaries by forwarding these documents on to England. Facing imminent charges, however, you employed a bit of cunning – you stashed this evidence in a security deposit box. You used it as leverage – collateral – to secure your acquittal at a secret court martial convened by the British military authorities.'

'Go on.'

'Your freedom was granted on the proviso that you kept your head down and went back to living a quiet life... Something, of course, you were unable to do. And last October, when the chance came again to poke your nose into the business of intelligence matters...'

He cut in, irked.

'What happened in London – the Russians – was not by design, I can assure you. You think I do this for fun?'

She sipped her drink again.

'A few weeks ago there was a break-in at a bank in Holborn, London, the very bank where you had stored those documents. The security box was opened, its contents were stolen. *Because* the contents were stolen, the powers-that-be called in their debt, specifically a gentleman named William Melville, head of the Secret Service, who enforced your recruitment as an agent of MO3. It is on their behalf that you are now in the United States on a dangerous mission... and as an expendable commodity.'

It seemed pointless denying it. It would ring hollow. She continued.

'Now here's where it gets interesting... The *contents* of the security box.'

'What about them?'

'Seems they amounted to a single Manilla envelope.'

He nodded.

'What *hadn't* been banked on was that within that envelope there existed no documents at all, merely a copy of *Music Collector*, a magazine for those who appreciate phonograph records...'

It was true. The joke was on them. Finch got an inner kick at his own punchline.

'Very clever, Captain Finch. But I'm sure you'll reveal the documents' true whereabouts eventually. And that, fundamentally, is what *we* want to know.'

'*We...?* You... You're German secret service?' he spluttered.

'*N-Abteilung...?*'

She laughed dismissively.

'Right, that's it... Up!'

He gestured for her to rise and tucked the gun inside his jacket again.

A waiter arrived with the soup.

'But, sir...'

'I'm sorry, my wife is suddenly not feeling very well – motion sickness.'

'I'll keep it warm for you, sir.'

Finch hustled her away and steered her back towards their cabin. This time, in the corridor, he made sure to ram the barrel hard into her back. Inside the cabin, he motioned her to the far end by the window.

He had no clue what to do with her and would have to improvise. He put another cigarette in his mouth and went to light it, but had left his lighter on the dining-car table.

There was a knock on the door. The waiter returning it. He reached to answer it with his back turned.

The short sharp stab of a karate chop to the neck felled him to the floor.

Standing over him was a seven-foot Native American with the skin burnt off down one side of his face, the flesh a contusion of scar tissue, pus and raw, flapping skin, matted in long bedraggled hair. His right hand was in a thick black leather glove.

Teetonka.

Finch was stunned. Pain shot up behind his ear. The acrid taste of fear bit in his throat.

I still have the gun…

It had clattered across the floor between them. The giant Amerindian moved, but the space was cramped, he couldn't stoop quickly enough. Finch beat him to it.

He was a big target. Finch aimed for the centre of the chest and pulled the trigger.

Nothing… She had emptied it.

The huge man leered down, baring his teeth, laughing at him.

Finch turned to Katia and raged up at her.

'So that's your game, is it? All you little rats in it together.'

Chapter 17

Teetonka smacked the gun out of Finch's hand as if it were a mere plaything. It hit the wall with a crack and the silencer sheared off, rolling across the floor. He raised his huge fist and prepared to rain it down on Finch's head. Finch flung up a pitiful arm in defence.

'Stop!'

The cry from Katia threw Teetonka.

'Leave him!'

There was a look of confusion on the oversized man's wounded face. Finch flicked his eyes over to Katia. She cast a sideways glance. She was on *his* side.

It gave Finch brief respite – nothing now but the rhythm of the train, thundering west at a tremendous lick.

The giant of a man changed tack and moved to her instead. He swung a forearm. It landed a smash to the side of her face. She crumpled to the floor.

Despite his own physical limitations, Finch struggled to his feet and leapt onto Teetonka's back. Burns like his would have been agonizing, he knew... *fresh* burns. He had treated enough of them in the field hospitals of South Africa. He sunk his fingers into the mess of flesh on the side of his face.

Teetonka gave a guttural groan and, reflexively, elbowed Finch hard in the ribs. It was like a kick from a mule. He flew into the door and doubled over, gulping for air, his diaphragm in spasm. The giant leather fist came down like a sledgehammer and caught Finch on the temple. He was flat out on the floor again, stunned, immobile, still gagging for oxygen, his vision disturbed, part blacked. And then came huge hands clamped around his throat.

Finch discerned movement. Katia was coming round, dazed. This time it was she who flew onto Teetonka's back, beating at him fiercely but ineffectually. The hands around Finch's throat loosened momentarily. But the huge Amerindian shrugged her off. She cracked her shoulder on the light bulb. The room went dark. And Finch felt the crush again. He clutched at the giant hands but they were immoveable, solid. There was only moonlight, but enough to see the man's gritted teeth and the psychopathic stare. The side of his face was now a bloody pulp.

Finch struggled to maintain consciousness but it was slipping. This time his vision went completely, a peripheral sense to be snuffed out on the way to complete bodily shutdown. He had been without sufficient oxygen for the best part of a minute already, he knew. It would not take much longer.

Visions flitted through his mind... of childhood... of school... of his doctor's surgery... of treating old ladies' bunions... of a shingle beach in Norfolk and a one-armed man... of Russians on the streets of London... of South Africa... the battlefields of the veld... of running for his life in Cape Town...

Of Annie...

And then he resigned himself to it... surrendered. He had cheated death more times than any one man had a right to. His chest heaved, the lungs sucking for the air that did not come...

Suddenly the hands were gone. He was convulsing, panting, moaning with every precious breath; nothing beyond that than the express, with its rocking and rolling and furious, monotonous *clickety-clack*.

It was Katia. The cord from the venetian blind – she had somehow reached up to get it round Teetonka's neck. She had crossed her wrists, locking them against each other, negating resistance. And he was doing everything that a fighter *shouldn't* – pulling at the ligature, scratching to get a thumb under the cord, instead of peeling off the arms that were inflicting the damage.

She knew what she was doing. He could see it in their combined shape. She was walking backwards towards the window, preventing Teetonka from establishing a defensive foothold. But the cabin was small and they slammed into the window.

'My bag,' she urged. '*Bullets*.'

She had removed them from the gun, knowing full *well* he would take the Luger from her, he realized. She had let him. She had gleaned more information from him as the subject of his stupid questioning than if she had interrogated him at the point of it. The same old trick.

With a blast on the whistle, they were into a tunnel. It was pitch black, the outside noise suddenly deafening. Then out again...

The Luger. Where was it? He was on his hands and knees feeling around. He could see she had wrapped her legs around him. They were toppling over backwards. It had skidded under the bed. He stretched his hand out to it. It was beyond his reach.

He breathed deep and extended into the stretch, finding another inch, then two. With broken fingers he dragged it out.

Teetonka was kicking furiously. Finch took a blow on his bad knee.

But there, on the floor... the bag. He fought to undo the clasp but another clout sent him reeling. Its contents scattered across the floor.

And then another tunnel...

When the moonlight returned, he could see the things that had spilled out: lipstick, a powder compact, keys... *and a magazine with rounds in it.*

'Flip on the safety. Pull up the peg,' she was yelling, as the big man's legs flailed like that of a hanging man.

'The *peg*?'

'It has two wheels – either side.'

He followed her instruction and lifted the lever. It ejected the empty magazine from the stock.

The Luger was an unconventional design for an automatic pistol. Its handle, which contained the magazine, sloped back from the breach at a sharp angle, almost 45 degrees – unlike a Browning, whose grip, like most handguns, aligned more perpendicular. Finch struggled at first, but rammed the fresh magazine home.

He turned to Teetonka and aimed the weapon.

'The silencer!' Katia yelped.

It had snapped off. It couldn't be re-screwed, even if he tried.

'A pillow,' she said.

She had meant for Finch to use it as a muffler, but he had a better idea. He grabbed one from the bed and held it over the big man's face, pushing down hard to seal off the air. It seemed to take for ever but eventually the legs switched from a kicking to a twitching.

And then… *nothing…*

Katia wriggled out from under him.

There was a knock on the door. A steward.

'Mr and Mrs Travers. Everything okay in there?'

Finch cracked the door a couple of inches.

'Thank you. My wife had a turn and collapsed.'

'You need a doctor?'

'She's okay now. It's the blood… her sugar… It happens sometimes.'

Katia called out, for extra effect.

'I'm fine now. Thank you for asking. We appreciate it.'

'Very good, ma'am.'

Finch closed the door. He looked down.

'What do we do about him?'

'We can lock the body in the bathroom… or get rid of it.'

'How?'

'The window – if we slide it down. It's dark outside.'

A sharp kick to the thigh sent Finch sprawling.

Teetonka… *He was still alive.*

Katia jumped on to him and smothered the pillow over his face again but he was simply too strong. He flipped her over. He fumbled to place his hands on *her* throat.

'Shoot him! Do it!' she wheezed.

Finch placed the gun to the back of his head. Then he remembered the pillow and paused to wrap it round the gun.

As they entered another tunnel it fell pitch black again, the echo screaming back in through a window with its vent still open. There was a flash, but the sound was lost. And when they exited, a man was dead.

It took a while for the snowstorm of feathers to settle, falling in the moonlight, thought Finch, like a surreal Dickensian Christmas scene.

Finch unscrewed the remnants of the main cabin's broken light bulb and replaced it with one from the small en-suite bathroom. Lit up now, the room was damaged and dented and there was blood spreading from under the gunshot wound. Katia was already busy. She had tied a towel round the Indian's head to stem the flow. She slid down the window and told Finch to kill the light.

'Okay, you ready?'

He was heavy. Way more so than the bodies they had hauled in the alleyway. They managed to manoeuvre Teetonka up and prepared to launch him, head first. Finch couldn't help but feel sorry. The burns would have been excruciatingly painful alone. What a miserable end.

'One... two... three...' she said, and they pushed him out partway.

Then they hit another tunnel.

There was a scrape and a thud. And, when the moon-light returned, Teetonka's head had been sheared clean off.

Finch froze.

'Again,' she said. 'Concentrate!'

This time, the large Native American was propelled out for good.

Finch pulled the blind down as best he could without its cord and turned the light on again. She urged him to clear up the feathers while she took a spare blanket to mop up the blood spillage and the bits of brain and tissue. Once done, she threw them out too.

'Your clothes. Turn around for me.'

He did as he was told. There were a few blood spots on his sleeve, but they could be washed off.

She, however... She had been wearing a dress and bolero jacket of pale blue. She was a bloody mess.

'My suitcase,' she said.

He hadn't noticed, but it sat above them on the mesh of the luggage rack. She had clearly planned this escape in advance.

She began stripping off and, by the time Finch had placed it on the bed, was down to her white cotton corset.

'This is no time to be bashful,' she said.

He sat on the bed with his hands over his eyes, but the attempt to avert his gaze was pathetic. She was in excellent physical shape, he admired – the body of a sportswoman. When she slipped out of her corset, too, he noticed a scar on her abdomen.

'Here,' he said. 'I'm actually a doctor, believe it or not.'

'I know.'

'I need to look at your neck.'

There were red marks, bruising had already begun to show.

'There's not a lot can be done. Ice, but that's not practical. Do you have a dress with a high collar?'

She nodded. It was a deep yellowy brown, like old gold. She wrestled it on.

They surveyed the patched-up damage to the room. It was presentable to a quick glance. And then she said words he thought he'd never hear.

'Thank you.'

There was another knock at the door, the steward again. Finch took a chance and opened the door a little more widely, allowing him a look in.

'I forgot this,' the man said and he handed over Finch's lighter.

'Thank you,' said Finch. 'You know my wife's feeling a little better now...'

He threw her a look and she nodded.

'I think we're ready to resume our meal.'

As they took their table, the train began to slow. After the rush of country air there came the smell of the city again. They were pulling into Philadelphia – 'Philly'. There seemed nothing out of the ordinary as the passengers came and went and porters scuttled along the platform, wheeling handcarts of luggage. He heard someone remark that one of the wagons 'may have hit a deer'.

They ate in near silence. Despite all that had happened, they were still ravenous. There were other people in too close a proximity for them to have a meaningful conversation.

After dinner, back into the night, and with the train having resumed its hypnotic rhythm, they retired to the bar. They ordered fresh drinks and lit up cigarettes and sat in the corner, safe from the distance of eavesdroppers.

'So,' she began. 'Ask me.'

And he did. To which she divulged more about Muller's grip on New York's population, his sponsorship of the American National Party and its leader, Abel Schultz.

'Don't underestimate Schultz. People like him, they have a way of stoking passions, whipping things up, playing on grievances.'

'How about that ritual – the one with me on the altar?'

'It's a pseudo-religious ceremony. Muller's a secret member of a mysterious cult called the Order of Teutons

– which mixes growing Germanization with Aryan mysticism and is proving popular among conservative members of the intelligentsia back in Germany. That cross they wear, it's called a '*sauwastika*'. It's actually an ancient peace sign – means "well being" in Sanskrit, would you believe – only the arms of the Aryan cross point in the opposite direction.'

'Nationalism is pretty easy to tap into. It's cheap politics. Basic demagoguery. You don't need mumbo jumbo like *that* to back it up, surely?'

She drew deep on the cigarette. The train wound on through the bends and horseshoes of the Alleghenies.

'You have to remember, Finch, Germany as a unified state is only 30 years old. It's having to forge its own creation myths – much like America's doing now with the "Wild West". You know, all those cowboy books, the Buffalo Bill shows, the "Western" cine-films it's starting to make. Turning away from Europe. Presenting itself as a land of pioneers and frontiersmen settling a New World. Manifest destiny.'

'You mean as opposed to being European colonists, topped up with a recent flood of cheap immigrant labour. Not to mention the extermination of the indigenous population.'

She nodded.

'It really has no other choice. The Civil War, that's a *huge* rift to heal… If it ever will. North and South, they're still different worlds.'

'But this Teutonic thing? Robes… human sacrifices…? I'm assuming that's the way Kimmel met his maker?'

She nodded.

'Don't get all holier than thou, either. It's not much different to what the Freemasons are up to in your country. It's rife in Scotland Yard, most evident in the prosecuting of the Jack the Ripper case. You should know that.'

She was right.

'Even Tammany Hall. You'll have heard of that?'

'I've seen it mentioned in the newspapers. I wasn't quite sure…'

'Superficially it's a political lobby, the Society of St Tammany, largely run by powerful Irishmen with a vested interest in the lot of New York's working class. But by origin it's an old Columbian Order whose roots are founded in the preservation of "American purity", whatever the hell that means.'

She sipped her drink.

'This stuff is everywhere. It's as if our modern age – the age of industry, of technology, of progress – it's all too much, all happening too quickly. It's sent people scampering back into the shadows, finding meaning in primitivism… in the occult. Spiritualism… mediums… seances… stage magic… even this fascination with Houdini… They're all part of it, an extension of something primal within us.'

'And Muller?'

'Muller's participation in the Teutonic rituals can't be proven – he's not *that* stupid. For him things work best when left open to interpretation – that hanging suggestion in the air; that element of fear. To know he tacitly endorses the Order is enough in itself. What he *has* done, though, is ensure a sadistic twist, using the Order to recruit his own youth movement, his own little army of foot soldiers. New recruits become complicit in some pretty gruesome acts – drugged to the eyeballs, forced to enter a code of silence and pledge their loyalty. If there's one thing sacred to the Germans, it's their damned oaths of loyalty.'

'"Their"? You're *not* German?'

'Captain Finch, I will continue to answer questions on one proviso.'

'What's that?'

'You don't ask anything about *me*.'

They were the only ones left in the bar when the train pulled into Pittsburgh. It was gone midnight. There were just a few passengers boarding this time. Finch had bought the remainder of a bottle of whisky and slipped the barman a hefty tip to leave them to it once he'd left.

'So what you're saying is that Muller, through selective brutality, exerts a hold over the local populace, but the Teutonic, mystical stuff adds something, spooks people, gives him a fear to wield?'

'Exactly, like he has some kind of magical grip – not that it can ever be proven. It pretty much gives him control over the city's German labour force. That's a hugely powerful lever to pull. Only Muller would never do something as unsavoury as get involved in politics himself. Not *big* politics. He prefers to be the power behind the throne... the kingmaker.'

'To Schultz.'

'Exactly.'

The whisky was a straight rye, *Old Overholt*. They were offered the obligatory mountain of ice to drink it over.

'Okay,' she said. 'Your turn.'

'My turn what?'

She reminded him that he'd already told her a lot, whether he liked it or not. Given events, he didn't suppose there was much she didn't already know. She was merely seeking confirmation.

He told her about the contraband heroin that Muller was supposedly trafficking, though, to his surprise this time, she claimed no knowledge of it. Again, he wasn't sure what to believe, though her ignorance *was* perhaps plausible.

The train left Pittsburgh and its huge bridges over its confluence of rivers. There were fires from the steelworks burning through the night. A train of Standard Oil wagons lumbered past, heading east.

'Property of John D. Rockefeller,' said Katia with an air of contempt. 'One thing you can say about America, Finch, a small amount of people got rich awfully quick – Rockefeller, Cornelius Vanderbilt, John Jacob Astor, J. Paul Getty and their kin. The United States eschews royalty, but it creates its own blue-blood dynasties all the same.'

Finch thought for a moment of Lady Brunswick and her own little golden circle.

He heard a guard saying they were now in West Virginia, the slender panhandle of the South that poked up between the Pennsylvania state line and the Ohio River. There were coalfields out there, Finch knew. You could glimpse the silhouettes of wheelhouses, the mounds of slag… spoil tips.

Eventually they were trundling across the mighty Ohio River. They were into the Midwest, hurtling towards Columbus.

'So, you clearly have a plan,' said Finch. 'Is it too much to ask where we are going?'

He recognized an edgy look – like she didn't want to say it but now felt obliged. She confessed she always had a plan, yes, a getaway contingency, but that was for her and her alone. She hadn't figured on bringing an extra.

'Then why didn't you just *leave* me?' he asked.

'Because you know too much, Finch. They'd tear you apart.'

She said she had a loose intention to either go out West or take a riverboat from St Louis down the Mississippi and a ship out from New Orleans.

'You seemed pretty cosy with Muller. Why the change of heart?'

It killed the conversation stone dead. Her eyes darted down then up again. It was the nearest thing he'd seen to her being sad.

'In my line of work, sometimes one has to do things that are...'

She chose her word carefully.

'...distasteful.'

'Your line of work?'

'I told you – not about me.'

He didn't know why he said it but he did.

'Was there ever anybody else?'

She was silent for a moment.

'I was married once. But love has no place in this life. You'll learn that soon enough.'

Columbus came and went.

'And you?'

'I'd rather not say,' he said.

She gave a wry smile.

'There was someone, *is* someone, isn't there? But you can't have her. She belongs to somebody else, right?'

He felt himself blush.

The train began to slow. You could hear the wheels creak and the clank of the couplings as the strain was redistributed. Then, with a judder, it came to an abrupt halt.

A steward came in to clear the tables.

'Excuse me, do you know what's happening?' asked Finch. 'I thought we were travelling now right on through the night?'

'The police are boarding and searching the train, sir.'

Finch and Katia looked at each other.

'Do you know why?'

He shrugged and went back to wiping the table.

Finch whispered: 'You think they found the body?'

'No, too soon,' she said. 'It wouldn't be discovered till morning. They were already on to us.'

Within two minutes they'd exited between the carriages and were running down the ruts of a ploughed Midwestern cornfield. Behind them they could see police flashlights sweeping around the train.

'So where *are* we going?' Finch asked.

He tried to stay with her but it was dark. They were stumbling.

'To different destinations,' she said.

And with that, she was gone.

Chapter 18

They were on the cusp of spring but the night was exceedingly cold. Finch staggered on over mounds of soft churned earth but, with no plan, no defined end goal, he was expending precious energy. He had no idea where Katia was. While initially he could hear her struggling through the mud some way ahead of him, he eventually lost her. He resisted calling out, lest the police were still on their tail.

He tried to get his geographical bearings. The train had passed through Columbus, Ohio, but he really did not have much idea where he was beyond that.

He carried on for what he thought must have been about a mile. In the moonlight there were the shapes of buildings up ahead – a farm. The lights were out. He knew the best use of his resources would be to bed down for a few hours and try and make sense of things at first light.

It was only as he plodded towards it that it suddenly hit him just how utterly exhausted he was. He hadn't slept at all in the best part of two days, and that was on top of all that he had endured both physically and mentally. He was shivering, as much through shock as cold.

There was a barn – a large wooden one. He eased open the door and crept inside. He struck his lighter then realized it wasn't the safest of things to do in such a place. Once his eyes had adjusted, he saw the ladder up to the hay loft. He climbed it. There was straw – bales and a welcoming loose mound. He buried himself deep, insulated against the cold.

His sleep was a surreal slumber in which he flitted in and out of dreams and memories. In some ways it seemed he had drifted off for ever… in others, just five minutes. Eventually he felt sunshine on his face and another strange sensation… wet, warm. His cheek was being licked… by a dog.

Blinking an eye open, he saw it was a border collie.

So they have them here too?

The friendly black-and-white animal was a reminder of home – of a different, simpler world – and he reflected on Katia's words about modernization and the pace of change. It backed away as he sat up and gave a friendly yelp, extending its front paws forward and leaning down onto them, wagging its tail. He reached to stroke it but it kept its distance. He held his hand out for it to sniff and gradually it edged back within his orbit. He ruffled the warm fur behind its ears and was, for a moment, lost to everything.

He wondered how the hell it had climbed all the way up to the loft. But there was a loading hatch, through which the sun was now streaming, and a gangplank that ran up from the ground. Eventually the dog went back its own way and Finch descended the ladder. He had no weapon. Katia had taken the pistol. He noted a pitchfork – there should things turn nasty.

There was no one around… for the moment. Even if he slipped away quietly, he still had to deal with the matter of his conspicuous appearance. He was in the middle of a Midwestern farm landscape dressed in a dinner suit.

The barn was of the 'prairie' design with the high Dutch gambrel roof, double-sloped on each side, almost rounded. He peered round the edge of the building into the yard. The dog appeared again, his new friend, and it followed him. There was smoke rising from the chimney of the main house and a door that was open – the kitchen. He could smell bacon.

The land was flat and seemed to stretch on for ever. On the breeze came the sound of a tractor far off across the field. He could see it, maybe half a mile away, lazily plodding up and down, turning at intervals. It was a great, steam-driven thing, pulling a plough. There was a cloud of birds circling for worms behind it.

They gave us grey squirrels, we gave them starlings.

He sneaked from the barn to an outhouse and reconnoitred further. To his delight there was a washing line. Clothes had just been pegged to it, wrung, warm and steaming, fresh out of the copper. They sagged with dampness, but they would do. He grabbed a thick woollen shirt and some work trousers. He could hear a woman singing.

There was a shed in which hung some outdoor gear. It smelled of creosote and oil. The odours transported him back to South Africa – the field hospital that had been set up at the Boer farm during the push on Kimberley. Alongside a workbench and a rack of tools, there was a thick, tattered corduroy jacket that looked too small. He took a chance on it anyway.

He gazed to what he judged to be the north and confirmed it with an old army trick, aligning the hour hand of his watch to the sun and drawing an imaginary north–south divide between the hands. There were telegraph posts in a line on the crest of a slight mound – a road.

'Hello,' came a small voice.

He turned. It was a boy. He was no more than about seven years old in a rough, home-knitted sweater and tatty knickerbockers. The dog nuzzled into his legs.

'Hello,' said Finch.

'What are you doing?'

He was curious, not accusatory.

'Oh… nothing.'

Finch put a finger to his lips, the expression of a secret that must be kept. It was lost on the kid.

'You talk funny, mister.'

'I do?'

'You want me to fetch Mommy?'

'No, it's all right.'

Finch reached in his pocket and pulled out a quarter.

'Here…'

He set it down on the workbench.

'…let's see how long you can go without making a sound. If you can count to 100 – slowly – the quarter, it's all yours.'

'Don't wanna.'

The kid ran off. Then he could hear him.

'Mommy… Mommy… There's a man who talks funny…'

Shit.

'…and he's stealing our clothes.'

Finch wrapped everything into a bundle and set off as fast as he could. He had put himself 100 yards clear of the farm buildings, beyond the whitewashed rail fence that surrounded them, when he heard a male voice.

'Hey… you!'

Finch ran. There was more shouting. He looked back. The man had a shotgun.

The first shot rang out and he threw himself to the ground. But evasive measures like that gave his pursuer a chance to catch up. He couldn't afford to stop. Finch remembered his time on the battlefield. When under fire, you zigzag. On he ran, weaving left and right, clothes under his arm like a rugby ball.

Another blast.

He prayed that he wouldn't get winged by buckshot. A third shot came but the man seemed in no mood to keep up the chase. He heard some expletives hurled in his direction, then the man turned back.

Finch eased off into a walk. His knee was killing him.

But now there was a horse buggy rattling up the farm track... It had two men sitting on it, one cracking a whip at the solitary beast, the other yelling and gesturing. The path was a hard, compact drive that headed in the direction of the main road.

Mired in the heavy soil there was no way he could outpace it. They would outflank him easily. But, up ahead, next to the path, sat a pile of long, stacked logs. Finch scurried as best he could towards it. There was a drainage ditch and he scrambled over it, before hoisting himself up onto the loose timber. They were rough sections of tree trunk that had been cut for farmyard use, each uniformly 12 feet or so in length. He heaved at the top log with all his might but it wouldn't yield.

Turning to put his back to it, using his whole body weight and what power he had left in his legs, he tried again. There was enough give this time to merit a third attempt and he summoned every ounce of strength. With a creak and groan, the uppermost piece of lumber wobbled for a second before giving way and clunking down, rolling to a stop across the path. Then he pegged it for all he was worth.

Hastening towards the main road, he heard the scrape of hooves and the horse whinnying at the obstacle. Because of the ditches either side of the path, it would be unable to divert around it. He cast a glance behind. The men had climbed down to haul the log out of the way. It had been merely a temporary block. There was a squeak and spring of suspension. The men were back in the buggy.

It was gaining fast and Finch stumbled down across the ditch, ploughing through the mud again. He was maybe 50 yards short of the road. In the distance was a black speck. He could hear the sound of a motorcar. As it hove into view he could see it was a truck, a flatbed – one in rather poor condition by the look of it and pootling along with a rattling engine that was belching out black smoke from the exhaust.

The horse buggy was heading fast for the road. The second man was bracing himself. There was another rifle…

Finch knew it instantly from the way the man pivoted down the 'repeater', the knuckle-guard lever underneath the trigger – a Winchester, far more accurate and, at that range, deadly.

A shot rang out – the phenomenal crack rolling across the plain – and a clod of soil shot up to his left. Starlings scattered into the sky. Finch threw himself into a deep rut and hugged the ground. The buggy stopped. Someone was on foot, charging towards him.

Another crack… A shot sheared off a chunk of mud just a yard in front of his head.

The truck on the road was Finch's only chance. The telegraph poles were strung at regular intervals. If he could make it to the nearest one for cover, then dart out, he could flag it down.

He decided to let the next round be loosed off. It would give him seconds. The shot came even louder, much closer this time. Then Finch got up and ran for his life.

'Hey!'

There was another shot, an explosion of soil by his left foot, and Finch pulled himself behind a telegraph pole, standing straight, keeping himself shielded.

A slug thudded into the wood, the other side of his head.

The truck was close. He dashed into the road and waved his arms frantically, hoping that no one dared shoot him dead in front of a witness. Indeed, the man with the gun was now scurrying back to the buggy.

The driver of the truck had no choice but to slam on the brakes. It screeched to a halt just inches from him. He could feel the heat of the radiator.

The driver leaned out. He was a middle-aged black man with a ragged, grey beard. He eyed Finch up and down.

'Now here's something you don't see every day,' he said.

Finch was not only in a ripped tuxedo but covered in mud.

'Any chance of a lift?'

The man looked over to the approaching buggy, which was now coming round, up onto the road behind them, the driver whipping the horse furiously. He seemed to take wry amusement at the prospect of throwing his own proverbial spanner into the works.

'Hop in.'

Finch threw his bundle of clothes in and scrambled aboard.

'Please,' he urged. 'Fast!'

'Don't worry,' said the man and eased up the throttle.

The truck was piled with scrap metal – bits of tubing, pipes, part of a bed frame, old rusty springs, gasoline canisters and some stacked crates of particularly vocal chickens, whose volume increased with their acceleration.

The horse-drawn buggy followed for a minute or so but, once the truck had moved up through the gears, gave up the chase. The man smiled to himself. He was wearing a beaten-up straw hat with a plaid shirt and a woollen jacket. He'd been chewing on sunflower seeds, their husks littering the cabin. He spat one out of the window. as they passed a road sign. It proclaimed they were in Wayne County.

'Wayne County?' asked Finch.

'Just like it says.'

'But *where*?'

'*Where…?*'

The man pulled a wide-eyed look of surprise mixed with curiosity.

''Bout 40 miles short of Dayton is where.'

'We're in Ohio?'

'Indiana… for the moment.'

'Is that where you're headed, Dayton?'

The man gave an 'uh-huh'.

He looked Finch up and down. He laughed to himself. It was a deep, infectious chuckle.

'A woman?'

Finch couldn't help but smile.

'I wish it were that simple.'

The man extended his hand to shake.

'Moses,' he said.

'I suppose,' said Finch, 'you should call me Travers…
No, *Collins*.'

The man chuckled again.

'Sounds like you got a story to tell.'

Chapter 19

'Listen, do you mind if I change?' asked Finch.

He indicated his bundle of clothes.

'Go right on ahead.'

Finch pulled off his shoes and wriggled out of his muddy tuxedo.

'You ain't from round these parts,' Moses mused.

'I'm from England.'

'Boston?'

'Not New England – *Old* England.'

Moses exhaled a whistle.

'This story gettin' bigger and bigger.'

Finch laughed, the first time in a while. In all that had happened to him, Moses seemed about the most sane person he had run into.

'Moses, I think I need to get to Columbus… to go back east.'

'The railroad?'

Finch nodded.

'From what I hear, the Pennsy'll take you all the way. New York?'

'No, Washington… DC.'

Moses pulled a face as if to say that this destination came with certain implications.

'Happy to take you to Dayton. You can make your way from there.'

He hesitated.

'You got money? 'Cause that's somethin' I *can't* stretch to.'

Finch patted his tuxedo, the wallet was still there. He transferred it to his new outfit. His passport too, which he tucked into the lining of the corduroy jacket, keeping it separate.

'Don't worry.'

The borrowed clothes were damp but fitted well enough for a passable imitation of a farmhand, what with the two-day beard growth, unkempt hair and the bruises and dirt from his scrapes.

'Moses,' said Finch. '*Thank* you.'

Moses gave a tilt of the head in appreciation.

'You took a chance on me,' Finch added. 'You know nothing about me. I mean, for all you know, I could be some crazed killer on the run.'

I am a crazed killer on the run.

Moses grinned.

'You don't look the type. And one thing's for sure, I never much cared for the folks that run that place anyhow. And when someone appears out of the blue dressed up like a penguin…?'

Finch laughed again. He rooted for his cigarettes.

'I'm not a criminal… Not in the traditional sense.'

'So, you're an *unconventional* criminal?'

'Let's just say I'm being chased by people who *are*. Criminals, I mean. Traditional ones.'

He offered Moses a cigarette, took one for himself, and lit them both.

He couldn't go into too much detail but felt obliged to offer some kind of explanation.

'The thrust of it goes like this,' he began. 'I'm a British citizen; I'm in the US on some quite important business. Unfortunately there are some people out there who'd rather I didn't *complete* that business. And somehow, due to an unforeseen sequence of events – *circumstances* – I find myself out here in the Midwest, bumping along a prairie trail in the company of your good self.'

'I see... Say, this a British smoke?'

Moses examined the cigarette between his fingers.

'Yes.'

'Not bad.'

He exhaled a lungful.

'Course when you grow up workin' the tobacco fields, you only appreciate the strong stuff.'

The land went on endlessly – dark ploughed earth, but with some fields of winter crops and some patches of long prairie grass in the fallow areas. And there were tall wooden towers dotted about the landscape, grain silos. But, above all, the landscape was flat – so flat the straight dirt road continued all the way to the horizon, the telegraph poles strung along it, with their sagging cables, almost boring in their uniformity.

'I'm sorry... You say you worked the tobacco fields?'

'In Kentucky. Yessir. Soon as I could walk and wield me a knife, I was out there a-cuttin'.'

For someone from the compact confines of the British Isles, the vast endless space, and the silence, felt perversely oppressive; the sky with its sheet of low grey clouds, weighing heavily. The only variation in sound came in the occasional crunch of the gears as Moses navigated his way round a rut or pothole.

'Seriously?' asked Finch. 'You started that young?'

'Yessir, me an' my kinfolk.'

He pulled up his left sleeve. The inside of his forearm bore a scar, like a large welt, an old injury of some sort. No... it was a burn, with its raised pink ridges of seared flesh, even on his dark skin.

And then Finch realized... Not a scar... a *brand*. Moses had been a slave.

'Freed when I was 14. Just as the War a-startin'. The Underground Railroad. You know, not like a regular railroad, like the kind you be takin'. A metaphorical railroad – trails and safe houses. Network o' good Samaritans spiritin' black folks from the South to the Free States. And a good many beyond that too, up to Canada.'

Finch simply didn't know how to react. He sat stunned for a moment before mumbling a platitude about 'being sorry' when the truth was he had never heard anything so shocking. For all that he had witnessed in South Africa, the fact that holding humans in bondage had occurred within living memory in a modern industrialized country like the United States, and that it was mentioned so casually...

'My Pappy, he long been sold,' Moses continued. 'Never see him again. But Mama? She *determined*. Got us across the river into Ohio. Folks from the underground sent over a raft. Hauled us back on a rope. Me, my little brother... It was winter. That water perishin' cold...'

He paused, wistful.

'He with the Lord now.'

The truck had a wing mirror. Something in it caught Moses's eye.

'Shee-*it*.'

He threw a thumb over his shoulder. Finch turned. In the distance was a cloud of dust.

'Are those our farmer friends?'

'No, sir,' said Moses. '*Worse.*'

The dust cloud appeared to be gaining on them.

'He hope to catch us before we hit the state line.'

'How far?'

''Bout another three miles. Hate to say it, but this ol' girl...'

He patted the dashboard.

'...don't think she got the legs.'

Within a couple of minutes the dust cloud had made considerable distance on them. It was close enough now for Finch to see that it was being kicked up by a motorcycle, a shiny black motorcycle – an incredibly noisy one at that. Soon it had pulled right behind. It was being driven by a policeman. He had a leather jacket over his uniform, but with the starred badge of authority upon his chest, and wore a peaked cap rather than a domed helmet.

'You might want to lose that,' said Moses and pointed to the bundled-up dinner suit. Finch stuffed it under the seat.

The policeman was waving an arm, indicating for Moses to pull over, but he pretended not to see. Next thing the bike was alongside, the rider repeating the gesture more emphatically.

They could determine the big green sign up ahead with the white lettering upon it, vaguely making out the word – 'Ohio'.

But the cop knew their game and pulled in front. There was no way round him and he slowed them down to a stop. He wagged a finger, meaning for Moses to pull the handbrake lever and turn the engine off. Moses obliged, though, noted Finch, he didn't kill the motor completely but set it to a low idle.

The cop parked his bike on its stand — it had a double-barrelled name, 'Harley-Davidson', saw Finch — and he made considerable theatre out of dismounting, then removing his goggles and long leather gauntlets.

He sauntered over, chest puffed. He wore khaki jodhpur trousers, like riding breeches, flared at the thigh.

'I told you to kill the engine.'

'Please, sir,' said Moses. 'You stop this motor now, it take for ever to crank the thing back up again. Maybe never.'

The cop thought about it.

'This your vehicle, sir?'

It took Finch a second to realize that the man was speaking to *him*, not Moses.

'No, officer.'

'This *your* vehicle?' he repeated to Moses, dropping the 'sir' this time.

Moses shook his head.

'You stole it?'

'No, sir.'

'Then whose vehicle is it?'

'My boss's, sir.'

He looked at Finch again.

'You his boss?'

'No.'

Any humour, decided Finch, had been beaten out of the man in childhood.

'*Who's* your boss?'

'Mr Downey,' said Moses. 'You know Downey's chicken farm over on West Grove?'

Finch noticed how Moses had changed his accent and demeanour, like he was playing a part — that of a supplicant — like he had been in this spot many times in his life.

'You live over there?'

'Yessir. Mr Downey. He a good man. There's a shack on the farm. He let me stay there. I take care his chickens for him, yessir, I do.'

The policeman got a notebook out and took his time writing this all down.

Moses whispered to Finch.

'You want me to break for the border? Once we're past that sign, he can't touch us.'

'What happens when you try to come back?' hissed Finch. 'Don't put yourself in harm's way. He knows where you live, for God's sake.'

'Then steal his motorbike and be on *your* way. I'll create a diversion.'

'I don't how to ride one.'

The cop looked up.

'Step out of the vehicle.'

Finch gave a reluctant shrug.

'I said, step out of the vehicle. *Now!*'

They complied, climbing down, wearily engaging their feet with the earth. Moses had bandy legs and something of a stoop, Finch noticed, and moved with the pace of someone broken by a life of manual labour.

The cop made them stand apart, their backs to him.

'Hands on your heads.'

'Is that absolutely necessary?' asked Finch.

'Just do it!'

They could hear him pacing behind them.

'What's your name, son?' he asked.

There was patronizing contempt in the way he addressed Moses. The cop was at least 20 years his junior.

'Moses.'

'Moses what?'

'Clotilda. C–L–O–T–I–L–D–A.'

'What the hell kind of name's that?'

His pencil scraped on the paper.

'My adopted name, sir. I was named after a ship.'

'A ship?'

'Yessir.'

'What kind of ship?'

'Kind that's lying on the seabed in Mobile harbour, way down in Alabammy.'

Silence.

'And you?'

'Me?' asked Finch.

'Your name.'

He improvised on the spot.

'Whitehall… *Melville* Whitehall.'

Finch hoped that the name would crop up on any arrest lists MO3 might be scrutinizing, alerting them to his ongoing existence. Moses raised his eyebrows in amusement.

'Funny, Whitehall. I've just come from a farm back on the main road. They said there'd been a thief. Stole some things from their property. His accomplice was a negro driving a Ford truck with a whole load of junk in the back. Am I ringing any bells here?'

They said nothing.

'Said the white man was about six feet tall, dark brown hair. Had stolen some britches, a shirt and a work coat – pretty much described as exactly the kind you're wearing right now. Guessing for all the crap you got back there it wasn't the first property you'd turned over, either.'

It was no good, the game was up.

'Look, officer, I can explain,' urged Finch. 'And the first thing I want to tell you is, Mr Clotilda, he's entirely innocent in all this. I was on the farm, yes, and I took some clothes. It was a matter of survival. I will happily reimburse...'

'You'll shut your mouth.'

'Please... Mr Clotilda, I didn't even know his name till a second ago. All he's guilty of is stopping to give a stranger a lift out of the kindness of his Christian heart. Please, let him go.'

'Okay, hands behind your backs, both of you...'

There was the clink of handcuffs being readied.

Finch thought fast. On a motorbike, the cop couldn't take them in. He had no means of calling for assistance, unless he knew some was already on its way. If he was reliant on a passing vehicle stopping, they hadn't seen anyone else the whole time – he could be waiting for hours. And he certainly wouldn't leave them alone in any interim as they were close enough to walk to Ohio, unless he chained them to a pole.

The fact that he consented to allow the motor to keep idling suggested he was going to put them in the back and drive them in to the police station himself.

The engine noise gave them cover.

'I'm gonna get us to Ohio,' whispered Moses. 'You disable the cop.'

'Disable?'

'Push his goddamn bike over. Time he's righted it and restarted it, we'll be clear.'

'No, Moses...'

The cop yelled at them again.

'Be quiet.'

'He's got no backup,' said Moses.

'He's got a gun.'

'You dodged plenty of bullets this morning. Figure it's your lucky day. On the count of three...'

'Fuck. No, Moses... *Please*...'

'One...'

'Quiet!'

'Two...'

'Put your wrists together.'

'Three...'

In an arthritic flash, Moses was climbing up to the cab. The cop dropped the cuffs and reached for the holster on his thigh. As he did so, Finch lunged at the motorbike and heaved it over, giving it a hard enough shove to leave a clear path ahead. The cop spun, taking the heat off Moses.

The shock of his shiny new steed now lying in the Indiana dirt threw him. Moses was already easing the truck forward and Finch ran to the blind side.

'C'mon!' Moses yelled and upped the engine hard into the next gear.

Finch glanced back. The cop had drawn his revolver and was pointing it his way in what seemed an over-exaggerated training academy stance. The chickens clucked like crazy.

Finch tried to leap up but it was beyond him. The truck was at a sprinter's pace now.

'Here!'

Moses extended a forearm and Finch clamped his own on to it. He yanked Finch aboard as the first shot whistled past.

'See... You're *lucky*!'

Finch scrambled in as the second clanged into the door. They were up to a full 30mph and hurtling towards the big green sign.

The motorbike revved. Finch ducked, turned and saw the cop stamp down on the pedal.

'Moses. What the hell? Why did you do this? They know where you live!'

He gave a great gurgle of a laugh.

'You think I'm gonna give the police my *real* address... And hell, that name I gave ain't no more real than yours. I live in Dayton with my wife and three kids. Why, you think I look like the kind of man who lives on charity in some ol' chicken shack?'

'I don't know, Moses,' Finch deadpanned. 'You played it pretty convincingly.'

Moses howled with delight.

'Moses *is* my Christian name, by the way. It's the other...'

'Clotilda?'

'Yessir. Name of the last slave ship that ever entered the United States. Little history lesson for our big-mouth lawman should he ever get the gumption to look it up. My little contribution to the well-roundedness o' his education.'

The bike was screaming towards them again but they had vital seconds to spare. They crossed the invisible state line that divided Indiana cabbages from Ohio ones. The bike revved down and stopped like it had run up against some magical barrier.

It was another idiosyncrasy of the United States, thought Finch. That each state functioned as its own entity, like a country – legal jurisdictions ending according to surveyors' lines of latitude and longitude or the courses of rivers. It was why, he had already surmised, that Federal institutions – like the NBI – deemed agencies of the capital's over-arching authority, were so mistrusted at state level. America was not a nation as such but rather a *concept* – a voluntary union of sovereign territories whose individual goodwill could be withheld. It explained a lot about the Civil War.

They rattled on into Ohio, the 'Buckeye State' as it had styled itself on the sign, Moses pointing out the occasional tree which looked, to Finch, just like a horse chestnut, and apparently yielded a poisonous nut, shiny reddish-brown, that fitted the exact same description of a conker. He told Finch too about the flying machines that had been spotted gliding hereabouts courtesy of the local Wright Brothers, and Finch thought back to where else he'd heard their names previously – in the company of a crazy American 'kinematographer', a man who made 'moving pictures', on a long painful train journey across the South African Karoo.

As he and Moses proceeded, they passed the odd farm wagon and one oncoming car, the only thing of note about it being the stand-off as they headed towards one other, each vehicle unclear as to whether it should pass on the left or right, things not being so regimented as the traffic of New York.

Eventually the road split, one fork heading south to Cincinnati, while they continued along the branch with the signs now showing 'Dayton' and 'Columbus'. Eventually there was a line of further buckeyes to break the monotony of the landscape, suggestive of a riverbank. Indeed, there was a slight hump in the road ahead as it crossed over a bridge.

But it was too late... Two police Model Cs had been angled in a shallow 'V' to block their passage. They'd been clever, knew Finch. They'd positioned themselves on the far side of the rise so that they weren't visible until one was upon them. He had a curious flashback to history lessons, the Duke of Wellington and his similar deployment of troops in battle.

In any case, word was out. Either the Indiana police had telephoned ahead to their Ohio counterparts, or there was a general manhunt on anyway.

Moses ploughed on but knew, within moments, he'd have to stop.

'Moses, I implore you. The only way for you to get out of this is to say that I forced you into this. Give them your *real* name this time. Tell them I jumped your vehicle – *hijacked* it. Everything you've done up till now is because I *made* you do it.'

There was reluctance, but Moses nodded.

'See, under the seat, my old clothes. It's evidence. You've done more than enough. Don't imperil yourself… your family.'

There were several policemen strung across the road behind the vehicles with a plain-clothes officer in charge. Moses slowed.

'How you jump me with no gun?' he asked.

There was a spanner on the floor, a wrench, Finch picked it up.

'Trust me, Moses. Do exactly as I say. Stop the vehicle short, right on the brow of the bridge itself.'

Moses thought for a second, nodded, then skidded his truck to a halt. Finch pulled Moses roughly from the cabin, pressing the spanner into his back, simulating a pistol. Moses complied with a struggle of resistance.

Finch yelled out: 'One false move and he gets it!'

There were several weapons raised in his direction. Two of the police had rifles. They were resting elbows on the hoods of the vehicles to steady their aim.

The plain-clothes officer called out: 'Put the weapon down. Let the negro go!'

Finch edged towards the bridge's low side wall. The river was wooded, its banks steep, and it ran southwards towards, on the other side, some rocks and boulders. It was maybe 20 feet wide with a rush of water to suggest sufficient depth, though there was no way of telling. It was dark, you couldn't see the bottom, which was at least a promise of it. It was a 10-foot drop from road level.

'Please, don't shoot!' cried Moses.

Whispered Finch: 'Thank you. For all that you've done...'

He'd already made sure to shove half the contents of his wallet into Moses's glove box.

Replied Moses, under his breath: 'Good luck.'

In a flash, Finch was over the wall and plummeting. There was a cold hard splash and he bobbed up, just thankful that he'd gauged it right.

He had jumped in on the upstream side and was washed under the bridge for a few seconds, giving him momentary cover. He merged from the darkness into a volley of gunfire.

He took a deep breath, dived, and let the current carry him, sensing the hiss of bullets all around him. He emerged again behind the first of the large, smooth boulders.

'There he is! Over there!' cried a voice. But it was Moses calling out, diverting the police to the bank on the opposite side.

For some reason, Finch was still clinging to the wrench and he threw it towards where Moses was pointing, creating enough of a splash to elicit more gunfire in its direction.

The current was moving at quite a lick and was tugging at his legs. There was a tree branch in the water, cruising by. He grabbed it and let it carry him. There was a bend ahead. The ominous crack of a rifle was followed by a ping off the rocks. But, within moments, Finch was out of sight, being swept along at the river's mercy.

There were more rocks up ahead, like small rapids, but he managed to cling on, kicking himself through the gaps. Through a swirl of foaming white, he was into more tranquil waters as the river widened out, sending him drifting sedately through the greenery.

He held on to it for as long as he could, but ultimately it was cold, too cold. His medical knowledge told him that he could only survive in water like this for so long. He didn't know how much daylight he'd put between himself and his pursuers, but when some shallows appeared, he kicked his feet and steered the branch to the shore.

He lay there panting, face down amongst the mud and pebbles, and he thought of poor young Moses and his flight to freedom. For a brief moment the clouds moved clear and a burst of thin sunshine took the edge off the cold. He wriggled his fingers and toes, then hands and feet, then moved his arms and legs. He had emerged intact.

And then he looked up. Just inches from his face was a pair of brown brogues.

The shoes belonged to a man in a double-breasted suit, wearing a fedora. He was flanked by two men who shopped at the same tailor but were bigger, broader – his muscle. If they *were* police, then they weren't – Finch guessed – part of the local crew back on the bridge.

'Okay, fellas,' the man instructed. 'Get him in the car.'

Chapter 20

Finch sat in the back, wedged between the henchmen. The main man sat up front with the driver. All Finch knew was that they were off the Dayton road now, heading towards Cincinnati. It was the same flat countryside – endless fields, endless sky.

They travelled in silence. Though Finch had asked a few questions at first, the repeated 'Shut your mouth' instruction on the part of the boss made it quite clear that answers would be unforthcoming.

It took about two hours, but eventually they turned off the main track and wound through wooded countryside to a long drive that led to manicured lawns, trimmed hedges and a grand brown-brick mansion. It was built in the colonial neoclassical style with a cupola atop the roof and white Greek columns at the front. There was a paddock nearby, surrounded by whitewashed wooden rail fencing, in which a pair of palomino thoroughbreds sauntered.

The car crunched to a stop on the gravel and Finch was escorted inside. The interior was just as impressive – the high ceilings and grand staircase, the looming chandelier... Folks round these parts, at least the ones with money, seemed to enjoy their sense of space inside as well as out.

Finch was shown into a large drawing room. It boasted a grand piano and Queen Anne furniture, a thick Persian rug, velvet drapes, potted ferns, and portraits on the wall of stern-looking colonial forebears and bucolic country landscapes. Finch had a blanket thrown round his shoulders and was deposited in a chair, an upright Chesterfield, his clothes still damp underneath.

'Wait there,' the leader said, in what, by his standards, was a lengthy monologue.

Finch hadn't been cuffed or tied. Indeed, there hadn't, for once, been a single weapon pulled, not that it was needed with the two gorillas either side. When the men departed, closing the door, Finch was left to his own devices. Tempted as he was to start snooping, sitting in comfort on his own, in silence, was the preferred option.

The room had another set of double doors leading into it on the far wall. And, eventually, they swung forth. She was just about the last person he imagined he'd see, but there she was, bustling into the room dressed in a long, dark green dress with a black shawl around her shoulders.

'Lady Brunswick?'

Instinctively he stood.

'Please, Captain Finch, sit,' she motioned, her tone brisk, businesslike.

She swished to the armchair opposite.

'Quite a pickle you've got yourself into,' she said.

She donned her lorgnette glasses and read down a list that evidently summarized Finch's adventures of the past 48 hours. She looked up again.

'You're lucky. I happen to be a friend of Mr Stanford White. He dropped into conversation something about meeting a "Mr Bradley Collins" at Madison Square Garden and you going off to the Bierkeller Club. MO3 were already monitoring police activity and tracked you via your arrest, then Muller's house, through to the Missouri Express. Our man on the train lost you, but then all that excited local police telephone chatter...'

She shook her head.

'"Melville Whitehall"... A flag for us, but none too subtle... The sharks will be circling. I'd already given up tickets to *Swan Lake* at the Met to head on out here – 600 miles at the drop of a hat, not easy at my age. I hope it's worth it. How's your knee, by the way?'

'Oh, you know...'

She nodded at his bandaged hand.

'It's not *all*, I see.'

He hadn't had a chance to nurse his broken fingers. Though the police medic had done a good job, he considered. Despite all that had happened, the dressings, the splints, they'd remained pretty much in place. As for pain, so much had happened that he hadn't even had a chance to think about it.

'It's fortunate that I know the owner of *this* sumptuous spread,' Lady Brunswick went on. 'Seemed a suitable place to bring you in, given your location.'

'Not bad,' said Finch, casting an eye around. 'Though not the sort of place one imagined existed in the Midwest. Feels more, I don't know, antebellum. You know, like we're on a *plantation*.'

She gave a wry smile.

'My dear Captain. Just because Northern landowners didn't *keep* slaves, it didn't mean that they didn't *use* slave labour. The Ohio River is a stone's throw from here. On the other bank lies Kentucky – the South. There's always been a brisk trade across it. Things are never as they seem, Finch, especially in America.'

She lowered her spectacles.

'Anyway, as I was saying… Stanford White. He gave us a lead… But it was only when we got word from our spotters on Miss Madeleine Foche that we really put two and two together.'

'*Madeleine Foche?*'

She took her time. She got up and went to the drinks cabinet, then came back with two large brandies.

'You must be cold. We'll get you dried off, but in the meantime…'

She raised her glass to his good health.

'Please…' he pressed.

'Oh yes… Miss Foche… *Mademoiselle* Foche. You'll know her better as Katia.'

There was an urgency to Finch now.

'Have you caught her yet?'

She smiled again, several steps ahead in a game in which, he felt, he was still left flipping through the rule book.

'Why on earth would we *catch* her?'

'Because she's possibly German intelligence.'

The upward inflection made it sound like a question. There came a wry smile and a patronizing scoff.

'*German?* No, Captain Finch, she's with the *Deuxième Bureau*, the French security agency.'

He sipped his brandy. It was pungent stuff. You could get drunk on the fumes.

'She does a very convincing impression of a German.'

Lady Brunswick explained how Madeleine Foche was originally from the borderlands – the town of Colmar in Alsace, once French territory, but annexed by Germany after the War of 1870.

'Her parents were murdered by the Prussians,' she added. 'Right in front of her. She was four years old.'

'Why do I get the feeling that everything in this business seems to boil down to the personal?'

'A facile interpretation, Captain. Would Mademoiselle Foche like the province of Alsace-Lorraine returned to France? Her loved ones avenged? Yes, of course. But her motive in this business, like ours, indeed like *yours*, though I'm not sure you fully comprehend it, is altruistic. It's to prevent another war. Or, should I say, prevent another war happening on Germany's terms. What you might call laying the groundwork in order to ensure a victory for the Entente. As I told you before, that means keeping America onside and away from the Kaiser's clutches.'

She explained to him that Foche/Katia had heard in advance of Finch's mission and hoped he'd keep away.

'The intelligence community is a small community, Captain Finch. Unfortunately, your intervention compromised her position – that is, of someone working undercover with Muller. It's not your fault. I can only express my regret that France and Britain… we did not coordinate our intelligence. That's something we need to correct.'

She offered him a cigarette from a large silver case and fastened hers into her long holder. Finch leaned over and lit it for her. To his surprise, his trusty lighter still sparked after all it had been through. He pondered whether it was his only real friend.

'Katia' had spent considerable time working her way into Muller's inner sanctum, she went on. She had provided a lot of information. Every morning she would go and buy flowers from her local florist, using a 'dead drop' en route to pass secrets to her French handlers.

'If we're all such bosom pals, then why did the *Deux-ième Bureau* attempt to burgle my bank's safety deposit box back in London? Steal the documents...?'

Lady Brunswick grinned.

'Let's just say such documents can be a useful tool when it comes to focusing diplomatic attention; France's way of ensuring that she and Britain are bound to each other. Don't worry, MO3 has plenty on *them* too. And, in any case, we know your documents are currently safe and sound, even if they're not where we all thought they'd be... *Right*, Captain Finch?'

'And the codebook?'

'Well, it's always useful knowing each other's encryptions and cyphers. The NBI are after the codebook for the very same reason. Let's just call it speaking each other's language. But yours was an old code we no longer use, a *plant*. Fortunately, when it comes to relaying misinformation, Delgado – the actual thief, by the way – was not a very good cryptographer. Gave himself away immediately when he tried to use it.'

'So Delgado, is *he* with the Germans?'

'Not exactly. He is NBI, or rather *rogue* NBI. Pretty much a freelance, a gun for hire—'

It was exactly as Katia had told him.

'—but a pretty nifty operator all the same – probably from his Pinkerton days – working all sides against each other. Or so we've now found out... On that score you've done sterling work, Finch. That was a secret objective of ours – for you to flush him out... which you *did*. We knew that third-party knowledge of a codebook would ultimately lead to it getting stolen. It's a trick we've tried before. But to lose it *on the first day*, Finch? That really is a record.'

He drew hard on the cigarette and felt a brief, light-headed wobble.

'Delgado is driven by greed as much as anything else,' she added. 'Cutting side-deals here, there and everywhere. Which is why he's of most use to *us* being left in play... for the time being. His knowledge of both NBI tactics and Muller's affairs will make him much sought-after by rivals. He may lead us somewhere.'

'Somewhere?'

'Hopefully to the source of Muller's new-found wealth. That *heroin* he's been trading. We understand there are three tons of it being stored somewhere in New York, with the Mafia. You've heard of *them* now...'

'Yes.'

'...and other crime syndicates eager to get their hands on it.'

Finch told her that Katia seemed unaware of the heroin.

'*Très amusant!*' spluttered Lady Brunswick. 'It was through the French that *we* found out about it. It's just a question now of locating it.'

The sun was shining. Outside, the greenery looked paradisiacal. Finch wished he could just walk outdoors with his brandy and sprawl on the lawn.

'And then there's the murders of MacLeish and Kimmel,' she was saying.

Finch told her what he knew. It seemed merely to confirm information she already held.

'MacLeish was protective of Kimmel, they were friends,' she explained. 'Now *that* had become personal, which always leads to trouble... something you already touched upon. Which is why MacLeish had gone beyond the bounds of duty in sniffing around this case. Unfortunately, curiosity killed the cat.'

Finch sipped some more.

'Kimmel was working undercover and had got himself in pretty deep by the sounds of it,' he added. 'I assume the savagery of *his* death can only be because Muller was pretty furious with him, which means he must have uncovered something.'

'In my experience, such things usually occur after an act of betrayal.'

'So, he was *exposed*?' asked Finch. 'Muller found out who he really was?'

She nodded.

'Quite probably on a tip-off – most likely from Delgado?'

She sighed. 'It's what we suspect, anyway.'

Finch downed his drink. He relished the burn at the back of his throat.

'If Kimmel's killing was ritualistic, there *must* be witnesses. I was in just such a room for just such a ceremony. There were maybe 70 people present at least – robes, chanting, the lot...'

'That's the intriguing thing. From what we know from Miss Foche, no one's talking. Muller's got a hold over the locals. They're scared. Complicit. And, in the case of the new recruits, drugged.'

Finch set his glass down and stood. He paced back and forth as the thoughts came to him.

'Please, be careful... the rug,' she said. 'The owner had it shipped at great expense.'

But he was in full flow.

'So, what do we know about MacLeish? His death happened quickly. Delgado must have alerted Muller right away – maybe even delivered up MacLeish himself if he's as duplicitous as you're suggesting. We already know that Delgado planted the bomb to do away with *me*. But why was MacLeish killed so swiftly? Did someone panic? And why was *I* suddenly thrown to the Teutonic lions?'

'Because you *survived*, Captain Finch. And when Delgado heard MacLeish was going to question Chang—'

'Chang?'

'—he knew he might tittle-tattle about that little crack-erjack bomb. It was Delgado who had commissioned it. Revelation of that fact would have outed him as a rogue NBI operator. Addicts are easily persuaded, easily manipulated. They tend to talk.'

'Chang's a heroin addict?'

She nodded.

'Delgado *was* operating independently in trying to kill you, by the way, nothing to do with Muller – that much *was* true. Delgado had his own motives.'

'You mean getting me out of the picture, not poking around in his affairs.'

'Correct. His connection with Chang was established during that Idaho bombing you may have heard about...'

Finch nodded.

'He did some time out West. Was involved in the investigation.'

She set her own glass down.

'It was careless of Delgado, though,' she continued. 'He should have been leading lines of inquiry *away* from the likes of Chang, not *towards* him. MacLeish was the unlucky victim, his head quite literally delivered up to Muller, as if done for a favour.'

'Wait, wait, wait...'

Finch paused in his pacing.

'MacLeish sought out Chang because he thought he knew who *might* have made the bomb, not that he made it *himself*. He's in prison, remember? No, there's more to this. It all suggests that Chang *knows* things. About Muller, about Delgado, maybe about the NBI...'

Lady Brunswick gave a schoolmistress's smile of satisfaction – at the B pupil demonstrating progress.

'Indeed,' she said, 'and we'd like to find out *what*. Unfortunately, we'll not get much out of Chang now. He's been drugged to oblivion and thrown in a psychiatric ward. But here's the thing, Finch. We know, back in New York, he did some work, before his incarceration, for an anarchist group called the Black Flag.'

'Black Flag?'

'A nasty little nest of vipers. No one knows quite who they are but they pop up here and there – the odd act of political violence... a stabbing, a shooting; the random act of destruction... a building torched, a police station attacked... If we can find out what *they've* been up to, it might yet give us a lead; something else to pin on Muller... and, by association...'

She stopped herself.

'I'm sorry, I shouldn't be too ungracious about our host.'

Our host?

It was only then that Finch got it – this was *his* house, Senator Schultz.

'Oh, don't worry,' dismissed Lady Brunswick. 'A case of keep your friends close, keep your enemies closer. Though he really is becoming such a frightful bore.'

She handed him a newspaper, the *Chicago Tribune*. He sat again. She pointed to a front-page story – a piece about Senator Schultz and his latest bit of Entente-bashing.

'His intention at running for the Presidency? I can confirm that from the horse's mouth. He's making an announcement in three days. It's why he's away now... Currently in Washington, preparing his nomination.'

'Assassination seems so simple.'

'As I told you before, we can't afford for him to be martyred. No, he needs public shaming... discrediting... exposing... We just need those final pieces of the puzzle to be put in place.'

Finch set the paper aside. He saw that Jules Verne had just died. He pulled his blanket round.

'So what happens now?'

Lady Brunswick explained that Foche – *Katia* – bravely, had decided to return to Muller.

'I don't know what was said between you, but she evidently changed her mind about fleeing Muller. At great risk to herself, she is now playing the abduction story and how she escaped from your evil clutches. She is a very resourceful young woman – she even robbed a gas station at gunpoint and stole a car. She drove to Cincinnati and telephoned Muller to bring her home. We and the French tried to dissuade her but she was most insistent. We are now obliged to go along with her yarn, doing all we can to "massage" facts and facilitate this version of events to maintain her cover. And that, by the way, has involved agents scouring the swamps of New Jersey in order to dispose of the body – and head – of a certain Native American.'

He felt himself blush.

'And me?'

'Well, you're a marked man now across a handful of states. The police... the NBI... Muller – daresay a number

226

of other parties, too – all expressing a deep interest in your whereabouts. Quite impressive, Captain Finch.'

He wasn't sure if this was sarcasm.

'We send you back to New York, they'll have staked out all the obvious places. That locker in Grand Central Station, by the way. Clever move.'

'Thank you.'

'That said... you, on the run... It does come with certain advantages... It's actually very useful to us – like a piece of bait thrown to lure some big fat fishes. More importantly, you being on the loose helps preserve Miss Foche's cover story. Which is why we need *you*, Captain Finch, to continue to play the part of the fugitive.'

He hadn't heard the henchman come in behind him.

By the time he did, the leather cosh was swinging down.

Everything went black.

Part Two

Chapter 21

Hell's Kitchen

The cramped cellar bar was airless, stifling hot, with a thick fug of smoke that clung to the low ceiling. Finch sat at the back and supped the beer he'd bought with the few pennies he'd managed to scrape together. He wiped occasionally at the sweat – his and others' – the sort that condensed on the ceiling, trickled down the walls and dripped from the beams.

Up front, the chairman was attempting to bring the meeting to order. With a whitening goatee and modish fiddler cap, he sighed, removed his round spectacles and rubbed at tired eyes.

'Comrades,' he announced. '*Finally*... a resolution.'

The party secretary read it out loud: 'Motion 12c... "We, the chapter of the 20th Ward, Manhattan, of the Socialist Party of America, recommend to Conference that we commence with urgent food and clothing collections, to assist the oppressed people of Russia."'

To a general hum of approval, the chairman blocked his papers on the trestle table, hung with the party banner – an image of hands clasped across the globe.

'I take it we've no need for a vote?'

There were nods all round, a tantalizing moment of unanimity. Until, to a collective groan, that accursed hand shot up again...

'Comrade?'

It was the same young man Finch had noticed at the previous mind-numbing meetings he'd sought out. He was up on his feet, thin, gaunt, blonde hair unkempt, his face a contorted rictus of hate, jabbing his bony finger of accusation.

'A clear distinction must be made between "historical materialism" and *"dialectic* materialism",' he was raging. 'Your action, by its very nature, is *inaction*.'

The chairman sighed and appealed for calm.

'Please, brother. We're just trying to find practical solutions…'

'Sit the fuck down!' shouted someone less charitable.

'True socialism comes not from food parcels but from *arms*!' the young man continued. *'Das Kapital*: "It is only achievable by the forcible overthrow of all existing social conditions."'

'You mean the *Communist Manifesto*…' someone corrected.

There was a smattering of laughter.

'Son, if you're gonna quote Marx…'

'Fuck you.'

A big man got to his feet, beer-drinker's belly accentuating his size. He towered over the young radical.

'No, fuck *you*, you little shit.'

Finch nudged the man next to him.

'Is it always like this?'

'Mostly.'

The party had come about through a recent merger, it was explained – between the Social Democratic Party and the Socialist Labor Party; theorists versus activists. They had more mistrust of each other than of capitalism.

'But if you want to see something that *truly* unites them,' he added, 'it's their contempt for *this* moron.'

He pointed at the young man, ranting away, spittle flying in the big man's face.

'Who is he?'

'Name's Max Sheldrake. Fronts for a group called Black Flag...'

At last.

'They show up at meetings all over the city, he and his cronies, trying to use the Party as cover, eat us away from within. Sometimes they just sit and watch, biding their time, looking for opportunities to exploit. But here, situations like this, the minute they sniff weakness...? Basically, they're just *anarchists*. Wanna piss all over everything.'

There was a gang of them, taunting the big man now, egging Sheldrake on.

'Emma Goldman and Alexander Berkman!' Sheldrake was shrieking. '*They* took the initiative – like they did with Henry Clay Frick. The only way to deal with fat-cat industrialists like that is to *liquidate* them.'

'Last I heard, Frick survived. And Berkman's in prison for attempted murder.'

'Brother Berkman was betrayed... by reactionary scum...'

He poked his finger right in the big man's face.

'Scum like you, *motherfucker*!'

That was *it* – the big man swung a sizeable fist, but he was slow. Sheldrake ducked. Meanwhile, his acolytes had sprung into action, gathered around him, snarling like rabid dogs.

'Please! Order!' urged the chairman. 'Division is the proletariat's true enemy.'

A beer bottle flew through the air and burst on the wall. The chairman ducked behind the table.

'Here we go,' said the man next to Finch.

There were fists, scuffles, more bottles – all the while Sheldrake goading his detractors from behind his protective cordon.

A young woman stood on a chair – a shrill, skinny, wild-eyed girl dressed in black. She clutched a copy of a revolutionary magazine, *Mother Earth*, whose cover bore a crude cartoon – a vicious Uncle Sam planting the Stars and Stripes in the open mouth of a prone Filipino native.

'Imperialists!' she screamed. 'The lot of you. *Imperialists!*'

Squeezed out from the ensuing mêlée, a body blundered into Finch and his neighbour. They shoved him off.

'And with that, mack,' said the man. 'I'm outta here.'

–

Half an hour later, after the Party diehards had crunched away over the broken glass, Sheldrake was left sitting in the middle of a circle, his ragtag of devotees pulling their chairs in close to hang on his every word.

It was obvious to Finch why such meetings were staged in places like Hell's Kitchen – the police were never going to trouble themselves here with something so mundane as breaking up a fight. In some ways an anarchic state had already been achieved.

He lit up a Lucky Strike he'd been forced to scrounge once Lady Brunswick's men had stripped him of his wallet – supposedly to ensure his 'authenticity' – before dumping him back into the city so unceremoniously.

He was still struggling to reconcile the contradiction between his own appalling treatment and yet his apparent vital importance to fulfilling MO3's overall mission – if indeed bringing down Schultz was the *real* endgame. Nevertheless, his own redemption… salvation – probably his *life* – still hung on the outcome. As, he knew, did Katia's. He had little choice but to swallow his pride and stick to the job in hand.

Choice has nothing to do with this, Captain. You were not selected without good reason.

He exhaled into the stale air, wedged himself in the corner and turned again to Sheldrake, unsure as to whether he was appalled or impressed at the sheer depth of love one man could have for the sound of his own voice.

'He's m-m-magnificent, isn't he?'

'What?'

It came from a small, fey youth, who had noticed Finch sitting alone. He seemed ridiculously fragile, oddly feminine and with a noticeable stammer.

'He's quite *something*,' Finch replied.

He studied Sheldrake once more – the hollow, intense eyes, the wisp of fluff on the chin; the sallow skin that hadn't seen the sun in some weeks.

'While the decadent Tsar sends his fleet to Japan,' he was raving, 'our brave comrades have been at the forefront of the struggle – the "permanent revolution" as comrade Trotsky puts it – doing as comrade Lenin bids…'

Finch wondered when Sheldrake found time to breathe. He was obsessing now about the Bolshevik–Menshevik split – hardly of deep concern to your average Manhattanite, Finch mused, nor to the downtrodden masses of St Petersburg with the Imperial Cavalry bearing down on them.

Said a red-haired kid, a youth who spoke in a voice that mimicked his master: 'We have friends elsewhere – Karl Liebknecht... Rosa Luxemburg... Taking the war to the enemy...'

Friends?

'Just like we did in London,' nodded Sheldrake. 'Our attempt on the Russian ambassador.'

Finch tried to stifle his snort of derision but failed.

If only they knew.

Heads turned.

'You think this is funny, old man?'

He was tired, aching, his clothes were filthy and, no doubt, he smelled. 'Old' was not unreasonable.

'It's your misrepresentations I find amusing.'

The lady friend was snarling now.

'He's a cop.'

'Do I look like a cop?'

'Then who *are* you?'

They were on their feet surrounding him, one of them a smashed bottle in hand, another armed with a chair leg. But Finch was not cowed.

'Someone,' he said, 'who wants to make a difference.'

And, for the next ten minutes, he told them... about the war in South Africa, the 'Great Imperial Struggle' and how, on his return, he had chosen to devote his life to the liberation of the oppressed.

'We don't need the likes of you,' someone snapped.

'But you *do*,' said Finch, addressing them all. 'You talk of war, but do you *know* war? Because I've seen war, seen it up close. And war is hell. It's not pretty. It's dead bodies. It's hacked limbs and spilled guts and plenty of blood. It's boys your age screaming in agony for their mothers and women raped and homes burnt to the ground and disease and starvation – a land of confusion and shit-yourself fear and people with dark skin treated as if they were animals. And all of it, every last drop of it – this, you can *always* be assured – will come dressed up in glory and flags and monuments and pomp and circumstance, be it Manchuria or Cuba or the Philippines or Transvaal or St Petersburg or, yes, New York City… And you can bet your bottom dollar every time on one other sure thing – of some fat capitalist getting rich off it.'

They were quiet now, some nods. Even Sheldrake was silent.

'So let me tell you, *all* of you, from someone who's been there. If you *are* serious about a war – a class war, against the people responsible for all this, right here in Uncle Sam's backyard…'

He nodded at the cover of the young woman's magazine.

'…you're going to need someone who's been in the heat of combat.'

They looked at each other, waiting for a cue from their leader.

'Can you get us guns? Weapons?'

'Yes,' Finch lied.

'What's your name?' Sheldrake asked.

He was in.

'My name…? What the hell is a name? Nothing but a label – a prison sentence, comrade – the words that dictate the life you're meant to lead… but don't have to if you don't choose it.'

They seemed to like that last bit.

His cigarette had gone out. He got out his lighter. They'd left him that at least.

The red-haired kid saw the initials – *I.F.*

235

'Whoa… Mr "If"…'

–

In Gramercy Park they stood outside a tall brownstone which, even in the dark, Finch could see, was an impressive property. There were eleven Black Flag members plus himself. Most of them were drunk, a couple of them barely able to stand.

'Sammy's place,' said someone. 'It's where we live.'

'Sammy?'

'That's m-m-me,' stammered the fey youth, the one who'd approached him earlier. 'Sammy Proctor.'

'This is *yours*?' asked Finch.

The young man with the red hair whispered in Finch's ear.

'His parents disowned him, man. Loaded. Moved out to East Hampton. Left him the run of it.'

A bottle rolled across the cobbles. There were flashes of light in neighbouring windows, twitches at curtains.

And now Sheldrake was on the steps, yelling.

'Sammy, get your ass up here and open the fucking door.'

Said the red-haired one: 'Watch this.'

In what seemed an effortless leap, Sammy was onto the drainpipe and shinning up it.

'He does this all the time, man.'

Then he edged along the first-floor windowsill, slid in a flat-blade knife, and popped the catch on the sash window.

Whooped Sheldrake: 'G-g-go-go-go, you stuttering little prick!'

A moment later Sammy was opening the front door from within. Sheldrake turned to the others.

'Now everybody, get your asses inside.'

Sammy's parents were of serious means, no doubt about it, observed Finch – with the trappings of the bourgeois life Black Flag so detested, though not so much that it prohibited their indulgence of it. They had expressed their theoretical disdain in other ways, the expensive wallpaper and paintwork daubed with crude words in red paint – 'HATE'…'GREED'…'ENVY'…

In the parlour was a beautiful Steinway grand piano. Someone had carved into its side, 'CHAOS'.

The kitchen was a mess, with its filthy piles of used dishes and saucepans – 'dialectic materialism' clearly not extending to the necessity of doing the washing-up. The rooms were strewn with greying mattresses, dirty blankets and stained bedding. There were burns everywhere, cigarettes being stubbed out on any available surface.

Finch held Sammy back.

'How long have you been letting them stay here, Sammy?'

'A while.'

'And until *when*?'

'Until the revolution.'

'You give them money too?'

'My t-t-trust fund…'

He was nervous. He gulped for air.

'I s-s-signed it over.'

Sheldrake leaned out from the master bedroom.

'Don't you talk your shit now, Sammy. You shut the fuck up.' Then to Finch: 'Help yourself to whatever you want, man.'

As Finch walked past, the girl was already snapping a rubber strap round Sheldrake's forearm. Finch saw the glint of a needle.

Sammy led Finch to an upstairs lounge.

'Look, it's okay, see,' soothed Sammy. 'Here, *you* have the couch. M-m-m-me, I'll sleep on the floor.'

Sammy offered a swig of cheap vodka, then got out a small tin, shoe-polish size, and tipped the browny-white powder into it. With a casual skill he added some kind of clear solution.

He lit the tin over a lighter until the smoke started to rise, swirling it to keep the liquid in motion, then began inhaling the fumes through the snapped-off stem of a clay pipe.

'This way's called "chasing the dragon",' he said. 'We had this Chinese guy here... Jimmy...'

Jimmy Chang.

'Hey, Sammy,' yelled someone else this time. 'Keep your fuckin' mouth shut.'

Sammy lay back and drifted off.

Then – Finch didn't know why – he took the pipe himself...

–

And then, finally, Finch got it. He understood – the bliss, the euphoria, the sheer golden ecstasy that was flooding through his entire body. He was an eagle, soaring high near the sun, then swooping down, in a great warm rush, to flash through cherished scenes of his own life, each glory, each triumph, each outpouring of love swelling to an opiated rapture, a state of transcendence that he never wanted to end.

Marx was wrong. Religion isn't *the opium of the masses.*

He didn't know how long he'd been gone – hours... days... weeks... months...? Time no longer had meaning.

But eventually, as the feeling began to subside, he could hear a voice, and feel a motion, a rocking… a beating, a drumming.

'C'mon.'

He was down in the dark, swimming, then crawling his way up a rabbit hole towards the light.

'C'mon,' the voice was going again. 'If you want to be part of this – to live *here* – you've got to prove yourself.'

He was up and out, a human soul once more, in an aching body – a body that now just wanted to sleep. He squinted to focus. It was Sheldrake. He was kicking the sole of his shoe.

'Prove myself?'

'Show that you're committed to our cause. Not just full of bullshit… Call it an initiation.'

Chapter 22

In the dead of night, the horse cart plodded down the lower end of Broadway, wheels creaking away till it reached the towering thicket of granite that constituted the Financial District of Lower Manhattan.

There had been a small group selected for the mission and they huddled in the back alongside Finch – Sheldrake, his woman, the red-haired kid, Sammy and two brothers, also part of the crowd who had been dossing down at the house. Twins or not, Finch had yet to determine but, amid the general silence of drunkenness and delusion, the pair were the only ones who seemed to speak on the journey – conversing in their own private language, grinning to each other as if over some shared secret. They were leaning back against a mouldy old wooden crate, part-covered with a horse blanket, that reeked of chemicals, petroleum of some sort.

The cart diverted off the main drag where the driver – a shaggy-haired man who went by the name of 'Moose' – brought his overworked beast to a halt, steaming and snorting in a narrow passageway in the shadow of the Federal Hall.

'Here we are,' said Sheldrake, and kicked down the tailboard with a nonchalance, signalling for them all to get out.

He motioned to the brothers.

'Clarence… Claude…'

The siblings, still half-intoxicated, scraped the wooden crate to the edge. It was about four feet long, three wide and deep, and clearly heavy. They grabbed the rope handles to dump it down on the sidewalk.

Finch was having trouble focusing his vision, but it was then, when the blanket was whipped off, that he saw it, that solitary word stencilled in black paint…

'*DYNAMITE*'.

'What the…?'

He tried to shake the fuzz that was still enveloping his thinking.

'Exactly what it looks like,' hissed Sheldrake.

The two brothers laughed their strange fraternal laugh.

'No, I mean how *old* is this stuff?'

The wood was mould-stained, rotten around the bottom.

Sheldrake referred the question.

'Moose?'

'Dunno,' he shrugged. 'My cousin brought it back from out West one time. Workin' on the gangs. Buildin' a dam in the Arizona Territory.'

'*When?*' spluttered Finch.

'Guess… maybe eight years ago… ten. Shit's been sittin' there in a lock-up in Fort Lee ever since. Figured it was goin'-a waste.'

Finch gestured urgently into the back of the cart.

'The crow bar…'

'The *what* bar?'

'Whatever you call it? The jemmy… the *jimmy*…'

One of the gurning brothers passed him the iron tool.

'What do you think you're doing?' shrieked the girl.

But Finch was already at work, carefully inserting the wedged end under the lid and gently prising it off, easing up the rusty nails that had been holding it down.

There was enough street light to see inside. Resting on old straw, the stack of eight-inch cardboard tubes were sticky with goo which had crystallized to a crust in parts.

'Jesus Christ. Do you realize how *unstable* this is?! Dynamite's only good for a year at best – and with regular turning to avoid chemical imbalance. This liquid seeping out—'

He pointed.

'—it's nitroglycerin. Just a physical shock – a small jolt – can set it off.'

Sammy was backing him up now.

'He's r–r–right, remember what Mr Chang said?'

Sheldrake cuffed him hard round the ear. He mimicked him cruelly.

'He's r–r–right. Will you shut up about the goddamn Chinaman. You've been warned enough. If the stupid Chink hadn't got himself locked up, we wouldn't be relying on *this* cheap shit.'

One of the brothers went to light up a cigarette.

'*No*, damn you,' snapped Finch. 'Put that thing away!'

'Hey, I give the orders around here!' barked Sheldrake. 'And what the fuck do you know anyway? What you told us – the army – you were just a *medic*.'

'I know enough that it's a wonder we're all still here in one piece.'

Sheldrake gave one of his smug, self-satisfied smiles.

'Then that's going to make things very interesting.'

He gave a signal to Moose and smacked the nag on the rump.

'See you at the pick-up.'

The horse clip-clopped off.

Finch came face to face with him.

'What the hell are you up to, Sheldrake?'

He grabbed Finch by the arm and led him purposefully to the corner, from where they could peer, from
behind the bronze statue of George Washington, across
Wall Street into Broad Street.

'*There.*'

In the full glare of Edison's electric street lighting stood
the tall, imposing white building with its marble portico,
soaring Corinthian pillars, and the triangular pediment
atop it with its Romanesque demigod statues: '*Integrity
protecting the works of man.*'

'Behold, the belly of the beast.'

Its name was carved in gold for all to see.

Finch spluttered through his own incredulity.

'You seriously telling me you're going to blow up the
New York Stock Exchange?'

Sheldrake nonchalantly extracted a pack of Bull
Durham plug tobacco. He pulled off a wad, tucked it
behind his lower lip and chewed it over.

'I'm not. *You* are.'

'I am *not.*'

'Well, if you don't...'

There was a sneer as he leaned in. He was holding in his
hand Finch's battered passport, part mangled from its dip
in that Ohio river, but still just about presentable. Finch
checked his jacket... the lining... If MO3 had missed it,
Sheldrake hadn't. He must have taken it from him while
he was out of it.

He lunged for it. Sheldrake whisked it back.

'Otherwise I'm sure there'll be some people very
interested in the whereabouts of a certain "Mr Bradley

Collins". People not necessarily known for their kindness, if you get my meaning.'

'What if I just walk away?'

'You're free to do as you like. But a man like you...? Says here you're the Managing Director of a corporation called British Nitrate. For me that doesn't quite square with being the anarchist you claim. Yep, I figure a man like Bradley Collins is hiding something – the *truth* most likely. Either that or he's on the run... So, do this little job for me – for *us* – and we'll talk. Then you can get back to procuring all those weapons you promised us... Unless, of course, that was a pile of shit too.'

Finch let out a sigh.

'I don't deny that Bradley Collins is a name I've used. One of several. My occupation is a cover. What I told you – about South Africa... my views on war... on empires – I meant every word of it. You think I'm slumming it with you just for kicks?'

'You're "slumming it" with us – if that's how you want to put it – for *something*.'

There was a scrape and a scuffle behind them. The brothers had ignored Finch's warning and were part-carrying, part-dragging the accursed crate towards them, the others in tow.

'Jesus. No!'

That was it, knew Finch. The confirmation. Black Flag were not a credible political group, rather just a personal cult – a vainglorious exploitative exercise on the part of some spoilt, feckless brats – and one almighty bullying brat in particular.

I must go along with them now regardless.

'So here's what we're gonna do,' instructed Sheldrake. 'You and Tommy—'

He pointed to Finch, then the red-haired kid.

'—you're going to take the crate and place the sticks around the main door.'

'Sheldrake, listen to me. Think this through. You have dangerous, unsafe ordnance. None of us is in a fit state. You can see from here, too, that the door's solid metal. Steel probably. You'll put a dent it for sure, but you're not going to bring the house tumbling down. What, exactly, are you hoping to achieve?'

'To show that capitalism's days are numbered,' snarled the lady friend on his behalf.

'And what about *him*?'

Ambling up past the building's steps was a policeman, whistling to himself, swinging his nightstick. He seemed like an afterthought in all this.

'There'll be more,' cautioned Finch. 'The Centre Street station is just round the corner. Trust me, I've been there… in a cell.'

Sheldrake looked Finch in the eye. Finch could see it now – not idealism, just sheer malevolence… *hate*.

'"What is genuine is proved in the fire. What is false we shall not miss in our ranks" – Karl Marx.'

'Actually it was Engels.'

Sheldrake faced Finch and lifted his own shirt. He revealed a long-barrelled Colt revolver tucked into the waistband, its stock resting on the hollow stomach below the near-emaciated ribs.

'I really don't give a fuck.'

Sheldrake signalled to one of the brothers, snapped his fingers, and he scampered off back into the shadows. Finch could see the brother darting along the front of the buildings, presumably off to create some kind of diversion at the other end of the street.

'Right… according to Moose's cousin, the fuses are good for sixty seconds. So Tommy – and *you*—' he said it sarcastically. 'Mr "*If*"… When you're ready…'

'You mean you don't even know for sure about the length of the fuse?'

The girl was agitating now.

'See, he's a counter-revolutionary.'

I have to do this.

'Look,' offered Finch. 'Why don't we go up the side of the building? That alleyway over there. No one will see us. We can sneak up. If this is about symbolism, the newspaper headlines will still announce that an attack was made on the New York Stock Exchange, plus you're less likely to get any innocent bystanders hurt.'

'The police aren't innocent. The more we take down the better.'

'Then for God's sake, just—'

'The front door. I want to blow capitalism's ugly face right off. Show her for the ugly bitch she is.'

Finch studied the crate. It would be a cumbersome exercise to drag it with them, not to mention highly dangerous.

'Then let us do it this way. You – Tommy…'

The red-haired youth turned to him.

'Take your jacket off. Carefully wrap four sticks in it. Then, when the policeman is distracted, we walk across. Note "walk", not "run".'

'What about the rest of the dynamite?' snarled Shel-drake.

'Leave the crate. The police will see it, recognize its volatility, and dispose of it accordingly. In and out quickly – you live to fight another day.'

The lady friend was agitating again, this time directly into Sheldrake's ear.

'You want me to do this or not?' asked Finch.

With reluctance Sheldrake nodded.

There had been little thought put into strategy. Before they were even ready to cross the road, Claude, the brother, had appeared at the far end of Broad Street, hurling abuse at the policeman. He was turning to march in his direction.

'Christ almighty,' yelled Finch, and motioned for Tommy to hurry. Finch himself removed his own jacket and lay four sticks in it, swaddling them like a newborn.

The constable was shouting back at Claude now, threatening him with immediate arrest if he didn't shut up and go on his way. Attention would already have been drawn.

Finch, with Tommy in tow, crept out from the shadow of the Washington statue. They hugged the wall along Broad Street, then, when opposite the Exchange, prepared to cross. Finch looked over. The copper had already drawn his nightstick.

'Tommy... Now... We cross!'

Tommy was struggling. His bundle was insecure. He fumbled a stick but caught it mid-air. Finch felt the trickle of cold sweat. But there was no time to waste. He used the cover of Claude's distraction and edged across the cobbles and up onto the marble steps, Tommy behind him.

There was more shouting, more abuse. Then the policeman blew his whistle. Two short blasts, the call for assistance. The response – *one* short blast – was already being echoed by several of his colleagues round about.

The whistles threw Tommy. He hesitated. There were the sounds of frantic footsteps then a 'Hey you!' as he was spotted, exposed in the street lights' glare.

As he turned, he lost his grip...

The next thing there was a blinding white flash and an almighty crash of an explosion, the blast reverberating around the narrow avenues of concrete.

Finch ducked behind the base of a column and threw his body over his own dynamite, cradling it as if it were a living thing. Stone and gravel rained down.

As the thick, acrid smoke began to clear, he could see that, where Tommy once stood, was now a small crater.

There was also a policeman who'd been flung to the ground nearby. He was getting to his feet now, dusting himself down.

A gunshot rang out. There, back by the Washington statue, was Sheldrake.

You colossal idiot!

He'd wrestled a handkerchief up round the lower half of his face in some styled approximation of an outlaw and was waving his revolver. A second shot followed. There was a shout. Another copper, the one who'd tussled with Claude, was down, clutching his thigh. Claude was running back towards the sanctity of his gang.

Another shot. In an instant, the downed copper had pulled his gun and had felled him. Claude took two, three strides, then tumbled over on his front, motionless. Clarence his brother was now screaming dementedly, trying to reach his prone sibling but being restrained by the others.

There were more whistles, more police heading their way.

Finch gently placed his deadly cargo where it could be seen, laying it all out for the authorities to find and deal with. He kept low and darted across the cobbles again. Screened by the smoke, he pulled alongside Claude and felt for a pulse.

He was alive… just.

But there was a bullet wound in his side. What it had hit within him, he simply couldn't tell.

Finch helped Claude up, draped his arm round his own shoulder and forced him to his feet, dragging him back into the shadows, ducking down just as another policeman clattered past.

The gods had a sense of humour, he sensed. They were sheltering under the J. P. Morgan building on the corner. He wondered what John Pierpoint would be thinking of his old dinner companion now.

'Claude… The rendezvous. Where is it?'

Claude groaned and clutched his side.

'Claude… Listen to me… I'm a doctor… When we get back, I'm going to patch you up, you hear me? Now tell me… the rendezvous.'

'He told me not to tell you,' he gasped. 'You were meant to take the fall.'

'Where?!'

'The Trinity Church… the rear…'

Finch had spotted it on the way down. It was just a couple of blocks.

'Claude. This next bit's going to hurt like hell. But here…'

He pulled Claude's muffler from around his neck and folded it.

'Press this to the wound with your free hand… hard… Claude, stay with me…'

He was beginning to pass out. Finch delivered a slap to his cheek.

'You hear me?'

Claude groaned and nodded.

Five minutes later they had staggered their way to Moose's horse cart. It was beginning to clop away. Finch heard a scream.

'Wait!'

It was Clarence, the brother, yelling at the driver.

Finch reached the cart and helped Claude up, to be pulled on board and embraced by his sobbing brother, the pair breaking immediately into their strange unintelligible language as Claude was eased down to the floorboards. Finch threw himself in after him. Numbed by adrenaline before, he was now acutely aware of the pain in his own knee.

'Clarence… Sammy…' he said.

They each nodded.

'Clarence, you keep talking to him. Keep your brother focused, awake. Sammy, the scarf. I need you to keep pressure on to stop the bleeding.'

They did as he said.

Finch looked out the back. Somehow – and he wasn't quite sure how it was even possible given the shambolic nature of the operation – they'd given the police the slip.

'Moose. You need to get us back to Gramercy Park as quick as you can. You hear?'

Moose twitched his whip and worked his old mare up into a trot.

'And you, what's your name?'

He was talking to the girl. The snarling revolutionary was gone. She looked young, scared.

'Lydia.'

'Lydia, can you put your first two fingers on his neck, like so…?'

He demonstrated.

'You let me know if the pulse drops.'

She nodded.

Finch sat back and sighed. He caught Sheldrake's eye.

'What's the matter, boss…? Surprised to see me?'

–

At the Gramercy Park town house, Claude was carried upstairs and lain on the master bed. Finch noted Sheldrake's selfish objection, as if surrendering his bedchamber was a threat to his supremacy. The patient was pale and sweating and with brother Clarence – confirmed by Sammy as a twin – almost feeling his sibling's pain by osmosis.

'Lydia… Sammy… Please. I need you to see whatever medicines, chemicals you can find… dressings too… I need kitchen cutlery… a sharp knife… a bowl… hot water… towels…'

There were others stirring in the house. They followed Finch's instructions to locate tweezers, tongs, a needle, thread… and the means to sterilize the equipment.

'I'm going to see what I can do. I can't promise anything,' said Finch. 'If this is beyond me, then there is no choice but to take Claude to a hospital.'

'He's been identified. The police will trace this back to us,' Sheldrake protested.

'I'm not going to argue, Sheldrake. *His* life comes first. If you're worried about him giving up your little organization and its part in tonight's fiasco, then so be it. You can move out of here right away and find somewhere else to hole up…'

Sheldrake snorted in derision.

'You've already got blood on your hands,' Finch reminded him. '*Tommy* – unless you'd forgotten?'

Sheldrake stormed off. Regardless as to what was about to happen with Claude, Sheldrake still held Finch's passport. He could not only be sold out, but now further implicated as an anarchist; as well as – in that phrase that Edmund Burke had coined – a 'terrorist'.

Hold your nerve.

The ad hoc surgery was arranged and Claude's abdomen cleaned up. There was no morphine but plenty of something else they could use, another opiate that seemed in abundance throughout the house... *heroin*. He instructed Lydia to prepare and introduce, intravenously, a generous dose of it.

Soon Claude was out.

And he was lucky. From his substantial experience on the killing fields of the South African veld, Finch knew a gunshot wound to the guts was not only the most painful, but almost always fatal. But Claude's left side, just above the hip, showed an entry *and* an exit wound. The policeman's bullet had passed right through him, grazing the wall of muscle that protected the abdomen but just missing the vital organs.

There was plenty of blood, and Finch had had a good root around to ensure that there was no debris lodged within the deep, dark hole. But, once he had sewed it up and applied plenty of iodine, it seemed that a second tragedy of the night had been averted.

Clarence looked over at him, clutching his comatose brother's hand.

'Thank you,' he said.

'Our job now is to ensure that no infection sets in,' Finch informed him. 'When he comes to, he's going to start feeling the pain again. You have to keep him calm. Make sure he drinks plenty of water and keeps still. We don't want that wound reopening. He needs constant monitoring – his temperature, his pulse. Understood?'

Finch retired to the other room and collapsed on the couch. Sammy followed him.

'Sammy. You've got to tell me something. Knowing what I know, heroin's not cheap. This house is awash with the stuff. Where do you get it all?'

Sammy looked nervous. He glanced over his shoulder. Finch motioned for him to close the door.

'Please, I *need* to know. You tell me and I'll get you out of all this. You're no anarchist. Just someone who's lost. There's only one way this is all heading and it's going to end up badly. You saw what happened out there.'

He reached for a cigarette.

'You get caught, you're talking prison for the rest of your lives. Or the gallows. The others here, they can all disappear, melt into the shadows. But you, this house, you're tied... The police will identify you soon enough. Sheldrake... his cronies... they're abusing you. You don't deserve it. Help *me* and I'll help *you*. I'll get you away from all this... or get them away from you. I promise.'

Finch stretched over. There was a drinks cabinet, a bottle of Scotch on the side, actual *Scotch* – a Glenlivet – Sammy's parents, evidently, were people of taste as well as wealth. He poured them both a drink and thought for a moment of young Private Miles, the soldier he'd been marooned with, supping from a flask in the no man's land of Magersfontein.

'Please, Sammy. You're safe with me.'

Sammy was sitting on the floor. He was reluctant at first, but then the words came, the stammer pronounced at first but lifting with the weight of the confession.

'The heroin… It's how they p-p-paid us,' he began.

'*Who* paid you?'

'I-I-I-I'm not sure. It came through an intermediary. But I think it had something to do with the German Mob…'

'Go on.'

'Because this man, Kimmel was his name, he came to the house asking questions.'

He got up and went to a drawer and came back with something which he pressed into Finch's hand.

'This was his…'

It was a small silver snuff box. Underneath was an engraving.

'*To Eloysius – Love Frances*'.

'…and we knew Kimmel was an associate of M-M-Manny Muller. You've heard of him, right? *Everybody's* heard of him.'

'Paying you in drugs is easier than cash, I'm guessing, especially if they're sitting on a ton of it.'

He nodded.

'We then sell it on the street. Not just the bums down on the Bowery – addicts on Skid Row – but Greenwich Village, wealthy users. It's easy money.'

'You mean now your parents' trust fund's been used up?'

Sammy said nothing. He didn't have to. Finch lit them both a Lucky Strike.

'And what was the payment for… this heroin?'

'A job we did.'

'Who's "we"?'

'I mean us… Sheldrake… Black Flag.'

'What kind of job?'

'I can't say.'

'Can't say or *won't* say?'

He looked up. In the candlelight, Finch could see his eyes were wet.

'Please… I've seen some bad things,' sobbed Sammy. '*Terrible* things. I know what can happen if you go against certain people…'

He thought about it for a moment, chewing over Finch's words.

'You can help me? You *p-p-promise* me that?'

Finch nodded this time. He exhaled smoke and gambled that he could trust Sammy with what he was about to say. He had to demonstrate his faith.

'I can't tell you exactly, but I'm not quite who I say I am,' said Finch. 'But in my official capacity, I have the power to help you – indirectly at least.'

'Who *are* you?'

'I'm not saying either.'

'Does Sheldrake know?'

Finch sighed.

'He knows enough. He stole my documentation… my passport.'

'Your passport?'

'Yes. Cut it out of my jacket…'

He flashed the lining and the slash in it.

'My official identification, to do with as he pleases. He had absolutely no intention of me surviving or escaping this evening. You see, he has the ability to blame everything on *me* as much as he does on you. We're *both* his convenient victims… his "patsies"… his "fall guys". Is that what you call it?'

Sammy nodded.

'Look, the heroin,' he said. 'If I can't tell you... What if I take you – *show* you.'

'When?'

'Now.'

'Sammy. It's three in the morning.'

'N-now. It has to be n-now.'

Chapter 23

In the dark, Finch found himself being led by Sammy past the pungent, empty halls of the Fulton Fish Market. Sluiced run-off from the wash-down glistened on the cobbles and carried the stink with it.

Sammy seemed to know every passageway, every cut round the warehouses and stores that lined the South Street Seaport. Finch watched the way the young man moved. He had the grace of a cat, slinking between the chandlers' stores, the sailmakers, the tackle suppliers; round the parked-up wagons, the barrels, the lengths of chain and the endless coils of rope.

Though only a mile away across Manhattan Island, the docks on the East River — with their battered sailing barques and rickety wooden buildings — seemed from a bygone era; certainly an age apart from what he'd experienced on the Hudson with its huge mooring piers and oceangoing liners. The reek of effluence, discharged straight into the water from the slums of the Lower East Side, accentuated the divide.

Finch was struggling to keep up.

'What are we doing here, Sammy?'

The reply was thrown back over a shoulder.

'You wanted to see the heroin… where it comes from, right?'

There were two ironclad windjammers before them, their masts and riggings silhouetted in the moonlight, the huge Brooklyn Bridge looming behind them. One, the *Cambuskenneth*, a former Scots vessel, was hung with the blue cross on red of Norway; the other, the *Antilia*, a steam hybrid, bore the blue ensign on the Bahamas. Their bowsprits and jib booms overhung the quayside and they edged beneath them, stepping over the ropes and cleats. After the fish market, between the bursts of sewage, the sea air was cleansing. The East River was a river in name only, knew Finch – it was really just an inlet of the Atlantic.

'And how do you know it's here?' asked Finch.

'Kimmel... Remember, I told you about him? Even though he was one of Muller's men, Sheldrake wasn't sure about him, didn't trust him. Thought he might be spying for a rival gang, maybe even with the police. You know, undercover... He asked me to keep an eye on him. One night I followed him... followed him down here.'

'Do you do that a lot, Sammy? Follow people? Sneak around? I noticed how you were pretty handy scaling your own building.'

He shrugged his shoulders.

'I guess... some.'

He beckoned to Finch. They squeezed in past the offices of the Munson Freight Company on Pier 17, whose signage proclaimed that it shipped to and from Puerto Rico. Beyond it was an anonymous warehouse. There seemed to be no one around.

'Here...'

Sammy indicated a door. It was the roll-up metal kind activated by a chain. It didn't fully reach the ground. There was a gap of maybe a foot. He got on his back and wriggled under. It was tough for Finch – with his accursed knee, plus the scrapes and bruises of recent days – and he made no attempt to hide it as he got down and rolled under.

Once inside, it was another aroma entirely that whacked them foursquare in the senses – the overpowering scent of roasted coffee beans. Finch switched on the Ever Ready flashlight that Sammy had found for them. There were hundreds of sacks.

Clever. Hide the drugs where no trained police dog can sniff them out.

From the labelling, the stock had been imported from the Pacific… On closer inspection from Samoa… *German* Samoa.

'What are you doing?' asked Sammy.

Finch was already over at the clerk's desk, the torch wedged under his chin, rifling through papers… documents… bills of sale.

'This…'

He waved Sammy over.

'See here…'

The invoice attributed the import of a large amount, if not all, of the Samoan batch – 300 x 224lb sacks, each the weight of a man – to a company called 'Herulian Holdings'.

'You know this name? Who these people are?'

Sammy shook his head.

Finch folded the invoice and stuffed it in his jacket and went back to pulling out files, flipping through orders.

But then, a hissing noise…

'Sammy, what the hell?!'

He swung the light over. The sound was that of coffee beans pouring out onto the sawdust and planks of the flooring. Sammy had produced a flip-open stiletto knife and was casually ambling down the walkway, slitting the sacks open.

'For Christ's sake!'

Sammy turned back.

'You wanted me to show you the heroin.'

'Not like this. We've got to be discreet… do this by stealth…'

As Sammy turned back to him, he could see that he was weeping openly, sobbing away.

'Sammy, please.'

Finch hurried over and embraced him, careful that the knife was pointed down. The boy's shoulders were heaving.

'Come on, put that blade away. Let's get out of here.'

He was slumping now, down to the ground. Finch couldn't hold him. His upset came in great convulsive waves as he curled up, hugging his knees, coffee beans cascading all around them.

'Tommy,' he was wailing. 'He was my friend, the only one who was nice to me.'

Opposite the coffee sacks was a stack of tea chests. Finch dragged Sammy away and propped him up against one. They were from China, bearing the name 'Ty-Phin', imports from German Kiautschou. Finch crouched down.

'I'm sorry,' he soothed. 'It must be a shock. But don't you see? That's why we've got to get you away. Not just for your sake, but so that there are no *more* Tommies. We can't let it happen again.'

'And not just Tommy.'

'Then who?'

He was beside himself, the stammer back.

'I-I-I-I've seen some bad things. Terrible things.'

'What are you talking about?'

'The Shooting Club.'

'The Shooting Club?'

'A b-b-build… a building… in Germantown.'

'Sammy, you're making no sense. I want to understand. Explain.'

He was clutching at Finch now, hugging himself into him, like an upset infant seeking comfort from a parent.

'Kimmel,' he said. 'I carried on following him. After here… Back and forth to Brooklyn… his home… to Muller's house in Greenwich Village… And then, an evening, a couple of days later, near Tompkins Square, some men, they grabbed him…'

'They took him away?'

'They dragged him to the Shooting Club. Down in the basement… Then, that night…'

His words trailed off.

'That night, Sammy. What *happened* that night?'

'I broke in… I watched… There were men in robes, hoods… And Kimmel…? They did terrible things to him…'

Finch embraced him. He stroked his hair.

'You poor kid. You saw all that?'

The sobbing came unbound, as if a great tide of emotion had been released. But then, with a burst of energy, Sammy had shrugged him off again. He was back on his feet, hacking away dementedly at the sacks.

The coffee beans showered hard and loud.

Suddenly, there were lights flashing around the other end of the building.

'Sammy, we need to get out of here.'

There was the rattle of a padlock, the scrape of a door opening.

'*Now!*'

But Sammy was facing him, standing still, a smile on his face.

'See...!'

From the last sack, tumbling out amid the coffee beans, were several brown waxed parcels, each about the size of a small bag of sugar.

Finch grabbed one, then yanked Sammy away by the collar, back towards the metal door and the gap underneath it. He turned his torch off as he did so. But now there was another beam of light swinging towards them. It caught them as they scuttled under the door.

'Stop right there!'

They slid out and ran for dear life across the cobbles of the wharf.

Finch glanced back. There was another man behind them, a fellow security guard. He already had a gun in his hand and he loosed off a shot, as much in warning as with intent, it seemed.

The man ran a few yards then gave up the chase as they wound their way back through the warren of passageways and up round the side of the fish market. They ducked back down behind a pile of crates.

There was a pink tint to the east. Dawn was breaking.

'Thanks, Sammy,' said Finch. 'What you showed me in there. It's important.'

Sammy said nothing, just reached into a pocket, fumbled around and pressed something into Finch's hands. It was his passport. He'd already stolen it back for him. Finch smiled.

But... the blood... on it... on Sammy's hands...

'Sammy. Are you hurt?'

There was a gurgle in his throat. He was coughing it up. Finch lay him down and ripped at his shirt buttons. He shone the light. The material was soaked a dark crimson. His chest…

'Sammy… please…'

Finch cradled him. He looked up, the blood pooling in his mouth tricking down his chin.

'Not afraid,' he spluttered. '…comeuppance… for what we *did*.'

'What you *did*? Sammy, stay with me…'

'Incendiary… device…'

'*Sammy*…'

And, with that, he was gone.

Chapter 24

The wind had picked up. The shadows of the clouds moved across the distant whitecaps of the Narrows. The Statue of Liberty moved in and out of the light, the sun glinting periodically on her torch, Finch still convinced she was blue. He sat on the grass on the high mound of the Green-Wood Cemetery just watching and waiting, staring out past the grand Civil War memorial with its soldier statues cast in bronze.

There was a small plaque nearby indicating that this spot had also been the key strategic point of the Battle of Brooklyn Heights, the first major engagement of the Revolutionary War. Throw in the War of 1812, the Mexican War, and the United States was a nation forged in blood, he mused; four major conflicts on its independent soil in less than a century – more if you cast back to the French and Indian War, the assorted colonial dust-ups, or the catalogue of exterminations it inflicted upon the Indians, continuing to this very day. The Civil War, with its million dead, made the Boer War look like a tea party.

Finch had located the grave at first light. It was new and well-tended with a small stone marker and cut turf that had yet to bed in fully. It stood back off one of the many paths that wound gently through the greenery and overhanging yews and lindens and maples; past the eclectic, ostentatious crypts and mausoleums that sat amid the carpet of everyday headstones.

Ensconced in his position, he had simply sat and waited till, as the noise of traffic rose, the working day beginning, a young woman, probably aged in her late 20s, wandered over to crouch down by the grave in question.

She picked off some leaves, then lay a bunch of purple irises before touching the headstone and hanging her head in silent contemplation. Then she stood up and smoothed down her long grey skirt, gave one last lingering gaze, before turning back to the path. Finch wondered when it might be socially acceptable to go and speak with her and waited till she had left the grave and was on her way back up to the main gate.

'Mrs Kimmel?' he asked, trying to strike a gentle tone. 'Mrs Frances Kimmel?'

She spun round as if his words carried threat. She had an attractive face, but with hair pulled back tightly, presenting herself as deliberately plain, he thought – unsurprising given the circumstances. There was a steely determination – an anger – behind the soft hazel eyes.

'Are you police? A reporter?' she asked.

'Neither.'

'Well, whoever you are, I don't have time… I need to get to the factory.'

He moved up ahead of her.

'Please…'

She went to sidestep him.

'I have two fatherless kids to look after… and not a red cent from my husband's employer.'

He followed her, acutely cautious of not wanting to harass her or to cause a scene of any kind. In the absence of a hat of his own, he'd taken to wearing a crumpled black felt gambler that he'd found. He removed it demonstrably.

'Mrs Kimmel, I'm truly sorry to approach you like this, and forgive the intrusion, but it's the only place I could think of to find you. I remembered mention of this cemetery. Believe me, if there were another way...'

She marched on with purpose, trying to rid herself of him.

'Please. You *must* hear me out. The work your husband was doing. I believe I can follow it up. Show that he didn't die in vain.'

She stopped and turned.

'Who are you? You're not from around here... Your accent...'

An elderly couple came down the path, nodding politely as they passed, though clearly sensitive to some kind of discord. He waited till they were out of earshot. He kept his voice low.

'I'm a British agent working with the NBI... or at least elements of the NBI I hope I can trust. My name is Collins, Bradley Collins.'

He thought he registered a slight flicker of curiosity. She threw a glance to his filthy, tattered clothes. He handed her his worn passport and she glanced at the details. He'd done his best to wipe off the blood.

'You don't look like Secret Service.'

She strode on again.

'Please, I must ask—'

'Don't overplay your hand, Mr Collins.'

'Mrs Kimmel. I'm sorry. I need to know. Your husband. Did he ever talk to you about his work?'

She stopped a second time.

'And why am I supposed to suddenly trust *you*?'

'I have no proof of my honesty. All I can tell you – with hand upon heart – is that the people who killed your husband, they tried to kill me too. I've been on the run.'

'Please. Just go away. I'm warning you now I can holler pretty loud.'

'Here…'

'What?'

He grabbed her hand and pressed the silver snuff box into it. She regarded it with bewilderment.

'Where… Where did you get this?'

She stroked it lovingly.

'From someone who was there. Someone who saw it.'

'You *know* about that? What they did to him?'

'They were going to kill *me* the same way. The same grisly ritual… I was fortunate… I escaped…'

She looked around. There was no one in view. Still she kept her voice down.

'In answer to your question, *no*… not officially.'

'The question?'

'You asked whether he talked about his work. But sometimes, my Eloysius, it was hard for him *not* to keep things secret – you know… names, his whereabouts. Plus, he talked in his sleep…'

She tucked the snuff box in her skirts and snapped out of her sentimentality.

'But *you* need to tell *me* why you need to know.'

Finch shuffled his feet.

'Look, I'll try and explain, it gets complicated… But what if I tell you that I know your husband was a very brave man. He had put his life on the line investigating the financial dealings of a gangster named Manny Muller.'

The name had power enough for her to put a halt to their conversation there and then.

'I can't say any more. Good day to you, Mr Collins.'

She bustled on her way. He followed.

'Please, you must…'

'Muller's not someone *anyone* should cross. I hear they got Angus too. He was a good man. And now I have to live with the thought of that bastard Muller every day—'

She hitched up her skirts to walk faster.

'—bankrolling politicians, presenting himself as some do-gooder, some great American patriot…?'

Her anger was such that she almost broke into a run.

'Please, Mrs Kimmel. There are other names. Did you ever hear of any of these – an anarchist group called Black Flag? Maybe a "shooting club"…?'

She said nothing.

'A company called Herulian Holdings? A man named Delgado…?'

She stopped once again and, this time, spat on the ground. She fixed his eyes with her own. The anger burnt in them.

'What do you know about Delgado?'

Finch took a deep breath. He'd budgeted for non-cooperation or, at best, reluctance. He was exposing himself more and more, though his instinct told him she was trustworthy.

'I'm pretty sure Delgado, a rogue NBI agent, betrayed your husband, blew his cover, leading to his death. He – Agent Kimmel – had worked his way in deeply within Muller's organisation and found out some important things, incriminating things – things that could still be used to bring Muller to justice.'

She laughed, disdainfully. It wasn't saliva this time but a word she spat out.

'*Justice*…? Where was justice for my Eloysius? He had to be sewn back together. No open casket for *him*. The police wouldn't go near Muller. He's got half of the NYPD in his pocket.'

'But not *all* of them,' Finch protested. 'I myself was interrogated at Centre Street by a Detective Copeland. He seems cut from the same cloth as MacLeish, a friend of his. Possibly a friend of your husband's also…?'

She shrugged. He wasn't sure if her ignorance was genuine.

'Maybe there's hope yet?'

'Hope?'

'Look, up till now, Muller had always been able to present himself as a legitimate businessman, someone of civic standing, enough to act as a backer… a patriotic benefactor to Senator Schultz of the American National Party…'

She gave a snort of derision at that name too.

'But what I also believe to be true is that Muller is securing a substantial part of his funds through a trade in illegal narcotics. Not just that but *foreign* narcotics, stuff he has to import. If there's one thing Washington won't buy, it's *that* – the fact that not just organized crime, but German-sponsored organized crime, is financing Schultz's likely run at the White House. This isn't just some local police matter but something *way* bigger… something worthy of Federal investigation and Federal indictment.'

She said nothing for a moment and Finch wondered whether he'd done the very thing that she'd just warned him about – overplaying his hand.

'You're asking the right sort of questions,' she replied. 'Yeah, sure I heard of Herulian Holdings. Black Flag too.

Herulian was something Eloysius was investigating. But you're not asking *the* question.'

She pointed to an impressive monument, a grand-looking obelisk mounted upon a square plinth. It reminded him to a degree of the banks of the Thames and Cleopatra's Needle.

'I have to go...' she said.

She gestured to some great chimney stacks that had begun belching soot.

'Domino... the sugar refinery.'

And with that, she hurried off.

Finch could not keep harassing her. It was highly improper. All he could do was let her go, watching as she stomped off up the path to finally disappear through the grand Gothic arches of the cemetery's entrance gates.

He walked over to the obelisk. It marked the final resting place of a Union hero of the Civil War, '*b. September 24, 1826 – d. April 14, 1894*'.

Henry Warner Slocum... *General Slocum.*

Chapter 25

The wind whipped up as Finch walked back over the elevated promenade of the Brooklyn Bridge, the threat of rain again in the air. The growing metropolis in all its living, steaming, cacophonous glory was stretched out before him. It was no surprise that New York City was the powerhouse of a titular 'Empire State'. If empires were about conquest, power and the pursuit of riches, then this – Washington Irving's fabled 'Gotham' – was an exemplar, riven with the same corruptive and Machiavellian politics of all the others throughout history.

Tired, cold, aching and hungry, Finch's head was still reeling from what he had just learned. Mrs Kimmel's reference to General Slocum could mean only one thing – the passenger boat... the one that had caught fire last summer and whose death toll had decimated the German community on the city's Lower East Side.

He reached Gramercy Park and walked the genteel side streets where nannies pushed perambulators, servants scrubbed steps and crocodiles of children were being led to kindergarten.

He was still in his filthy, smelly clothes – garments that had once hung on an Indiana farm clothes line. He wondered what kind of madness had led him across the Atlantic, across the States. Service to his country? His country hadn't served *him* well at all. It had put a gun to his head.

Poor Sammy, in his final hours, had referred to something shameful that Black Flag had been asked to do, a job for hire, and for which their payment, their reward, had been a batch of heroin – *Muller's* heroin. It had already been established that the group were involved with bomb-maker Jimmy Chang, someone who had known them well enough to fraternize with them at their commune. Black Flag's leader, Max Sheldrake, had frequently hushed Sammy's loose lips, but the poor boy's dying words had got to the nub of it – 'incendiary device'.

Agent Kimmel clearly knew what was afoot. He had got in deep with Muller's organization only to be rumbled, probably betrayed – almost certainly by Delgado. Detective MacLeish had begun putting the pieces together by himself but had met with a similarly grisly fate.

The fact seemed inescapable… No matter how hard he pushed it away, it all came back to one overriding probability – that Muller had commissioned the firebombing of the passenger ship *General Slocum*. To serve his own ends, he had wilfully brokered the deaths of the men and, in the main, the women and children of Germantown, well over a thousand of them. Politics had no scruples. Finch had long abandoned any notion of nobility on that score a long, long time ago.

But *this*…?

As unthinkable as it might be – as profound the tragedy – it made perfect sense. The *Slocum* Disaster had engendered a state of instant victimhood on the part of New York's German–American community. A vulnerable people needed hope, needed purpose, needed salvation, needed leadership.

It had put them in Muller's pocket. That was a powerful commodity – a hugely charged one – to manipulate to his own ends. Or, by using the fig leaf of civic responsibility, to offer up to a Senator, a would-be President, one who was already whipping up and playing upon nationalist sentiment amongst America's huge German-immigrant population. Schultz's success would bring Muller, the kingmaker, great power and influence – and protection – in return.

Was Senator Schultz in on it too? Nothing should be discounted.

Conjecture was one thing. Proving all this – *attempting* to prove all this – was, thus far, a guaranteed sentence of death… a slow, agonizing, protracted death. And with the police, the NBI, even MO3 not worthy of full trust, who the hell would he prove it *to*?

In his own mind, Finch still had some kind of credit with the Black Flag anarchists and could at least use time with them to uncover more information. He would have to explain where the pair of them had got to for the remainder of the night but believed he could bluff his way out of it – Sammy, after all, had a penchant for going out, sneaking around. Plus, they needed to know the solemn fact – that he was now dead.

Or did they even care? He began to doubt it himself.

As he turned the corner, his mind was made up for him. There, outside the Proctor residence, were several New York Police Department officers, and they were manhandling the ragtag remnants of the Black Flag gang, hands on heads, into three Black Marias. The muslin curtains of the neighbours were twitching. The more adventurous had come out onto their stoops to watch, no doubt with relief. Sheldrake was yelling something about oppression and revolution to an officer whose level of political engagement amounted to casually whacking him on the back of the head with his truncheon before shoving him inside.

There is more law at the end of a policeman's nightstick than in a decision of the Supreme Court.

The neighbours enjoyed that too. Finch ducked back out of sight and pondered as to whether the raid had come as a result of the discovery of Sammy's body, or if Black Flag's number was simply up. It, surely, had only been a matter of time? Although they would jump to the inevitable conclusion that it was *he* who had ratted them out, especially after having stolen his passport back... maybe even killed Sammy himself. It was a line they still might peddle to the police.

There was now only one thing for it – to find the only person who could possibly understand.

–

Finch stood on the corner of Christopher Street. He remembered what Lady Brunswick had said, that, in the morning, she left her neat Georgian house to go for a stroll and buy fresh-cut flowers. It took a while but, a little after ten o'clock, Katia appeared, in a deep burgundy dress. Unfortunately, she was accompanied by two muscular-looking men, Muller's goons, wearing crombie coats and derby hats, who followed just a few feet behind.

If Katia were playing a part then she did so magnifi-cently – the stoic, icy exterior betraying nothing of the emotional tumult she must be going through. Muller's

Ford stood at the kerb. He had not yet left to conduct his shameless, nefarious business.

There was no way Finch could get to Katia, he knew; no means to converse directly; so he followed, hanging back some 20 yards, bobbing and weaving and crossing the roads back and forth so as not to arouse suspicion. She soon turned onto Greenwich Avenue with its pedestrians and street traffic and the florist's store up ahead on the corner.

And then Finch saw it – so cleverly and artfully done amid the activity, that her escorts did not have a clue. There was a brick wall, an old one, crumbling slightly, with some of the mortar having fallen out. She brushed her hand against it, lightly, just for a second. You had to look hard, but as he passed the spot, Finch saw the folded piece of paper pushed deep into the crack. It was the 'dead drop', the point of communication with *Deuxième Bureau*.

The exterior of the florist's store was festooned with brightly coloured bouquets, blooming nicely in their baskets and buckets. The two men stood outside and lit up cigarettes as she entered. But he would not be able to speak to her without attracting attention. He lingered by the window but she didn't look out.

He doubled back on himself and hurried, as best he could, to the end of Christopher Street. He saw the trio re-enter the house, Katia now armed with a large bunch of daffodils. There was nothing then but to wait.

He found a discarded *New York Times* in a waste bin and half watched the door while flipping through 'all the news that's fit to print' according to the newspaper's covenant – something not evidenced by its obvious editorial bias.

American newspapers were a curious beast – so very similar to British, or indeed European ones, yet so very different. On Fleet Street, without question, the papers were just as subject to the political prejudices of their proprietors, but news was still news, regardless of geography, not split into domestic and 'world', with the latter reported almost as an afterthought. It seemed strange that the ongoing Russian Revolution, an event of potentially seismic proportions, should receive just a few lines of coverage.

Maybe it was fear of contagion. Domestic affairs were rife with court rulings on labour laws and word of a massive and deadly violent Teamsters' union strike that was now underway in Chicago. Another new socialist movement had been founded in the same city, Industrial Workers of the World. Mob rule and demagoguery were meat and drink to the likes of Senator Schultz.

It took over an hour, during which time he'd read every item, including a baseball report – of the New York Giants' walloping of the Boston Beaneaters at the Polo Grounds, something he didn't fully understand but appreciated for its poetry. Eventually, the front door opened and Muller and the two goons got into the red Ford and drove off. Approaching by the main entrance was not an option. Instead, Finch moved up the alleyway that ran behind.

They hadn't fixed the gate. It still hung off its hinges. Having staked out the rear of the property, scanning for movement, he determined that the only activity came from the study on the first floor – the room where she had shot North stone dead. It had a small balcony – more for show than anything practical. He didn't know how but, with a flood of adrenaline, he found himself climbing the drainpipe.

She was sitting alone in a chair, reading. The door was closed. He tapped lightly at the window, upon which she slammed down the book and rushed to it, her face a mix of relief and anger.

'What the hell are you doing here?'

She released the catch on the French door and let him in.

'You're going to get us both killed.'

Danger didn't need to heighten the senses. She was, knew Finch, highly desirable to him, something both amplified by what he knew about her, yet tainted by knowledge that she had prostituted herself in the line of her work. That she didn't touch him, kiss him on the cheek or show any sign of anything physical couldn't be attributed solely to his current wretched state. It only added to the confusion. But she had no time for anything as frail as emotion, she'd already declared that. She was protecting him, he understood. He was, as she had also warned him, too innocent for the harsh realities of the intelligence game.

'Please, sit,' she said, and poured him a bourbon, which he downed in one and she refilled. 'Muller's not here. I'm alone, but for how long I don't know. There are two of his men...'

'I saw.'

He pointed to the vase of daffodils.

'You *followed* me? Damn you, Finch. Were you born stupid?'

'Let me explain.'

She was reading Henry James's *The Golden Bowl*. He thought of the last time he had seen that book, in Annie's room at London's Savoy Hotel.

'Keep it short and to the point,' she said. 'They'll be back to keep an eye on me. Trust is in very short supply around here. I'm under virtual house-arrest.'

She lit them both a cigarette from a long silver case while Finch told her of his theory regarding Muller and the *General Slocum*. Her face betrayed nothing.

'I wanted to inform you that the heroin – the heroin you claimed to know nothing *about*, by the way – is being smuggled in in coffee bean shipments under the cover of a company called Herulian Holdings... I've seen it with my own eyes.'

He took out the brown paper parcel that had been pressed deep into an inside pocket. He handed it to her and she examined it.

'In order to link Muller – and by association Schultz – to these drugs,' he continued, 'we need to find physical evidence... *documents* pertaining to such a company.'

She gave it back.

'*We?* Why do you assume that I'm on your side?'

He tucked the parcel in his pocket again.

'I think *you* need Muller to be put away as much as I do.'

He wondered whether he'd overplayed his hand again – tipping her off that he knew who she really was. But then if she knew that *he* was working with MO3, and was still trusting *her*, there was every chance he might.

She stood and paced.

'It's true, I did know – about the heroin – just not the "how" or the "where". Muller kept that a closely guarded secret. But his papers are kept in a safe. If there *is* any evidence of this "Herulian Holdings", it would be in there.'

'A safe? Where?'

'The next room. This is the study, but in there…' she pointed, 'is his private office. He keeps it locked at all times.'

'You have a key?'

'To the private office? No, but I know where it's kept.'

'And to the safe?'

She shook her head.

'It's a combination lock. The only ones who know the code are Muller and his lawyer, Krank, a man I despise even more than Muller himself, if that's even possible. He's the person who trusts me least of all. He's already told me so.'

'Are you sure? About the code…? The ones who know…?'

'Yes, I'm sure.'

'Then do you know a safecracker… a safebreaker?'

She rolled her eyes.

Were you born stupid?

'I mean… is there someone trusted we could approach who *does*?' he said. 'You know, in a professional capacity?'

'Trust…? You mean on top of the not insignificant business of then having to smuggle said safecracker in and out of the house?'

He sipped his whisky.

'Then what do you suggest?'

She thought for a moment.

'Muller, every day – every *week*day – he comes home… three o'clock… remember?'

Finch nodded his understanding.

'Most days the pair of them – he and Krank – open the safe while attending to their business. They leave it that way, taking papers in and out.'

'And you think you can get in there with them?'

'No… Not in *there*. Like I say, the private office is small. They tend to come into *this* room to do their work. They sit either side of this desk here, spreading things out. The safe isn't unlocked for long, but it's unattended. I'm often around to pour them a drink or whatever. My presence wouldn't be unusual.'

'And what about the bodyguards?'

'Up here? No way. Their place is strictly downstairs.'

Finch rubbed his chin.

'It sounds like a risk. Is there another way?'

'None better than this.'

'And if you get caught?'

The silence said it all. She stood.

'You need to go,' she urged. 'If I find what I need, I will let the relevant people know. You have to trust me on that.'

'That word again.'

There was the faint trace of a smile. She motioned for him to leave, then hastened him down the stairs and out the back.

'Goodbye, Captain Finch.'

She shook his hand. It felt final.

There was a noise at the front door.

'Tweedledum and Tweedledee.'

It was the first time she'd made a joke. Then her face darkened again. There were some dollar bills and loose change in a brass saucer on a shelf. She scooped them up and pressed them into his hands.

'You need to get out of here.'

–

Back outside, Finch made his way to Greenwich Avenue and turned towards the florist's. As he walked past the brick wall, he saw the note still wedged into place. He wondered whether to read it but decided not to.

Instead he crossed the road and, with his new-found relative wealth, he smartened himself up enough to go into an Italian café. It had been so long since he had eaten. He was not only enticed by the aroma – it also afforded a good vantage point.

He bought himself a slice, as if from a giant flan, of something called a 'pizza'. It was made of a crisped dough base with a thick tomato sauce and ground beef and assorted vegetable toppings, added according to the various random nods he gave to the server. He then stood at an outside stand, fashioned from a large barrel, and observed how the others ate, folding the slice in half and manipulating it by hand. It was, he determined, at that very moment in time, the most delicious thing he'd ever consumed. A second slice later, with a cup of coffee to wash it down, he found himself just leaning, watching, waiting.

It was done so discreetly that it was barely perceptible, but eventually a short, fat man with a moustache in a drab business suit and homburg walked past, briefcase in hand. Barely breaking stride, and certainly without even looking down, he had filched Katia's note out of its hiding place.

Finch wolfed his coffee and set off after him. As he crossed the road, he saw that the man had not only retrieved the note but put a new one in its place, on yellow paper rather than white. And now he was marching off – the anonymous little fellow in the humdrum uniform of the office clerk.

He was anything but, of course, and Finch watched him undertake the professional manoeuvres of his kind – the criss-crossing of the road, using the cover of vehicles, or stopping in doorways, checking reflections as he made his way eastwards.

There was a streetcar clanging towards them. Though it looked to be of no interest, in one darting movement the man moved behind it, using it as a screen while he crossed the road, scuttled to the cast-iron cupola and down the steps of the new Bleecker Street subway station.

Finch followed him underground amid the beautiful blue ceramic signage and sculpted tulips, a nod to the area's Dutch heritage. He stood back while the man bought a ticket at a wooden booth and hastened towards the Manhattan Main Line. Finch rooted for five cents and did the same, handing the pasteboard ticket to the gate attendant, who slotted it into the 'chopper box' and allowed him through to the platform.

There was an immediacy about the New York Subway compared with the London Underground, he observed. It was right there, literally, 'cut and covered' by the street, its grilles venting right up into the sidewalk – not seemingly miles beneath the earth in a subterranean warren. There was an electric Uptown train pulling in and the man climbed aboard. As he moved down the aisle, easing past passengers, he gave no impression of having seen Finch, no hint of eye contact, although he couldn't be sure.

Finch hurried along as best he could and climbed into the red steel carriage. But then he saw the man step off at the next set of doors, just as they were sliding closed. Finch managed to squeeze out again just in time. The man hadn't looked back, so Finch pursued him once more, back up the steps and into the street.

They continued for several blocks north and west back into Greenwich Village until the irregular slants of the roads gave way to the regular grid street pattern and with

Finch so far back he occasionally, briefly, lost sight. Finch had no idea where he was now – the Chelsea district, he thought – but found the man again and watched as he turned off the main thoroughfare into a side street, and then left again into another.

But it was a trap – not a street but a dead-end alley, clearly part of a well-rehearsed manoeuvre, the very kind that Katia had employed on the way to their escape by ferry, evidently a trick out of the *Deuxième Bureau* manual. The man stepped out from nowhere, right behind him. And he was brandishing an automatic pistol. The clip hung open on the briefcase in which he'd been carrying it. There was nowhere for Finch to go. Instinctively, he put his hands up.

The man's voice came in a monotone; neutral, without a trace of emotion.

'Stay away from her, Captain Finch.'

With his left hand he eased his hat back. He was, saw Finch, quite bald.

'Muller too. Your very presence has already put a number of people in very grave danger. Myself included.'

'I just…'

He raised a hand to silence him, then reached into the briefcase, pulled out a silencer and began screwing it on.

'Trust me, Mr Finch, when I tell you that, according to protocol, I am supposed to terminate you right here and now…'

He raised the gun and pointed it at Finch's head.

'And believe me too when I tell you I have done such things several times before, including twice right here on this very spot. We've found it to be a most convenient location.'

'But…'

He casually squeezed the trigger and, with an innocuous click, a bullet was loosed off, thudding into the wall behind.

'That *is*, if it weren't for the fact that your death would bring unnecessary attention at a critical juncture. This will be your only warning. Do you understand?'

Finch shook like a leaf, but nodded.

'You will count to one hundred before leaving.'

Finch thought of the kid back on the Indiana farm.

And with that, the little man was gone.

Chapter 26

At one minute to three o'clock, Katia heard the rattle of the car engine and the ratchet of the handbrake. The two goons were downstairs, smoking, drinking coffee, casually – and too loudly – discussing acts of physical violence they had committed in the line of duty. It was for her benefit, she knew – to let her know of the consequences should she stray from the fold.

They were pathetic, she thought. Little schoolyard bullies. Indeed, the scrape of the key in the front door induced an instant servile reaction on their part – springing alert; their menace mere child's play compared with the sort of terror that Muller could visit upon them... or anybody *else* for that matter. It reminded her of something she had been reading about the Nobel Prize and the study of its latest recipient, the scientist Pavlov, who'd been conditioning responses in dogs.

Krank and his pompous *basso voce* reverberated up the stairs, following Muller as he ascended. She stepped out onto the landing to greet them and was met with a light impersonal kiss from Muller and a look of veiled scepticism from Krank. Muller signalled for her to fetch them drinks – schnapps... *Kirschwasser* – a sign, she knew, that they had had a good day. She had been careful to wash and replace the tumblers that she and Finch had used, remove the cigarette butts, and had brushed away any evidence of his entry via the window.

Muller unlocked the private office next door and, right on cue, clanged open the wall safe. Dutifully she went to the drinks tray on the sideboard in the study and poured two shots.

I could poison you both right now if I wanted to.

When they entered the study, Muller gave a slight flick of the head, indicating that she should leave. Krank issued one of his supercilious grins.

'Would you like anything else?' she asked, employing a suitably subservient tone. The silence told her that they did not.

She went to close the study door on her way out.

'Leave it open,' commanded Krank.

From the table in the study you could see the landing mirror which, ordinarily, gave a reflected view into the private office. She had made sure to place the vase of daffodils on the occasional table below it, part-obstructing the view, affording her a critical blind spot. Downstairs, meanwhile, the two goons were behaving themselves, just compliant foot soldiers.

Now… It has to be now.

Muller and Krank had commenced with a discussion about the economic standing of the Bierkeller. Funny, she thought, despite the raging criminality and sadistic brutality, they still talked about prosaic matters such as profits, turnover, overheads, staffing levels and taxation. Krank seemed most exercised about the colour scheme of some new upholstery.

The door of the private office was half open. She nudged it further. The room was small, just a strong room, a castle keep. It had a single window, the only one in the house with bars, and a small rosewood davenport with a blotter and inkwell – the modest inner sanctum of Muller's nefarious underworld.

Behind the davenport was a false bookcase. It hinged like a cupboard, the spines of the books merely fake. And there, set into the wall, mounted at chest height, its capacity about the size of a small suitcase, was the safe. And its door was hanging open. Tantalizingly so.

Now!

She took a deep breath and entered the room.

Despite the solid steel and the combination wheel, the safe was quite unassuming, just another repository for paperwork, its interior lined with the sort of green baize they used on pool tables. It had a shelf that split the interior into two sections. There were some bound bundles of dollar bills in the rear – not an extraordinary sum of cash. In front of that, piles of neatly stacked papers and brown cardboard folders – three on the shelf itself and three below it.

She removed the top left-hand pile, placed it on the davenport and began rifling through. There were invoices from the Bierkeller and other businesses; bills of sale; a certificate of health from the sanitation department; some documents pertaining to a court case regarding a disputed liquor licence.

As she proceeded through the mound of innocuous admin, the chances of finding what was required were beginning to diminish. She wondered whether there might be a better way of doing this… maybe go through the companies register at City Hall?

'Katia!'

The voice induced a cold shiver. She shoved the documents back and dashed to the landing, pretending to rearrange the daffodils in the vase. There was the reflection from an adjoining parlour of the *sauwastika* that hung on the wall.

Muller appeared.

'What was the name of that city councillor?' he asked. 'The one we met at dinner the other night... the one who came over and introduced himself? Johnson? Johns? Jacobs?'

She looked up.

'I'm not sure,' she said.

She cast a furtive eye while Muller re-entered the private office, watching him in the mirror. It had been inevitable that he would return to the safe. He took something. Then, to her horror, paused in confusion.

Had he noticed?

'Krank... did you move...?'

'Jacobson,' she interjected.

'What?'

'Jacobson... That was his name.'

He shouted the name back through to Krank, who uttered something profane and contemptuous at its mention. Then he shrugged to himself, put the papers back, and returned to the larger study.

I have to move quickly.

She noted the positioning of everything in the safe this time, careful to leave it all exactly as she found it, then resumed leafing through the papers, flipping methodically – the top-left pile again, then the centre one, then the right. There were maybe 100, 200 papers in each. She sped through them looking for one thing only, senses primed for any movement in the room next door.

Finding nothing of relevance, she replaced what she'd gone through, then began work on the bottom shelf.

The first pile, the fourth in total, yielded nothing. But then, in the next, about midway through a bunch of bank statements, it leapt out at her. The figures were in a handwritten ledger beneath a typed heading...

Herulian Holdings.

–

With the sun setting, Finch gripped the rungs of the ladder that descended from the skeletal structure of the incomplete Queensboro' Bridge. He had no head for heights and the prospect of edging down what amounted to a series of wooden ladders lashed together over a drop of 100 or more feet put the fear of God in him. But with insufficient cash now to pay a ferryman – at which he cursed himself – it was the only way possible to access Blackwell's Island.

The ladders bowed under his weight and he fought to maintain his grip. Worse, it had started raining, whipping at him in great icy sheets and making the rungs slippery.

'Hey!' called down someone from way up high.

But Finch was lost in the shadows.

Up till then it had been surprisingly easy. He had simply walked round the wooden barrier and worked his way along the girders that framed the prospective bridge's outline. There were still some workmen around, packing up tools to go home, but he had been inconspicuous enough.

With darkness falling, the buildings were cast in silhouette while the lighthouse light winked on the north end of the island. You could hear the shouts from the penitentiary, the screams from the asylum.

There was, he knew, only one other person who could confirm his theory about the *General Slocum* – Jimmy

Chang. Given what he knew about the US legal system, there was a chance Chang could barter any information for leniency. Finch would do what he could to both elicit the information and promise to vouch for Chang's compliancy to the relevant authorities. That in itself required a huge amount of trust.

From what he had been told, Chang had been moved to the asylum. If New York was anything like London, such places were a living hell… bedlam. Anyone incarcerated there would do whatever they could to get themselves out of it.

The chaos of the asylum also meant Finch just might bluff his way in – far easier than he could into the actual prison.

Finch padded around the bushes of the perimeter of the grim Gothic edifice. There was no way he could approach via the front entrance. At the rear he found a pathway that led from a jetty on the East River, where a tethered empty supply boat, a large rower, bobbed on the evening tide.

The path led up to the swinging double doors of a trade/delivery entrance, with laundry carts in a row under a covered area. Next to them were a man and woman in conversation.

The man, big and muscular and dressed in grubby white overalls, was an orderly of some sort – physical strength, Finch knew, being a crucial part of the job in a place like this. The woman, by contrast, was skinny, haggard, hunched, smoking a cigarette and with a look of desperation about her. She wore a tattered evening dress and, even in the fading light, Finch could see the harsh make-up – the overly rouged cheeks and garish eyeshadow. She was almost certainly a prostitute.

After some kind of negotiation, the orderly looked this way and that, then helped the woman into the laundry cart and covered her over with fresh linen. He wheeled it inside.

Finch walked low behind a screen of laurel bushes till he got close. He wondered whether he should just try and make his *own* way in – though that came with problems.

About fifteen minutes later the man reappeared. Finch approached.

'Hey... Excuse me... Sir?'

The man spun round.

'Who the fuck are you?'

He was huge – bear-like but with the look of someone who enjoyed the less seemly aspects of his work. He had the stink of the institution about him... and of the institutional bully.

'Someone who wants to make contact with a man inside.'

The man paused to light himself a cigarette.

'You a cissy?'

'No. This is business.'

He exhaled at leisure, knowing he held all the cards.

'Good. 'Cause I don't help no cissies.'

'Can you get me in? And *out* again?'

'That depends on your business.'

'I have to get a message to someone.'

'If it's a message, *I* can take it.'

'A discussion, something I need to do face to face.'

The man thought about it for a moment.

'Ten dollars.'

'Ten dollars... I don't have ten dollars...'

Finch didn't see from where he had produced it, but with a deft move, he had flicked open a stiletto knife.

'Then you better find it.'

'Look, get me in and I promise I…'

He waved the knife in Finch's face.

'Ten dollars.'

He pointed down to the dock.

'You got about an hour till the last laundry consignment comes in. Boat picks it up at the 59th Street dock.'

A man was climbing down into the boat.

'*He'll* take you back across. Be there for his return…'

He prodded a thumb at his own chest.

'Tell him you're with Ernie. You're doing me a favour.'

'Have you heard of someone called Jimmy Chang?'

The man's laugh was a mocking one, a great faux belly guffaw.

'We got 2,000 crazies in there.'

'The one I'm looking for *isn't*.'

'Yeah? That's what they all say. And by the way, you try and make your own way in there, without going through *me*, you won't get out again…'

He gave another spluttering laugh.

'You'll know crazy, sure enough.'

He flipped his cigarette onto the path.

'But if you *are* serious about locating this one guy, this Chang? There's a desk clerk on the second floor does me favours.'

'Thank you.'

'But that'll cost you ten extra.'

He folded his knife away and gestured down to the jetty.

'You got one hour.'

Katia scanned the Herulian Holdings bank statement. It was less than a month old and showed a balance of over $100,000. The figures meant nothing in themselves. For all his unpleasantness – and even Muller could only tolerate him in moderation – Krank had already proven a master manipulator of money, someone who ran both a series of legitimate concerns and other ventures that conferred superficial respectability to Muller's shady dealings – a nexus of out-of-state accounts, pseudonymous holdings and acquisitions and shell companies. 'Money laundering' as the Federal investigators had taken to calling it. She often wondered why Muller, a natural businessman for all his faults, didn't just concentrate on his legitimate enterprises. He'd still have been filthy rich.

She didn't know whether to take the statement or leave it in place. Would there be other means to tie Muller to Herulian Holdings?

Heruli… The ancient Germanic tribe… Scourge of Imperial Rome.

She doubted whether Krank would leave his boss so exposed. Neither man's name was evident as an account holder. The address was given via a US Postal Service mail box.

But then…

Down amongst the weeds, amid the columns of figures, there it was – a company, a payee registered to a holding called 'Gerta'. It proved nothing in itself. But, she knew, Gerta was Muller's mother's name. Coincidence? Or had he got uncharacteristically sentimental?

Gerta… yes, she had seen the name already, somewhere in amongst the documents already viewed.

She returned to the start. Yes, Gerta, Gerta, Gerta…

About halfway through the first pile she found it… a letter. It was from a real estate office in Downtown Manhattan which had corresponded with an endowment trust set up under the title 'Gerta: Discretionary'. It had a forwarding address in Columbus, Ohio's state capital. And the company had been established with Krank as a trustee. It was, she knew, enough of a lead to pursue – one that potentially tied Schultz into dealings, too.

She folded the relevant documents, then tucked them into the deep pocket in her skirt. She began putting everything else back exactly as it was.

I must get the hell out of here.

But when she pushed the last pile in place it caught her eye. She had not noticed it. At the rear of the safe was a small baize tab. When she tugged at it, it was evident that it pulled open a panel. There was something behind it.

She listened out. Muller and Krank were still deep in conversation.

Quickly she removed the papers again, set them on the davenport and slid out the shelf. She pulled on the tab and a false wall hinged down, revealing a hidden compartment. There, tied up with a black ribbon, was a further bundle of documents.

She retrieved them and undid the bow. A drop of sweat landed on the paper. She hadn't realized it but her brow was dripping. She wiped at it with her sleeve and began sifting through – they were housing deeds and leases for properties in the East Village… St Mark's Place, First Avenue, Tompkins Square, the Bowery, Avenues A, B, C… Second Street, Third Street, Fourth Street, Fifth… Sixth… Maybe 60 or 70 altogether. And *all* in Little Germany.

But it was the dates – July 1904… August 1904… September 1904 in the main, though with other contractual exchanges running up to only two weeks previously. *All* had been transacted in the past nine months… And *all* properties or property leases had been purchased because the owner or principal tenant was suddenly deceased. Sometimes the lease pertained to a business address – a store or workshop – but mostly they were for domestic dwellings, with the surviving, *grieving* family then forcibly evicted if they couldn't meet the drastic rent hike.

This was no coincidence. She would wager that every single death, every eviction, had come as a result of the *General Slocum* tragedy. Judging by the timeline, some of the soundings had even been initiated, speculatively, in *advance* of it.

There was no 'Gerta' this time, no office in Ohio, not that she could see. But again there was that signature, 'Bernard Krank'.

She felt numb… sick. Finch had only been half right. This knocked the drug dealings and everything else into the shade. Muller hadn't just commissioned the fire on the *General Slocum*, ripping the heart out of the local German community, manipulating them to his own ends; he had done it, too, as a cynical land grab, a means to expand his own property portfolio – a sleazy get-rich-quick scheme – meanwhile blaming it all on others.

There were too many documents here to steal. She pulled off the top one and stuffed it in her pocket with the others. When it came to property, a search through the city's archives would surely throw up copies.

Hands trembling, she tried to redo the bow but could only manage a knot…

Get out. Now!

…then placed them back in the secret compartment.

But she'd missed something… there, right at the back. She reached in and took it – a thick piece of paper, near parchment in texture, with a photograph pinned to it.

The blood pounded in her ears. The photograph was a standard portrait taken of her at the *Ministère De L'Intérieur* in Paris some five or six years ago. And the sheet was the *original* registration card, neatly typed by the brisk Ministry secretary while she had sat in the vestibule on her first day of basic training for the *Deuxième Bureau*. It contained particulars – the name, address, the physical, personal and educational details for one Madeleine Foche.

They had known all along.

Muller's voice cut right through her.

'Find anything interesting?'

She froze, then turned. There they were, standing in the doorway – Muller with a Luger in his hand, Krank behind him with his haughty, overbearing smirk.

–

There was no alternative, Finch had to make his way to Grand Central Station. The risk was high, but his locker was the only place he could access money. He no longer had the key, it had been tucked in his wallet, but his passport gave him a means of identification and he hoped that whoever was on the desk there would grant him access.

The darkness and the onset of what they called the evening 'rush hour' would give him some cover. Being soaked to the bone would make him more indistinguishable, less unpresentable, too. Everyone was drenched. He fought his way into the station amid the hordes of commuters.

Despite his hurry, there was a sudden comfort, an anonymity afforded amid a crowd. Though sizeable, the station still seemed ill-equipped for the numbers, running at over-capacity. He could see now why the Vanderbilts had commissioned a new super-station to be built on the same spot. The ongoing building works, as old parts were demolished and replaced by colossal blocks of marble, only added to the chaos.

The left-luggage lockers were exactly as he remembered them and he proceeded to the desk where a weary jobsworth of a clerk recited chapter-and-verse company policy with reference to lost keys and how Finch would have to fill out a form and come back tomorrow.

Finch produced his passport but the document was of mere curiosity to the clerk, who preferred something more native. It was only when Finch promised him a financial inducement that the clerk trooped off and returned with a spare key.

'You bring this back and the five dollars for the privilege, y'hear? Otherwise I holler for the police and tell 'em you stole it.'

Finch nodded.

He stood to one side and watched the bank of lockers before approaching. To his eye, the coast seemed clear. There were enough people pouring past in either direction to afford cover.

Swiftly, he moved to locker 774 and inserted the key. There, just as he had left it, was his bag. He sighed with relief.

No sooner had he reached for it, than he felt something pressed into his back, the unmistakeable hard menace of a gun barrel.

'Turn around slowly,' came the voice.

Finch complied.

'*Delgado?*'

'Okay. You, me, the boys…'

A man stepped forward either side of him – mid-height, stocky and of Latin complexion.

'…what's say we go for a little drive…?'

Chapter 27

The gun in Delgado's right hand was concealed in his coat pocket, poking at him with the ardency of an excited lover.

While he screened Finch, the two men moved to pat him down.

'So, Mr Collins... I'd like you to tell me everything you know about Muller and his heroin.'

He said it in a leisurely way, as if the story would unfold eventually.

'What the hell are you playing at, Delgado?'

He smiled and made a palm-down gesture with his left hand.

'Please... For the sake of decorum, let's keep this down.'

'I put my life on the line for you!'

'Please, I'm touched.'

'MacLeish too.'

The sarcastic smirk gave way.

'That was regrettable. If he'd stuck to his job... not tried to play the hero...'

'And Kimmel? Does that go for *him*?'

The lover jabbed his ardour into Finch's midriff.

'The heroin... Muller... You know the drill... Start talking.'

'I know nothing.'

He rolled his eyes.

'You got some moxie, kiddo, I'll give you that.'

One of the heavies whisked out the small brown parcel. Delgado smiled.

'You know, for someone in the intelligence game, you do betray a distinct lack of it.'

The heavies guffawed at his 'funny'.

Were you born stupid?

He motioned to them again and, discreetly, they strong-armed Finch out of the station, keeping each arm in a stiff lock against the elbow.

The car was idling at the kerb, a black Cadillac, its canvas top up against the driving rain. Delgado got in beside the driver, twisted round, his revolver pointed at Finch who was now sandwiched in on the back seat, between his two escorts.

The gun was of a curious design – it had no trigger-guard. Delgado caught Finch looking at it.

'Ah, you're admiring *this*,' he said, waggling it for effect. 'The Italians call it *coscia d'agnello*... Did I get the pronunciation right?'

The heavies grunted a yes.

'The "leg of lamb". See, the shape... A "Bodeo 1889", if you prefer. So much more stylish than those industrial German monstrosities or our clunky American ones too for that matter.'

He twitched his head in self-admonishment.

'Please, forgive me. Introductions... These fine gentlemen are Luigi and Carlo.'

Each heavy touched the brim of his fedora. Carlo, to his right, had a scar on his nose, as if someone had once slit his nostril.

'And this here—'

He motioned to the driver.

'—is Rafaelo… You've met before.'

It was the same bearded, toothpick-chewing thick-neck who'd picked them up at Central Park, then been with North outside the NYPD HQ.

'They are Signor Morello's men.'

'Morello?'

The car pulled out into the Midtown traffic. The windshield brush beat valiantly but ineffectively against the torrents.

'So,' snarled Finch. 'You're dealing with the Mafia now *too*?'

Delgado winced.

'Please, remember, we don't like to use that word, do we, fellas?'

They shook their heads.

'It's not just disrespectful. It's so…'

He searched for the word.

'…*vulgar*.'

'I'll tell you what's vulgar, Delgado…'

Delgado raised a palm.

'Please, Captain Finch, a clumsy sequitur. And so contrary to the aesthetic.'

He prodded the gun for emphasis.

'Allow me to get to the point. We don't have much time. As I was saying… Muller… the heroin…'

'What about them?'

'I have word from an informant, a longshoreman, that a recent shipment, a *sizeable* shipment of the drug, has arrived via a pier on South Street… and that a consider-able amount of this consignment still lies concealed in a warehouse.'

The car cruised down Park Avenue, turning to splash through the puddles on the eastern side of Union Square. A distracted pedestrian dived out of the way.

'And?'

'And, Mr Collins... Due to your exploits with that tedious band of revolutionaries Black Flag... and especially now that we've caught you with *this*...'

He waved the parcel of heroin.

'...naughty, naughty...'

The heavies both laughed.

'...it seems with 100 per cent certainty that you know where that heroin haul might be located.'

Delgado got out his Lucky Strikes, offered one to Finch, who declined, then lit himself one.

'We would have beaten it out of one of the kiddie communists themselves, with great pleasure when it came to that little shit, Max Sheldrake... but unfortunately, when we went a-calling, we found the poor darlings had all been carted off to jail.'

'What's it to you, Delgado, anyway?'

'What's it to *me*? Quite a bit actually. Signor Morello and I, we got ourselves a deal. I find the heroin stash for him, I get a little cut of the action... along with these gentlemen too for their trouble. Call it a finder's fee. Right, boys?'

The 'boys' sniggered.

'If it weren't for you, Finch, poking your nose around, I could have found it for Morello working from the inside; gotten a hook into Muller's whole network. I should be sunning myself in Havana, drinking rum, having a roll with a couple of *mamasitas*, out of this godforsaken hellhole. Instead you survive my crackerjack, thanks to your little French friend, and now I'm exposed. I gotta split.'

Finch knew that he must have reacted at the mention of her name.

'Oh yeah, Mr Collins – or should I say, Captain Ingo Finch – Miss *Madeleine Foche*? I filled Muller in. Gave him all he needed. He's known the truth for a while, by the way. Been playing her along. And now I'll get what's mine. And you – and *her* – you'll get what's yours. As you say, just like Kimmel, just like MacLeish. He'd been in the NYPD long enough. Should have known when to turn a blind eye, when to walk away. *Your* only chance of survival, Finch? Tell me what you know.'

Finch began to struggle. The two heavies pinned his arms.

'Not unless you ensure her safety.'

'Too late for that. Not my business. Gave it the big kiss-off. And seriously, you'd trade yourself for *that* little *putain*? Oh yeah, Finch, don't be kidding yourself she was exclusive to Muller... Me, Krank, even the dumb old Injun, we all got a taste.'

Finch strained hard this time.

'You bastard!'

He was beaten back by Delgado's hard, stinging slap across the face.

They were under the arch of the Brooklyn Bridge approach now. When they emerged, the South Street port was before them, the forest of masts stretching down to the tip of Manhattan.

Declared Delgado: 'And here we *are*.'

Three other automobiles waited on the cobbles. More of Morello's men.

'You notice anything, Finch?' said Delgado.

'You mean other than your carfuls of goons?' replied Finch.

'Cute... I mean no police. Let's just say they're smarter than MacLeish. Know when to make themselves scarce. Know when to take a hike.'

As they pulled up, the Mafiosi saw them and began disgorging from the vehicles. They huddled in the rain, sawn-off shotguns and heavy revolvers barely concealed beneath the flapping raincoats.

Delgado used Finch's distraction to reach over, grab his collar and ram the leg of lamb into his cheek.

'Okay, my friend. Time to spill the beans. Failure to cooperate and I'm afraid Carlo and Luigi will be taking you for a midnight swim, only with some cement round your ankles to make sure you get the full immersive experience.'

The heavies laughed again.

Delgado withdrew the gun and they pushed him forward in his seat, tugging his arms behind him. Finch felt the rough rope yanked hard around his wrists.

'This is your moment, Finch. What's it gonna be? Play ball or sleep with the fishes?'

Finch said nothing.

'Ready boys?'

They pushed open the door and went to drag him out.

'Okay... Okay, Delgado... you win.'

He felt the cold barrel of the gun again, this time in his ear.

'So... I'm listening.'

'The warehouse – Pier 17 – next to the Munson Steamship Line. There's some tea chests... fresh in from China – "Ty-Phin".'

'Ty-Phin? You sure?'

'Yes, I swear... T-Y-P-H-I-N. Stencilled on the wood. I was there two nights ago. I'd say there are about 20 or 30 chests... Comes in from the Kiautschou Bay Concession. You know, the colony the Germans have on the Yellow Sea. The heroin's buried deep within the tea leaves. Parcels just like that one I had.'

Finch was dumped back in his seat while, on a nod, the heavy on his left, Luigi, got out and ran the message to one of his colleagues waiting on the dock. The man scuttled off into the shadows, revolver drawn, to sneak down the quayside and snoop around the edge of the warehouse, peering in through a window. A couple of minutes later he returned. Luigi nodded back up to Delgado.

'Well, well, Finch,' he said. 'Seems there's hope for you yet.'

Delgado got out along with the driver, leaving Finch alone with Carlo, the one with the scar. The heavy produced his own revolver for good measure, keeping Finch pressed to his seat. On a signal, the men began fanning out along the waterfront and down the jetties either side of the warehouse, taking cover behind the crates and barrels and carts.

Finch watched as Delgado and his cronies crept cross the wet cobbles. The rain thundered hard, spray splashing everywhere. He didn't know what they had in mind, but the pair of security guards on duty were in for a rude awakening. Weapons poised, the Mafia men darted into the open, ready to bust their way in.

And then... CLICK!

From the warehouse roof, a huge searchlight was switched on.

Then a second, then a third...

Delgado and his men were lit up like performers on a vaudeville stage. They froze, utterly blinded by the white-hot glare.

The sound that came next was one that Finch hoped he'd heard the last of on the killing fields of the South African veld – the clunk of a bolt, followed by the deafening, sickening *clack-clack-clack* of a maxim machine gun.

The Mafiosi started firing back, loosing off their shotguns and handguns, but it was random, unfocused. Delgado, Rafaelo and Luigi, who were the most exposed, crumpled. The others ducked for cover but were felled in quick staccato bursts, some plunging into the water. The two or three that survived were left crawling for refuge while others on the roof, hidden behind the blinding lights, picked them off with single shots.

Carlo-with-the-scar jumped out and, using the cover of the Cadillac, began firing wildly, drawing attention to himself. As the maxim swung in their direction, Finch, with his wrists bound behind him, threw himself behind the front seats, hugging himself to the floor. In a banshee-wail and a hailstorm of lead, the windshield exploded and rounds slammed hard into the car's body, the vehicle sinking down as the tyres burst.

There was a shriek. Carlo had been hit. Finch saw him clutch his shin then, somehow, manage to limp off, stray bullets pinging after him.

A shout went up, the shooting had stopped. It had been over in mere seconds. Finch heard a groan followed by a shot – one of the wounded being put out of his misery.

With the car door open, Finch could see Delgado, his body broken, crawling pathetically through the wet, barely able to plant one elbow in front of the other. A man strolled up, stood over him, legs astride, casually racking back the breech on his Luger. Then he emptied a round into Delgado's head, the lone crack echoing round the docks.

Finch pulled himself in tight but it was no use, they knew exactly where he would be. The same man was striding over, purposefully, expensive Oxfords kicking through the wet, young acolytes trailing in his wake. There were hands under Finch's armpits. He was yanked out and dumped into the oil and grime, staring up while his victor casually wet, then lit, a cigarillo.

'So, Captain Finch,' said Muller. 'We meet again.'

Chapter 28

The room was dark, Finch's senses alert only to the waft of smoking greenery and the low resonant hum. There were dots of light that swirled... dancing. He willed himself to focus, to harness them, to bring them under his control.

He was on his back, shirtless, he could feel *that*. He tried to speak but the words sat fat and unformed on his tongue. There was a difficulty in propelling them beyond his lips. They hung, disconnected from the thoughts in his head. Despite the strangeness, he felt warm, calm even, when he knew he shouldn't be. He recognized the sensation, the comfort, the incongruous feeling of euphoria that coursed through his veins...

Heroin.

He willed himself to concentrate and to force the emotions, the reactions, to come; to experience the sensations that had been smothered in a warm anaesthetic syrup. The lights were candles, he knew, borne amid the wall of cloaks and hoods that surrounded him. He stared hard and made them coalesce.

And then there were his limbs – a tightness at his wrists and ankles... a roughness... coarseness. Rope... *Twine*... And their angle... He had been spreadeagled, hands and feet bound, stretched across the rough wood of what he knew to be the altar. He turned his head to his left and, in the dim glow, there *she* was too, stretched on a second slab, motionless, just gazing upward.

He couldn't lift his head sufficiently, not enough to see forward, but the familiar voice was booming, deep, resonant. He had no doubt now, from what he had learned, that the man, the high priest, was Krank. And that, somewhere out there, too, was Muller.

The heavy staff banged on the ground three times. The room hushed. The man took his time.

'We are here to denounce the two parties brought forth before us today...' he was instructing. 'And for whose crimes we seek atonement.'

He raised his arm towards Katia.

'Behold the *Ausländer* – the French harlot who was secretly working against us.'

Then he pointed to Finch.

'Behold, too, the British agent, colluding with the Federal Government and in consort with that turncoat Delgado to bring the dregs of Italian organized crime against Mr Muller's legitimate businesses... Enterprises that have filled the pockets of all in this room... that have sustained families, put food on our tables, that have fostered the health and vitality of our dear *Kleindeutschland*.'

There was a muttering – a chorus of disapproval.

'Both parties have been responsible for the squalid and immoral deaths of a number of friends from our community, and for which there is no excuse, no apology.'

The chanting resumed, swelling. Finch yelled for all he was worth.

'You're insane, goddamn you. Muller, I know you're here... *All* of you, you've been used, abused, forced to torture, to kill, just so that he *has* something on you… can demand your loyalty.'

'Silence!'

But his words, he knew, were streaming in a slobbering, incoherent babble.

'Muller… Fire… *General Slocum*… He killed your loved ones!'

It made no sense.

'SILENCE!' denounced Krank. 'Enact the sentence.'

The room hushed – just the crackle of candles, the shallow nervousness of breath and the ominous soft shuffle of footsteps as the executioner stepped forward. Not Teetonka this time but a proxy, another weaponized thug for whom permission to carve open a bound captive was akin to a civic honour.

He came to a halt before Finch and, with a harsh metallic swish, and to a gleeful gasp from the onlookers, unsheathed the great knife. He raised it to the room, the candlelight glinting on the curve of the steel, on the ancient swirl of runes etched into the blade.

It was the sign for the ritual to enter its final grisly act, for Finch to lie still, spreadeagled, while the razor-sharp edge did its work, piercing the skin beneath the ribs, then being drawn down, deliberately towards the navel, cutting progressively deeper, slicing through gut, severing organs. Abdominal wounds were the most painful, he knew – he'd seen plenty of that in his time on the battlefield and in the field hospitals – the wounds that cannot be salved, cannot be tended, just the excruciating pain and the slow bleeding out while brain, lungs and nervous system still functioned; while the heart still kept on pumping.

There was a call and response from the throne to the gathering. Then the chanting began again, imperceptible at first, but soon rising in volume and tempo, amplifying to a viscerally disturbing pitch as the weapon was hoisted high and hovered over Finch's chest.

It was then, amid the cacophony, that he heard Katia yelling now too. To him, they were noises that made no sense, just like his had been. But there were two words he caught… 'MacLeish'… 'Kimmel'…

Only this time Krank was raging back.

'So-called lawmen who thought they knew better… We swatted them like annoying wasps.'

Whatever she said next struck home, for he rose and was waving his arms out wide, a departure from the script.

'STOP!' Krank commanded.

The room fell silent again. Confused looks were exchanged.

'Do the girl first.'

Then, as the executioner began to move towards *her*; as his soft shuffle crept away from Finch; the brain-addling guttural chant was issued again, more forcefully than ever.

Finch turned his head. Two men had appeared at Katia's side.

'No!' he screamed.

There was ripping… a white bodice.

'Not her, *me*! ME!'

The chanting swelled to a crescendo. The knife rose to its apex, hanging there.

'NOW!' bellowed Krank.

Then it came… slicing down on its final, fatal arc.

Finch dug deep within himself, mustered every ounce of strength, every fibre of his being.

'NOOOOOOOOOOOO!!!'

He didn't know what happened, but the arm froze mid-air. The executioner stopped, staggered, the hood falling back to reveal eyes locked wide open, his face set in a grimace.

And then… he toppled over.

The shot had been lost amid the noise but heads were turning now sharply in one direction.

Up high… through a grille… a rifle…

There was a second shot, this time from the floor, firing back at it.

Then came shouting, running, ducking, chaos… a panic, a stampede for the exit. More gunfire – from where, Finch couldn't tell. And there were whistles, the searing screech of police whistles.

The smoke blew thick. A brazier had been knocked over deliberately. Finch was struggling to breathe. He called, not for help, but for Katia. But when he turned, he couldn't see her – just uniforms, flailing truncheons and then Krank, on his knees, his hood back, face pink and pudgy, firing wildly with a Luger, clearly unused to handling a firearm, before being shot in the arm himself and falling.

A cop was over him, his revolver ready to finish the job, smirking.

'No,' cried someone in charge. 'We need this one!'

Detective Copeland was in the middle of the room now, barking instructions.

There were hands… a pocket knife… cutting Finch free.

–

Next thing Finch knew he was outside, sitting on a stoop, a police medic shining a light into his pupils. There were trucks in the street, men being herded away… more shouts… more truncheons.

He saw her again, resting against the tailboard of a motor ambulance, blanket round her shoulders, Copeland standing by her. The detective called to Finch and led him over to her, gently guiding. There were enamel mugs... strong black coffee...

He lit them both cigarettes and then struck up one for himself. Slowly the madness began to dissipate.

'We acted on a hunch initially,' Copeland was explaining. 'I wasn't sold on what you said, but I know enough to tell when a man is speaking the truth... or, in his own mind, *believes* he is speaking the truth.'

The first truck revved and pulled away.

'But as we started monitoring movements, some of the things you told me, Mr Collins—'

Mr Collins, still.

'—had started to ring true. And then at the end... we just had to wait for some kind of admission of guilt regarding Kimmel and MacLeish.'

Finch sucked in the night air. It was as if he were somewhere else, looking down on this scene of chaos. It made no sense... and every sense.

'Thank you,' he said, slowly, careful to enunciate, his full consciousness still yet to return.

'Actually, it's thank *you*,' replied Copeland. 'But if you want to bestow your gratitude on anyone, it's *this* lady...'

Finch had no clue what he meant. He wasn't sure where he was supposed to be looking, like his eyes belonged to someone else. He didn't recognize her at first. She had been standing behind the detective. She was in the same dull factory clothes.

'Mrs Kimmel?'

'She sought me out. Trusted me with what she knew... What you told her,' said Copeland. 'It was a risk on her

313

part. She's been through enough already. But it was a worthwhile one.'

Finch wanted to reach out… to hug her… she had saved his life… but it felt wrong.

'Thank you,' he said again.

Frances Kimmel nodded.

'Thank you,' echoed Katia.

If he felt close to Katia amid all this, his comrade in arms, it was not reciprocated. There was no eye contact, even though he willed it, just a flat logical inquisitiveness.

'What will happen now?' she was asking Copeland.

The detective took a drag on his cigarette.

'Well,' he enthused, 'we can get Muller's organization on racketeering, money laundering, narcotics, not to mention numerous counts of murder.'

This time there was a flicker of a glance from Katia – a quick, almost imperceptible exchange.

They don't yet know about the General Slocum.

'Don't worry, we'll get the information we need…'

He nodded over. Krank was being led out, clutching his arm, booming about his rights. With his big puppy-fat face he seemed like an overgrown baby.

'…We have ways of making him talk.'

Finch suddenly floundered: 'Wait… no Muller? You didn't get *him* in there?'

Katia almost spat with frustration at his and their naivety.

'All of you,' she scoffed. 'You think Muller is fool enough to get himself caught in a charade like that?'

'It's only a matter of time,' assured Copeland.

She sighed.

Were you born stupid?

'No, Detective. Men like Muller *always* get away... only to return somewhere else... and twice as dangerous.'

Chapter 29

Washington DC

It was crisp and cold but the sky was cobalt blue. The sun glinted on the dome of the Capitol building and the obelisk of the Washington Monument in the distance, at the far end of the trees and wild greenery of the Mall.

When Senator Abel Schultz appeared at the top of the steps that led down from the building's west entrance, it provoked the usual clamour on the part of his fervent supporters, who waved their placards and their American National Party banners, giving vociferous encouragement. A line of policemen, linking arms, leaned their backs into them, keeping them in check.

When Schultz descended, it was with less theatricality than usual and the assembled news reporters and sketch writers – always appreciative of the colour, regardless of the message – sensed it right away. This time there was no pausing to greet the faithful, they noted, no double-handed pressing of the flesh. Instead, with his minders in tow, he strode straight to the Edison microphonic device that had been set up on the concourse – purposeful, determined, steely-eyed. He waited for calm.

'My friends, thank you for coming,' he began, in his measured expository tone. 'As you know, there has been much speculation of late as to whether I, on behalf of the American National Party, would put myself forward as a candidate for the highest office in the land, that of President of the United States...'

There were shouts of affirmation.

'...To submit my application when nominations open...'

He reached up, made a clasping gesture and pulled down.

'...To ultimately take power in 1908 and put an end to the shameful and disreputable, imperialistic ambition that Mr Roosevelt, the butcher of Cuba, has foisted upon this country, in open violation of the manifesto drawn by its Founding Fathers.'

If his face were fixed, knew the newsmen, it had not diminished his thunder. The volume rose, the words more piercing.

'Well, I can tell you now, I will fight with every fibre of my being to ensure that neither he nor his Corpulent Crown Prince, Mr Taft – a man whose sincerity seems inversely proportional to his girth – succeed...'

There was a burst of laughter. He nodded to himself.

'...Nor, for that matter, Taft's likely running mate, James Sherman, whose decisions would decimate the land as surely as his uncle's troops tore through Georgia.'

He afforded himself a grin, the fire was back. He turned to point to the building behind him. This time he boomed.

'...And don't get me started on that lickspittle Democrat, William Jennings Bryan!'

Even the press were smiling now. There were more cheers.

'But my friends, there comes a time in every man's life...'

He was changing the mood, adjusting the tone, dropping down – the diminuendo before the rise... to the swell... the big crescendo.

'...when he is impelled to make an irrevocable, life-defining decision.'

The men of the press were leaning in. Was this the moment?

'It goes without saying that the first order of politics, of public service, is sacrifice. I speak not of myself, of whose tribulations have been a trifle, but of my wife – for over thirty years – and latterly, that of my three children... who have all surrendered their lives to our cause... The long, hard road that has been hoed.'

There were nods, barks of approval.

'Which is why... after a great deal of thought... soul-searching... now is the moment... the *perfect* moment...!'

This was it. The declaration. The applause soared from a ripple to a thunder.

'...The moment... for me to stand aside...'

Heads were turning. Confusion.

'...Yes, at this critical juncture in our nation's history, to stand aside for a new man to lead us into the sunlit uplands...'

The crowd was a-buzz.

'And while I, Abel Schultz, shall for ever have the name of the American National Party engraved upon my heart, and will, till the day I die, work tirelessly as its most humble servant... I hereby tender my resignation as its leader with immediate effect.'

To cries of 'Senator!... Senator!...' he turned on his heel.

It seemed an unnecessary flourish to Finch, the reading out of the news item from the *New York Herald* confirming Schultz's withdrawal from politics. Lady Brunswick did so in the manner of a schoolmistress, poring over every word, thrilled that one more skirmish in the epic war of attrition had been won.

It was, knew Finch, if not a Pyrrhic victory, then one that had still come at a cost. Yes, the American National Party was such a cult of personality that its chances of success had been severely damaged. On the other hand, both the NBI and MO3's operations had been exposed. And Muller was still at large.

'Are you enjoying the smoked salmon?' she asked.

'Yes.'

'And the eggs? Eggs Benedict is a signature dish. Invented by Oscar, the maître d'. A hangover cure, you know. *Very* popular. Then there's his Waldorf Salad and his Thousand Island Dressing...'

Finch muttered his approval.

'...A very small act of gratitude. Merely a token,' she went on. 'Of course, we can't begin to thank you enough for your service. You really did think on your feet. One of the reasons we recruited you, Captain.'

She gave a smile of satisfaction.

'We apologize for the predicament we placed you in, but it was necessary for the success of the operation. You may not realize it but you were being watched every step of the way. Washing our hands of you – or at least *appearing* to wash our hands of you – was the only way to throw them off the scent.'

'Throw *who* off the scent?'

'I'm afraid I can't say.'

She set aside her cutlery.

'Always make sure to use your knife, Captain.'

'My knife?'

He was still eating. He didn't imagine a private dining room at the Waldorf – or rather the whole of the lower ground-floor restaurant sealed off for their own purposes – should be something to be sniffed at. The truth was he just felt numb.

'The Americans have a frightful habit of chopping everything up then switching their fork to the right hand, using it like a shovel. I feel there are certain standards we have to maintain.'

She winked. Try as he might, humour was eluding him.

'Lady Brunswick, I thank you for your generosity, here as on the *Baltic*. It is not every day one is accorded such a privilege. But I fear you are buttering me up. Preparing me for something... something for which I have no desire.'

There was a slip in the mask of joviality, which he knew was only for public show. He was well aware what the private face was like.

She gave him a good hard stare.

'What *do* you desire, Captain Finch? Whatever you wish, we can arrange it. Some rest and recuperation, perhaps?'

He gave no reaction.

'Maybe see a little more of America before going home? A trip out West...?'

He wiped his mouth with his napkin.

'I want to know what happened to Katia... *Madeleine*...'

'I thought you might.'

She nodded to his packet of Navy Cut lying on the table. Alongside the tailored suit he was now wearing, she had made sure to leave a welcome basket of creature comforts in his new room here, including these cigarettes and a bottle of Talisker.

'May I have one of those?'

He proffered them and she inserted it into the holder. He lit hers, then his. She referenced the engraved initials of the lighter.

'I. F.' she said. 'We should have thought that through. Clumsy.'

'Where *is* she?'

'I should imagine indulging some similar hospitality as we speak, only with *her* people in Montreal. She was spirited there as soon as the *Deuxième Bureau* got their hands on her. She is to be highly commended. A remarkable woman. We need more like her.'

She exhaled.

'Good thing about Quebec, Captain. The cuisine's of exemplary standard wherever one may dine. One doesn't have to seek out places like *this*...'

She raised her palms at the surroundings, then mock-asided in a whisper...

'Better here than next door, the Astoria. In my opinion, of course.'

She tapped off some ash.

'They hate each other, you know.'

'Who?'

'The respective owners, the Astor cousins, William Waldorf Astor and John Jacob Astor IV. Only now their two hotels are linked by a walkway – hyphenated – the Waldorf-Astoria... effectively joined at the hip.'

She nodded again around the room.

'All this Renaissance-style architecture in honour of their ancestral home, Walldorf – two "L"s – a nondescript little *Stadt* in the Rhineland.'

She looked him in the eye.

'Ah yes, those Germans again. As I'm sure you've come to understand, Captain, a thousand years of high culture – Holbein, Bach, Beethoven, Goethe, even *this*—'

She threw her arms wide.

'—can be undone in one errant moment, a spasm of national vulgarity. Something that seems more and more possible by the day.'

He took his time. She didn't like silences.

'You haven't answered my question.'

'Miss Foche? I'm afraid that's all there is to tell. It's really all I know at this point. And *that* is the truth.'

She beckoned to the waiter who'd been standing over in the corner.

'Tea, coffee, Captain?' she asked. 'As you will also know, the tea here's terrible, deliberately so. America became a nation of coffee drinkers in protest at *us* during the Revolution. They delight in making it badly.'

'I'd prefer something stronger.'

'Very well. Brandy?'

'Why not?'

'Two cognacs, please… Rémy Martin… Large.'

He flipped his cigarette with his thumb.

'You asked me what I desire.'

She shrugged her shoulders in a 'go ahead, surprise me' manner.

'I want to get Muller.'

She smiled as if at some private joke.

'Impossible.'

'He's still at liberty. What Katia said was right. He'll pop up somewhere else causing yet more trouble. And when he does...'

'Muller's a gangster. He's of no interest to MO3. Not any more.'

'I had a telephone call this morning from Detective Copeland. Seems no coincidence that, the night of the warehouse raid – the night they killed Delgado – Jimmy Chang went missing, sprung from the asylum on Blackwell's Island... a man whose technical know-how could have devastating consequences...'

'Fanciful thinking.'

'Sprung, it would seem, with Muller's sponsorship... Were you hoping to keep *that* from me...?'

He could tell he'd thrown her, though she did her best to wave it away.

Finch strained to keep his voice down.

'Then at the very least let me help bring Muller to book for the simple reason that the man got away with murder,' he snapped, 'including, almost, my own. And as for the *Slocum* bombing, and the property scam... I can't think of a more cynical, heinous crime... a capital crime... Though it remains curious to me why the police made no mention of *that* on Krank's arrest, nor indeed when I spoke to Copeland on the phone.'

The brandies arrived in oversized bowl-glasses. She whispered from behind her hand.

'If this country's temperance movements are anything to go by, *this* won't be permissible for much longer.'

She gave a mock shudder, a deliberate distraction.

'*Please*,' Finch urged.

She dismissed the waiter and held back till he had gone.

'Look, you should know by now how intelligence works,' she said.

She rolled her glass and stared deep into it.

'Information is power. It is something to be deployed judiciously; to be held back, traded if necessary. Of course, our friends in the NBI are privy to broadly the same intelligence, especially when it comes to the question of Muller's culpability. But I ask you this, Captain, the deliberate destruction of a pleasure craft... Does revealing it to the American public serve any purpose...?'

He cocked his head to one side, unsure.

'...To tell the loved ones that all those lives were lost *not* through accident, but as part of a callous criminal act... It would provoke a scandal causing untold pain, yet more grief, yet more outrage.'

She sipped. He did the same. He knew she was right.

'No, we'll keep that up our sleeve for the time being. It is a card best played at a more opportune moment.'

'*Did* Schultz know about it... the *General Slocum*?'

'It doesn't matter. That Schultz knows that *we* know is a good enough start. We had a quiet word. It achieved its desired result. Plus, his links with Muller and, by association, Muller's other criminal activities, will soon be a matter of record.'

She raised her glass to Finch.

'He's gone. For that we should be thankful. A case of "mission accomplished".'

She pointed to the newspaper, the reminder.

'Which brings me to something else, Finch.'

He had sensed it was coming.

'No such thing as a free brunch,' he quipped.

She ignored him.

'As you know, the question of the USA's military adventures, its expansionist designs, have proven controversial. But we should not overlook the fact that, just as America has been asserting its imperial ambitions, so too has Germany. Neither are in a position yet to challenge the naval might of Britain, nor even France. But the worm is turning.'

She undid the clasp on her leather handbag and produced a large brown envelope.

'Open it.'

He unfolded its contents, the cerulean photosensitive paper of a blueprint, the white creases of the quarter folds rendered the same white as the architectural design etched upon it. It was of a warship, a large warship – a battleship – but of a size and scale, with its revolving turrets and massive guns, that even Finch could recognize as a behemoth… something more impressive than the Royal Navy or certainly the French *Marine* currently possessed.

'HMS *Dreadnought*…' she enthused. 'The hull is about to be laid down at His Majesty's Dockyard, Portsmouth. Look at the dimensions…'

Finch took a large sip of the cognac, his eyes wandered over the lines – 527 feet long with a projected displacement of 20,000 tons; 10x12-inch guns, an array of some 32 other powerful armaments; armour that was a foot thick; a speed of over 20 knots.

'It will be the largest battleship ever built, quick too, and with enough firepower to make everything else instantly redundant. *Everything*. It is a game-changer. The greatest single weapon ever invented. And we have more to follow.'

She took the plan back and folded it up.

'And so?'

'And *so*, Captain Finch… nothing remains secret for very long. The French, the Americans… the *Germans*, will soon be copying us, building their own *Dreadnoughts*. In fact, we know the Germans already *are* – they're in the process of designing four. We find ourselves in an Arms Race. Nothing more, nothing less.'

She leaned in. She lowered her voice.

'Needless to say, such weapons, in German hands, are a direct threat to the sea lanes of the Empire…'

He nodded.

'…but there's a giveaway.'

'There is?'

'These vessels require extra-large docks. With their Pacific acquisitions in mind, the Americans are already enlarging their West Coast ports at our insistence – San Diego, and a new one at Long Beach – to accommodate our new visiting warships… and their own ones, of course, eventually.'

He sipped longer.

'Meanwhile the Germans are undergoing a rapid colonial expansion – German East Africa… Kamerun and Togoland… German South West Africa… Then there's Tsingtao and the Kiautschou concession in China… Samoa and New Guinea, along with the Solomons, the Carolines, the Marshalls, the Marianas and numerous other Pacific Islands. And it's a safe bet there will be new, wide, deep-water docks built among these territories, too.'

'I see.'

'Only *they* don't signal their intentions so easily – like to keep things under wraps, disguising their military engineering by using civilian contractors.'

She tucked the envelope back in her handbag.

'We have to work out *where* those docks are to be built, Captain Finch. And we need *you* to find out more.'

'Why me?'

'Because one of the main bidders for the work, rather shamelessly, is a Pacific shipping company... a company run by an Australian gentleman named Edward Pointer. He's already got his fingers in the Long Beach expansion and has been using his acquired expertise to embark on a world tour, drumming up more business, under the cover of this new passion for ocean liners that we're all so guilty of.'

It took a moment for the penny to drop, but then that name hit home... *Edward Pointer.*

He saw her scanning for his reaction. He could tell by the flicker of a devilish smirk that she was enjoying this – tying him into an ever-expanding nexus of espionage where everything seemed interconnected; linked, in this case, to a man, moreover, he'd not only met previously, but privately loathed... not merely for his boorishness, not *just* for his smug countenance at being – whichever way he dressed it up over the South African conflict – a war profiteer...

'Fortunately, we have a plant, an insider, both high up and very close to him,' she continued. 'Someone *else* I believe you already know.'

She didn't need to say it.

Annie.

Lady Brunswick smiled, set her napkin down and moved to excuse herself.

'We will be in touch, Captain Finch.'

She bustled out with the same efficiency with which she had bustled in.

And of course, he knew, it made such perfect sense… That everything was part of some grand design; that Annie, too – fellow fugitive in the Cape, his unwitting accomplice, partner in crime, the woman he'd held a candle for over all these years – should have been ensnared in the same dark machinations as himself.

It explained why Annie, defying all reason, had become *Mrs Pointer*. It was why she had warned Finch away on their chance encounter in London last year, doing her utmost to keep him at a distance. She had been married off to the shipping magnate at MO3's behest, a fellow pawn in the Greater Game.

For all the extraordinary things that had happened in the past few days, he had not envisaged that he and Annie might somehow be teamed again. Nor that his mind would now be filled with the face of someone else, whose image he could not shake, no matter how hard he tried. A woman currently somewhere in Montreal.

He sat alone in the empty dining room, drained his glass and signalled to the reappearing waiter for another. Then he lit himself a Navy Cut, leaned back and turned the trusty monogrammed lighter in his hand. He stroked the engraved initials.

Ingo Finch… *IF*…